FIRST LAST CHANCE

E.H. HUNTER

www.BOROUGHSPUBLISHINGGROUP.com

FIRST LAST CHANCE
Copyright © 2022 E.H. Hunter

ISBN: 978-1-957295-10-7

To all romance lovers…

And to my Corner Café Writers Group: Stephanie, Elaine, and Kathryn Kern—
thank you for your suggestions.

FIRST LAST CHANCE

CHAPTER 1

Tired, in a bad mood, and in need of a stiff drink, Gabe rubbed his eyes as he waited at Cheyenne Airport for a woman he barely knew. Not for the first time, he wished his younger brother had never invited Professor Ashley Roberts, his late wife's best friend, to use their cabin on High Peak Lake for a few weeks. Then Jason had the nerve to ask Gabe to collect her and take her back to Coulter Creek Ranch first since Gabe was in town anyway.

He let out a pent-up breath as he paced in the lower level of the terminal. Since his father's death, the responsibilities of the family ranch hit him hard, which is why he never ran for a second term as the state's Governor. You'd think spending time in Cheyenne, debating with senators would be second nature by now, but when he fighting for his family's interests instead of the state's the stakes were different. Today he'd spent the day trying to get a cadre of senators to bring a bill to the floor that would keep ranch land in the hands of ranchers. Developers had overrun the state over the past few years, and it needed to story. Talking to these senators came with back-door dealing, and he'd gotten tired of trying to figure out who was left to trust.

Four weeks earlier, Senator Stanton had agreed to bring Land-Use Bill 482 to the senate floor for a vote, and now he was waffling. It wasn't like the senator to be so indecisive. Something was going on and Gabe needed to get to the bottom of it.

He stopped pacing and checked out a crowd gathering around a luggage carousel, then glanced at his watch for the third time. *Damn.*

Flight's forty minutes late. He turned toward the escalator then spotted a blonde standing near the baggage carousel, her gaze skimming the luggage on the conveyor belt. Over the years, he'd stared at a photograph over his brother's fireplace of Ashley smiling alongside his late sister-in-law. Some the tension eased from his shoulders when he saw Ashley's familiar face.

He took a deep breath, trying to shake off some of his weariness. Amazing what looking at a pretty woman did to lift a man's spirit. He continued to stare while she carried on a conversation with a woman next to her. Ashley always had a warm, infectious laugh, which made him smile. No one in his family had been doing much of that lately.

He headed over to say hello, but she seemed focused on the crowd, as if she was searching for someone, no doubt Jason. No surprise Jason had forgotten to mention someone else would be picking her up. But Gabe forgave his brother. His head was still buried in grief over losing his beloved wife, Susan.

"Professor Roberts?" Her gaze met his, and a frown creased her brow before her eyes widened. He offered his hand as he went closer. "Jason wasn't able to make it. I'm Gabe Coulter. We've met a few times, but only in passing. Welcome to Wyoming."

She smiled, shook his offered hand, and said warmly, "Thanks for meeting me, and I remember you. Is everything all right?" Concern tightened the soft lines around her eyes, and Gabe tried to ignore it. Grief over Susan's death had been a heavy blanket the family hadn't been able to shake. Today, he didn't want to go there. Especially not with her best friend.

He gave Ashley a nod. "S'all good, considering. Jason had an appointment with one of Cody's teachers. I was here for business. It made sense for me to come." With her soft hand in his and her kind smile, the moment they'd shared came with a warmth he wouldn't mind exploring. Slowly, she pulled free, and he stepped to the luggage carousel. "Which one?"

She pointed to a large, dark bag, which he grabbed then set it on the floor next to her. "That it?"

"Yeah."

Gabe took Ashley by the hand and guided her out of the airport. "This way." He eased through remaining crowd and headed outside to his car. He had to drive them to the hangar to get to his private plane.

***

Ashley had never been in a small plane before, and as they made their way over to it, her palms sweated at the thought of flying to the ranch in a Cessna. Gabe must've noticed since he held her hand. Which he'd done pretty much since they met. *He's being friendly,* she told herself, though not convincingly.

After he stored her luggage, he opened the door for her to board. She rubbed her hands on her pants and tried offering a distracted thank you, then buckled in and kept her gaze on him as he did a quick walk around checking external lights, then he removed the blocks under the wheels. He had to be well over six feet, but his movements were smooth and self-assured.

He hadn't needed to ease through the crowd in the terminal. He gave off the governor vibe, but stuck to his rancher roots, wearing jeans and a jacket. Yet, everyone stepped out of the way when he walked by. He commanded attention even though he didn't demand it.

After he climbed into the pilot's seat, he looked at her. "Your first time?" He settled in and buckled his seatbelt. "You all right?"

She sat on her hands. "Yeah." She forced a smile. "Guess it shows, huh?"

He chuckled. "A little. You've paled up a bit."

"Sorry. Can't be good to have a nervous passenger looking as if I'm ready to jump out without a parachute."

"You'll be fine once we're in the air. We've got some stunning views coming up." He went through a checklist before contacting the tower for permission to start up and taxi to the runway.

The engine kicked to life, and as they taxied, she grabbed onto his forearm. He looked down at her hand, then to her face before he rested his warm hand over hers. After a few comforting moments, she found the calm to let go.

During takeoff, she held her breath and kept staring out the front window, but within minutes floating above the gave her a feeling of freedom, and exhilaration. Tension eased in her body. "Wow, what a view," she said softly, then realized she needed to speak louder for him to hear. "It's beautiful from up here."

He nodded. "I fly this route so often sometimes I forget to enjoy it."

She kept her gaze on the landscape. "Were you able to make it home often when you were governor?"

"Not often enough." He angled the steering yoke and the plane leaned slightly to the left.

From up here, the land looked more compelling, showing every dip and curve. Homes cozied up to pastures, and forests stood tall along the rivers.

"I was sorry to hear about your father's death." So much grief had hit Gabe's family. She pulled her hands from under her legs and put them in her lap. "Unlike Susan, Jason said no one had a clue he was ill."

"He was a proud man. Never wanted to trouble anyone." He glanced her way. "Your family lives in Cincinnati?"

Okay, so he doesn't like to talk too much about what hurts. So noted. "My brother Nathan and his wife. My daughter's attending the university in Columbus."

"And your parents?" He pulled a case from the door pocket and slipped on sunglasses.

Ashley took a deep breath. She enjoyed watching the clouds' shadows dance over the rolling land as they headed north, but it was hard for her to talk about certain things too. "My parents died in a plane accident."

"Hey." He reached over and touched her hand as she rested on the seatbelt buckle. "It'll be okay. This plane's pretty safe."

She looked down and her stomach fluttered in all the best ways. Gabe spoke through his touches, and they slid easily into her personal space. "I know," she muttered. "I'm sorry. I read up on Cessnas after Jason told me we'd be flying to the ranch in one. You're experienced handling me…it, aren't you?" A blush worked itself from her chest to her face. "Um," she stammered. "I mean… You're used to handling small commercial runs with people."

He chuckled. "Yeah. I know what you mean. I've flown since I was fourteen, and we're used to visitors commuting to and from the ranch."

Ashley breathed a little easier. "I'm glad Jason and the kids moved back home to be with family." She brushed a hank of hair off her face. "Lisa loves the ranch. It's hard to believe she'll be graduating soon."

"I enjoy having them home. It gets lonely out there. I'll miss my niece when she leaves for school next year. She's got opinions she doesn't mind sharing." He chuckled and pushed forward on the yoke and the plane dipped a bit.

Huh. Ashley flicked him a quick look. She'd have never believed Gabe was lonely. He seemed to've had a full and active life. But since Susan and his dad died, she guessed his priority was Jason and the kids since. She understood since she missed Susan something awful. "Has Lisa decided which school she's going to attend?"

"I think so. We talked about it last week." He flicked a lever on the panel to ON. "Do you like working at Xavier College? Jason said you'd recently been awarded tenure and you're working on a grant proposal."

The question caught her by surprise. She'd wandered into a bit of fantasy, wondering if he'd flicked ON something in her. Embarrassed, she gave him a shy smile. "I love it there. It's a great place to work. I don't think I could teach anywhere else. I've been there for six years, and the university has become my second home. With Abby away this year, I served on several committees and found I enjoy working closely with my colleagues. We're hoping to receive a grant for our department." She shifted slightly, burying the simmer he'd somehow kindled in her.

"Jason invited me to visit him and the kids, and I thought the cabin may be a good place to work on outlining our proposal." She shook her head, trying not to make it so obvious she needed the distraction. "There's no rush, though. My colleague's traveling for a couple of months. I thought this would be a good way to wrap my head around what we're asking for."

"The guest cabin and lake are great places to gather your thoughts. I drive up from time to time to sort things out and do a little fishing. I've arranged for a car for your drive there."

"I'm feeling lost." She hadn't meant to be blurt that out. It sounded desperate, and she hated she'd said anything. "Sorry, not here, I meant in general."

He offered a soft smile. "We've all been there at some point."

She focused on the terrain below. "Susan loved staying at the ranch." She smiled sadly. Susan had passed away eight months earlier. It had cut Ashley deep. She could hardly imagine how Jason and the kids were still taking it. Gabe too. "If it's anything like what we're flying over I understand why. It's gorgeous."

"Yeah. Yeah she did." He gave a rough sigh, and the sound sent chills down her spine. Clearly, he was holding in a lot of grief. Through Susan, Ashley knew Gabe had gotten divorced eight years ago. She didn't remember hearing about anyone else his life except his family. She could imagine he dated, but kept it casual and discreet. He wasn't the kind of politician who trotted his personal life around in public.

"Susan was a special woman," he said. "She loved the ranch." He left it at that, shutting conversation down for landing procedure.

Warm but remote.

Gabe walked a tightrope of emotions.

***

Gabe landed the Cessna on the narrow, private runway, and taxied close to a hangar and cut the engine before climbing out and going around to Ashley's door to help her down.

"Thank you." She paused before taking his hand and giving him a smile that he felt in his gut.

"C'mon, our ride's over there." He got her luggage and led the way to a black Tahoe parked alongside the hangar. He put her bags in the back, warmed up the SUV, then turned onto a two-lane road curving west. After a few minutes, the peaks of the Bighorns appeared, rising high above the valley and river.

Ashley's gaze was trained on the mountains. "This is really something."

"I never get tired of it." He glanced her way and this time a softer smile played her lips.

"I can see how you'd miss this while living in Cheyenne. You're a homeboy, huh?"

With one hand on the steering wheel, he rubbed the back of his neck, a little unsure how to take that smile. It seemed friendly yet...more. Maybe she felt a connection to men who came back to their roots, to family. "I missed the ranch." He lifted his sun visor for a better view of the mountains, needing time to try to figure her out.

"You didn't want a second term as governor?"

He shook his head. "Politics can be a dirty business. And with Susan... It was time I got back home."

She fell quiet, a frown playing her brow. "Well, from our calls, Lisa certainly loves having you back at the ranch."

Gabe chuckled. "I think her new boyfriend has more to do with her mood these days. But, yeah, the ranch is in her blood. Her brother's too."

Ashley let out a sigh. "Cody. Such a sweet kid. I've missed him so much."

Gabe nodded. "They've missed you too. Lisa's surrounded by men, except for Ruth, who's more like a grandmother than housekeeper."

Ashley shifted nearer for a better view of the mountains, and his heartbeat hitched.

"I'm sure Ruth looks after them," she said distractedly.

"You've met her?"

"At Susan and Jason's wedding, then Susan's memorial service. Remember? We keep up by phone."

He clenched his jaw. He'd missed seeing Ashley at the funeral, but then he'd missed most of everything that day. "We all miss Susan." As the Tahoe sped over the road, the losses the family had taken hit him hard. His mother first, then two years later, his father, and then Susan. "How do you—"

"Stop," Ashley shouted.

"Huh?" Gabe slammed on the brakes, then pulled to the side of the road. "What's...?" His heart slammed in his chest. "What's wrong?"

Instead of answering, she turned and eased onto her knees to grab the small bag she'd thrown into the back seat. Gabe couldn't see what she was doing since her skirt rode high over her brown boots as she reached farther into the bag, offering him a view of the back of her thighs. He should've looked away, but he couldn't help leaning over for a better view. Ashley didn't fit any profile of a professor he knew, not with those legs.

"Got it." She slipped from the Tahoe with a camera in hand and headed into the field to climb a rocky knoll, then stood holding her camera firmly at her side as the wind blew her long hair about.

Gabe climbed out following, thinking she'd spotted a deer or possibly a wolf. "What did you see?"

She pointed off to the high, snow-capped mountains. "There. It's enough to take your breath, isn't it?"

"That's what got you out and running wild?" He kept the thought to himself as a smile played his lips. *Love at first sight*, her expression said it all, and damn his soul, he'd lost out to a mountain range, of all things. He buried a soft laugh, especially when her hand found his.

"We have nothing like this," she said quietly. "The peaks...they're old...so old, yet you never feel really alone with them watching over you."

He tried to concentrate on the peaks, not breast peaks, only mountain. Only the touch on his arm did so many...things to his body.

Focus. He loved this land, but it'd been quite a while since someone he knew had this type of reaction to it. Her unbridled need to get out and explore seeped through her touch as her gaze swept the landscape.

He'd hoped his ex-wife would've held the same passion for the land, but after six years of marriage, she'd asked for a divorce, took their son, Lucas, and left. The stress of politics and Gabe traveling without her for weeks took its toll, and she'd let him know what she thought about his deficits. She loved having friends and neighbors nearby and missed Boston. It had gutted him. He'd thought if she'd taken a little time to settle, or maybe if he hadn't gotten so lost in work, they would've had a chance. He didn't fight her taking Lucas. He knew he didn't have the time or focus to raise a child alone, and she was a good mother. But he missed his son something fierce, and lamented how empty the house and his heart felt without him. His business trips and career weren't ever meant to come at the price of his wife, and certainly not his kid.

Eight years later, he figured he'd never find a woman who could appreciate the beauty of the green valleys, the rushing waters of the rivers, and the mountains standing guard over them.

As Ashley shifted next to him, lost in the scenery, maybe she was going to change his perspective. Hell, maybe she already had. Seeing his land through her eyes gave him a new appreciation for it.

Her rosy lips stayed slightly parted, as her cheeks glowed, and her emerald eyes reflected the bright sun. But his gaze kept sliding back to those lips. He'd never seen a mouth more inviting.

One thing was for sure: her ex-husband had been a damn fool for letting her go.

CHAPTER 2

Ashley breathed a quiet *wow* at the sheer size and luxury of the ranch house. It looked more like resorts she'd seen in magazines rather than a working ranch. Gabe's home was tall with two wings and a second-floor balcony. Resting on a slope, the beautiful house had a stunning view of the mountains to the west. "This looks more like a vacation lodge than a home."

Gabe parked the SUV in front of a five-car garage. "Our granddad remodeled the old house to resemble the lodge where he and our grandma spent their honeymoon. She loved it here."

"I can see why. It's stunning."

"Yeah, it is. The contractor did a good job."

They entered the house and were in a wide foyer. A chandelier hung from a high ceiling showing off the superior woodwork that extended to the stepdown living area where the far wall was all glass showing off the view of the valley below.

"I could eat," Gabe said as she stood gawking. "You?"

He placed her luggage by the door and helped her remove her coat. His large hands brushing her shoulders and back. His touch took her breath away. Catching his eye, she sent him a smile over her shoulder, and made it last before he hung up her coat next to his jacket. "Breakfast was hours ago." She laid her hand over her stomach. "I'm hungry."

He winked as he said, "Let's see what Ruth's got in the fridge, then."

Trying not to look at his bitable ass, she followed him into an elegant, modern kitchen with dark wood cabinets, a few glass-fronted, and dark granite counters with gold veins running through them. As he made his way to the wide fridge, he turned and asked, "I should show you to your room first, right?"

She moved to him and buried her smile. She guessed, after being governor, he wasn't used to doing for himself, and she doubted had to show too many people around his home. "Food first. I'm starved."

He didn't step aside, and rested his arm over the fridge door almost inviting her to step close. He pulled out a casserole, and she moved away as he dished their servings onto two plates, then stuck them in the microwave.

She eyed the food as she pulled out a chair surrounding the wide dark wood kitchen table. A noise from down the corridor made her look up. Jason walked in with Cody close on his heels.

"Hey, Ash." Jason came over and gave her a hug and kissed her cheek. "Sorry I wasn't able to meet you."

"That's okay." She placed her hand on the side of his neck, keeping him close. Jason's gaze had lost its sparkle and humor, and the lines in his forehead had deepened. He appeared smaller, and his hug felt sad. "I'm so glad I came," she said softly. He was still a handsome man, but he didn't embody the energy and passion he used to have. Not surprising after he'd lost so much. Ashley knew she was a reminder of that and was why she'd waited so long to come out and visit them.

After Jason headed for the fridge, she turned and gave Cody a hug. He'd changed too. He'd grown taller and his legs were long like his dad's. But his smile was all Susan's, and it seemed as if he was trying to hiding his grief. "You're going to be taller than your dad soon."

Cody puffed out his chest. "You think?" He grinned. "I need to avoid the gray hair though."

Jason laughed. "Sit down, son. I'll get us some lemonade."

"Yeah, steer clear of the gray." Ashley picked up her fork. "How was soccer this year?"

"Fun. We came in third in the regionals." He took his drink from Jason.

She took a bite of the casserole. "Mmm. This is so good." She smiled, glancing at Gabe, who seemed transfixed on how her fork hovered close to her lips. She didn't think this was the right time to dwell on the "moment," and shifted the conversation to Cody. "What position do you play?"

The kid scooted his chair closer to the table. "Left midfielder. Dad came to every game."

Ashley turned and gave Jason a gentle smile then rubbed his back.

"How are things with Abby and Nathan?" Jason put his drink down and leaned in close to hear about her daughter and her brother.

"They're good. Abby loves her classes, and Nathan's working hard as usual." She sat back. "He and Kathryn will be celebrating their twentieth anniversary soon. I need to look around here and get them something for it before I go."

"Nathan's older than you, right?" Gabe took a forkful of casserole.

"Yeah. Nathan's older by five years."

Gabe nodded and seemed to communicate something to Jason before he said, "I'm sure you two need to catch up." Gabe got up and then took his empty plate to the sink. "You want to take Ashley's luggage to a guest room? I need to get back to ranch work," he said to Jason.

"Sure, not a problem." Jason started to eat. "Before you go, what did Senator Stanton have to say?"

Gabe scowled and stuck his hands in his pockets. "He didn't bring the Land-Use Bill to the floor. I need to see what I can find out. It looks like the Ranchers' Association has called a meeting for tomorrow morning." He glanced at Ashley then back to Jason. "Want to come along?"

"Well, I promised Ash I'd show her around tomorrow." Jason paused and looked down at his plate. "But I can take her around the ranch later. If that's okay with you, Ash?"

"No problem at all." She waved him off. "You two do what you need to do."

Gabe said softly, "It's good to have you here." He started for the door, then stopped as if he'd forgotten something. "Where's Ruth? I have a meeting in a few days and I need to sort things for traveling."

Jason swallowed a mouthful of food. "Lisa called earlier. She's driving Ruth to visit a sick friend."

"Lisa's driving her around?"

"Now that she has her license, she volunteers to drive Ruth all over the county."

Gabe winced as Cody pushed to his feet.

"I'm out too." He followed Gabe from the kitchen as Ashley focused on Jason.

"What's this bill you're hoping to pass?"

Jason pulled Cody's plate on top of his, then took care of Ashley's before offering a smile her way. "C'mon. I'll show you to your room and explain on the way."

***

As Ashley unpacked, her mind wandered to Gabe. His soft looks and touches made her feel alive in a way she hadn't anticipated. It'd been a long time since she'd let someone get close. She was wary of getting involved, especially with a man who made her heat up like the sun. The signs were subtle, but clearly there.

He was different from what she'd expected. From what Susan had told her. She'd pictured an arrogant, smooth-talking ladies' man, not a friendly, passionate-about-family, personable guy. He seemed such a far cry from his reputation as a tough governor who had been featured on the covers of major national magazines. But then everyone wore public masks to keep their private lives to themselves.

She closed her eyes and took a deep breath, then carried on putting her sweaters in the antique dresser drawers and hanging her shirts in the cedar lined closet.

As she turned from the closet, a soft knock came at her door. "Come in."

The door eased open, and Lisa walked to her and pulled Ashley into a hug. "You're here. I've been waiting for you." She sat on the bed. Her auburn hair and dark eyes were Susan all over, and her smile lit up her face like her father's when he used to smile. She had her dad's height. At seventeen, she was over five eight. Even though she seemed to be a typical senior, Ashley knew she was trying hard to keep that shine in her eyes. "How are you, sweetheart?"

Lisa shrugged. "There's a lot to do this last quarter of school." She sighed and leaned back on her elbows. "But I'm dating. His name's Michael."

Ashley sat on the bed and listened with a grin as Lisa took her through dating the most popular boy on the basketball team. Then she switched topics to the upcoming spring dance and the car Michael's father was letting them use for the big night.

"Will you go shopping with us Saturday?"

"Hmm?" Ashley teased. "Sure. Where are we going?"

"Dad promised to take me to Cheyenne. I want to get my dress for the summer dance next week while you're here to help."

Choosing a dress, that was a mother and daughter thing, and Lisa's quiet call for that type of support hurt Ashley's heart. "Sounds so good." She wrapped her arm around her best friend's daughter. "We'll look for the perfect one."

Lisa held on a little too tight, then looked up. "Abby loves her classes. She called me Monday."

Ashley smiled. "She's having a good year." She kissed Lisa's head, keeping her close.

Lisa tried a grin. "Next year I'll be in California. The change might be good."

Maybe. It could be she wanted to run from her grief, but she was right. A change could lift her spirits. "Gabe said you've already chosen your college."

Lisa's phone rang, and she shifted to glance at the screen. Her face brightened, and she got to her feet. The goofy boyfriend expression.

"Yep." Lisa didn't look up from her phone. "He helped me decide. But I still want to talk with you about it later," she replied before she headed out the door.

She left Ashley missing Susan in yet another way she'll never have her friend. They'd never talk about Lisa growing up and Ashley's experiences with her daughter, who was only a few years older than Lisa.

Ashley sighed and got to her feet to remove the last clothes from her luggage. She was glad to be here for Lisa's big high school dance to lend some sort of mom support.

Once everything was put away, Ashley stepped around the glass table close to the French doors and walked out onto the balcony overlooking a landscaped courtyard. Few flowers grew this early in the spring, but she recognized some early purple hyacinths. She inhaled deeply and a strong aroma of mint teased her senses. Maybe Ruth had an herb garden among the flowerbeds.

After taking it all in, she got out her phone and left a brief message on Abby's voicemail to let her know she'd arrived in one piece before calling her brother.

"Hi. How's Wyoming?" Nathan sounded busy.

"Hey, there. It's beautiful. I saw a great view of the Bighorns. The peaks are snow-covered and rugged. I wish you could see them."

"The wilderness... Not really my thing." Nathan laughed softly. "But explain your decision to spend time in Wyoming working, hiking, and being in the wilderness instead of somewhere exciting like New York. I'm worried about you." She grunted.

Her friends told her she was going through empty-nest syndrome, and maybe that was part of it. With Abby away most of the past year, Ashley missed her. But there was something more. She felt lost in the fog of everyday life and was looking for a way forward. During the last four years working toward a doctorate and dealing with a teenager, she'd had little time to explore what she wanted, allowing the fog to become thicker. She wasn't even going to dredge up the darker trails of her breakup with her ex-husband.

Since she'd had this conversation with her brother already, he took the grunt clue and switched topics. "How's Jason and the kids?"

"They're good as can be expected." Ashley rested against the balcony banister. Then decided to give him the deeper explanation so he'd understand where her head was at. "I wanted to get away from Cincinnati before Gloria started calling." Gloria was department dean at Xavier and knew she could rely on certain faculty members for last minute assignments, either to pick up a class or help with administrative matters. Ashley didn't want to compromise her leave.

She walked back to the sliding door. "I guess I needed a place where I could hear my own thoughts."

"Well then, you're in the right place. Take care and try to enjoy your stay."

"I will. See you soon." After hanging up, she stood on the deck, breathing in the fresh cool air while watching white fluffy clouds slide across the sky.

***

As Ashley padded into the kitchen, Ruth met her with a hug.

"It's so good to see you again." Ruth grabbed two cups from the cupboard. "I wanted to thank you for keeping in touch with me and the kids." She added water to the tea kettle and placed it on the stove. "Drop in here and have tea with me over your stay, okay? The kids are keeping so busy lately, it gets too quiet." They both knew why the kids kept themselves busy and avoided the quiet around here.

"I'd like that." Ashley rested against a unit. "Thanks for keeping me up on how they've been doing."

Ruth wiped her hand across her face. "Susan was special, that's for sure."

"She was." Susan had been lucky to have such a loving family. Ruth and her husband, Pete, had been with the Coulters for most of their marriage. Pete started working at the ranch for Jason's grandparents shortly after their wedding. He'd brought along his young bride, and a few years later when the Coulters needed a housekeeper and cook, Ruth had taken the job. They'd become part of the Coulter family, though Pete had passed away ten years back.

Now Ruth ran the kitchen while Pauline, whose husband worked as a ranch hand, handled the housework.

"I hope you're staying for a while." Ruth took folded napkins from a drawer as the kettle boiled.

"Jason invited me to use the High Peak cabin anytime I want. I'm hoping to drive up and do a little hiking. I want to try out the new camera my brother gave me for my birthday."

"I gave up celebrating birthdays a few years ago." Ruth gave her a smile. "Not the same when you're on your own." She pointed behind her. "The water's hot. I know you and Gabe finished off the casserole, but what do you say to a cup of tea?" Ruth placed the cups on a tray and filled a small pot with tea and hot water. "And what about a slice of banana bread I made earlier today?"

"Yes to the tea, please, but no thanks to the bread." Ashley looked around. "Gabe hasn't found you yet?"

"He was looking for me?"

Ashley nodded. "No doubt he'll catch up soon." But she felt a little disappointed he wasn't here. "Anything I can help you with?"

"No, I've got this." She piled everything on to a tray. "Follow me. We'll take this to the sunroom and enjoy the view."

Decorated with a flowered sofa and two overstuffed taupe chairs, the sunroom was warm and cozy. A green rug lay atop the honey-colored oak floor, and a wall of windows offered a striking view of the wide valley and imposing mountains beyond.

Seeming happy to have a house full of Coulters again, Ruth took a seat and affection stayed heavy in her eyes. "Gabe… I think most people are disappointed he didn't run for a second term, but Jason wasn't ready to take over the ranch after Bert passed away, so that left Gabe." She shook her head. "He's always been the responsible one and certainly knows what he's doing." She leaned over and poured the tea. "He's good with the kids too, and they love him."

Ashley took the one Ruth offered over then took a sip. Strange how talk had come around to Gabe, and Ashley winced. Had she been that obvious with her look around for him, Ruth was into matchmaking now? "How are Lisa and Cody really coping?"

"Lisa's too much like her mother when it comes to will: she's the strongest, but she hides under her smile a little too much. She's a pleasure to have around. Cody is a little withdrawn. I'm hoping the Boy Scout troop he joined will help pull him out of his shell."

"And Jason?"

Ruth fell quiet for a moment. "He hasn't been out on a photography assignment since, well, y'know." She picked up her cup and took a sip. "He's up and down with the kids." She pressed her lips together. "He's been too used to bouncing ideas around with Susan when it comes to them, but he's a Coulter. He's getting there. Gabe's a good sounding board. Between them, they're coping. Gabe got them their own horses and goes riding with them to talk or distract, whatever they need at the time, or if Gabe and Jason start to bite into each other, which they do at times."

Ruth steered the conversation back to Gabe, and Ashley tried not to react. Gabe cared for his family, she knew that, but was still maybe a little lost to his own grief too. The contradiction made her stomach flutter in all the right ways. Maybe. She still couldn't decide.

After emptying her second cup, Ruth got to her feet. "I can't put off work any longer, unfortunately." She offered Ashley a smile. "Would you like me to leave the pot?" She placed her cup on the tray.

"No, thanks. I'll finish this one."

"Okay. I'm just back through there." She pointed back at the kitchen. "I need to prepare dinner for tonight. That little bit you two ate earlier won't hold Gabe." Ruth picked up the tray. "Put your feet up and rest for a bit. You must be tired." She got to the door and turned back and winked. "The library is behind the stairs if you want to grab a book."

"Oh?" Ashley perked up, and Ruth smiled knowing exactly what she'd just said. Ashley didn't go anywhere without a novel. "Thanks."

Shadows shifted over the mountains as dusk settled in, but the view was still spectacular as trees swayed with the wind. Ashley put her cup on the small table by her chair and closed her eyes, easing into the soft cushions. She was glad she'd taken Jason up on his offer to visit. The ranch was amazing, and she already felt comfortable here in her grief. Her days at the cabin should be good for reflection, past, present, future. She needed to come to terms with them all, and a taste of Susan's natural stability helped.

As for Nathan, he had followed in their father's footsteps and started working in their father's law firm right out of law school. Their father and Nathan had worked together for many years. Her brother was lucky to have had that time with their dad. Time had flown by. Nathan and Kathryn were celebrating their twentieth wedding anniversary and making plans for a dream vacation.

Ashley had her work and if the paper she submitted last quarter on student involvement in curriculum development was accepted, she may have greater opportunities to apply for private research grants in that area in the years ahead. But she questioned whether it was what she truly wanted. She'd worked hard to get to this point in her career, but felt something was missing. She needed change.

With a long sigh, she stretched, then lifted her feet to the ottoman, falling asleep as twilight descended over the Bighorns.

CHAPTER 3

Gabe moved from his desk to the large window overlooking the snow-capped peaks. This office had been his grandfather's, then his dad's, and now it was his, along with the ranch. It surprised him today how Ashley had naturally fitted into all of that, and he fought back a smile at just how naturally he'd wanted to see how she could slip into…something more comfortable. She'd caught him looking at how her fork had touched her lips and… He laughed softly and tried to force her out of his mind.

Despite how the ranch had come alive around Ashley, the connection to his past and his legacy weighed heavy on his shoulders. Both former Coulters had been successful, and he was determined to keep that success going. He wanted to pass on the land to Lisa and Cody—Lucas if he wanted it.

But now rumor had it that his neighbor, Sam Frasier, owner of High Mountain Ranch, had racked up a lot of debt and was looking to sell a piece of land and Evan Development was looking to buy it up. The ranchers' meeting tomorrow morning should clarify what was going on with them trying to buy up ranch land in the valley.

Gabe stuck his hands in his pockets and leaned against the window frame. He'd definitely have a talk with Sam.

To get the bill passed, Senator Robert Stanton's vote was essential. The legislation would overturn the law allowing ranch land to fall into the hands of private developers like Evans Development that wanted to build resorts. At the last rancher's breakfast, several of the younger landowners were as concerned about allowing development near their ranches as the old timers.

"If Bob doesn't back this damn bill, it'll be dead," he muttered to himself. Even with his help, the senate vote would be close. Too close.

Maybe he'd fly back to Cheyenne tomorrow afternoon and check in with Bob again.

He wandered into the kitchen, where Ruth stood at the stove. "You need something?" she asked without turning.

"Nope."

She twisted around, lifting her brows. "Then are you after me or...someone else? Ashley said you needed a word. Are you still hungry?"

"I did, and yeah on the more food front." As for Ashley...? Ah. He blushed. Busted.

She shook her head, then glanced at the time on the stove. "Dinner can be ready in an hour. Can you last that long?"

"Sure." He turned to leave, then stopped, not really sure why he felt so restless. "We have a ranchers' meeting tomorrow morning."

"You want breakfast early?"

"That a problem?"

"Of course not."

"Thanks." He scratched his head. "On second thought, we'll eat after the meeting. Jason will want to have breakfast with the kids."

Ruth watched him for a moment, then offered a smile that seemed to know too much. "You could have called and told me that, right? Go on. I think Ashley's still in the sunroom. She might want to freshen up before dinner, if you're struggling for an excuse to give her for going in there."

Gabe laughed and waved her off before he left the kitchen.

A few moments later, he entered the sunroom—then froze halfway between the door and couch.

Ashley lay stretched out in the fading light, the rise and fall of her chest so light as she slept. Leaving came to mind. It was the right thing to do, but he stared a while longer as she lay with her head nestled into the back of the chair. She looked young for a woman in her forties. In the vanishing light reflecting around the sunroom, her skin appeared smooth and flawless. Strands of blonde hair had come loose from her clip and curled around her face.

Gabe's gaze lingered on her full lips. God, he wanted to kiss her, but it was a line he'd never cross. He was tired, resistance was low, and he'd had one hell of a day that accounted for wanting to do just that, but Ashley was definitely someone who no doubt needed more than a kiss to win her head before she even offered her heart. No... one of Ruth's dinners and a good night's sleep were what he needed. It looked like she needed the rest too, and he hated having to disturb her. But the cup teetering too close to the edge of the small table next to her looked set to do that, so he moved and reached over to grab it.

He brushed against her arm—then froze as her eyes came open.

***

Something invaded her space, and Ashley jolted and reached to push whatever it was away, but jaw stubble met her touch, and a huff answered her rougher handling.

"Gabe?" She jerked her touch off, regretting she'd tried to shove him away. It hadn't worked. "Sorry."

"S'okay. I didn't mean to startle you. Your cup's on the edge of the table, ready to fall." He pushed it back and stepped away, breaking eye contact.

"My fault. I...I didn't realize I'd fallen asleep."

"You enjoying the view?" He glanced at the window, his awkwardness clear, but then she had tried to shove him away like a stalker caught high on Sleeping Beauty syndrome.

Guilt crept in, and she wanted to try and take that...awkwardness from his brow. "Um... The sunset was..." What? She was too lost in

Gabe. "Beautiful. It was really beautiful." God, that sounded as awkward as he looked. "Relaxing," she said with a softer smile.

The tension eased in his shoulders, but only a little. Politicians and scandal…had he ever really escaped the threat of it, even in his own home? "You should see the sunsets during the winter months," he said eventually. "Being this far north, they're more colorful." He sounded just as painfully awkward.

"Maybe you'll have to show me." What the hell? She'd not only invited herself back to the ranch, but flirted with it when she hadn't meant to. Gabe smiled down to his feet, perhaps picking up that she hadn't meant to, and the tension between them fell away.

"Maybe I could. Any time." He stared out into the darkness before he found her again. "Ruth, she…well… She wanted me to let you know dinner will be in an hour if you'd like to freshen up." He pushed his hands into his pockets.

"Thanks."

He seemed to be waiting for her to say more, and when she didn't, he took a step back. "See you at dinner, then." And with that, he turned and headed out.

Ashley ran a hand through her hair, then winced when she caught her clip. It hadn't hurt, she just tried to bury how much of a train wreck she must have looked. Gabe had stepped right out of her restless dream, and she… she must have looked like a cavewoman throwback. She groaned, then stretched and rose from the chair before heading back to her room. Looking through her sweaters, she selected a green cashmere turtleneck and black pants. She grabbed a silver chain from her bag and placed it on the bed before washing up and returning to the bedroom to dress. A few minutes later, she stood before the mirror, applying a little foundation and mascara before brushing and pulling her hair back into a clip. With one last glance in the mirror, she smiled, knowing exactly why she was so concerned with how she looked.

She needed to feel confident to deal with a family dinner and…Gabe.

***

Ashley smiled at Gabe as he pulled out a chair and let her take her seat. Despite the offer of ranch, outdoors, and horses, he smelt good, his cologne enough to turn her head and glance back. He returned her smile, then took his seat at the head of the table, Jason to his right. Ashley sat next to Jason, and Lisa and Cody took their places across from them. Ruth had chosen to eat in her small apartment off the kitchen.

As the food was passed around the table and Ashley started to put a little on her plate, Jason glanced across at Cody. "You decided about soccer camp?"

His mouth full, Cody swallowed after a moment. "I want to go. Thomas called. He signed up."

"You'll enjoy it. I always enjoyed summer camp."

Gabe chuckled, and Ashley wondered just what knowledge that chuckle held. It was far too private, but left her smiling nonetheless. "You always enjoyed co-ed summer camp," he added.

Jason lifted his wine glass. "They were more fun."

Yeah, Ashley *really* wanted to know what they'd been up to there.

"When Dad and I spoke with the camp coach, he said he was an admirer of yours, Uncle Gabe, didn't he, Dad?" Cody reached for a roll, and Ashley pushed the bowl closer to him to help.

"He might've done some campaigning for you." Jason turned to Lisa. "You're driving Ruth around now, huh?"

"Sometimes. How else can I get experience?" She looked to Ashley. "If Dad gets busy, I could show you around Willow River."

"I'd like that. Thank you, honey." Ashley picked up her water glass, trying to figure out why Gabe never spoke too much about politics at the dinner table. He hadn't replied to Jason. She'd been Susan's best friend, and hadn't really paid too much attention to the details surrounding Gabe's breakup with his wife, but his quiet and reluctance to discuss campaigning perhaps called it out for him. He didn't want it to distract from family because maybe it had already cost him too much.

"I can show you a good place for a haircut or trim." Lisa took a drink from the tall glass of milk. "Now, Ash, tell us again what Dad was really like in school."

Ashley nudged Jason's shoulder but kept her gaze on Lisa. "What would you like to know?"

"Since you and mom were college roommates, you must know what she thought when she first met dad. What he was like?"

Gabe chuckled again, and Ashley couldn't fail to grin behind her glass, her gaze holding Gabe's for a moment. His laugh rode deep into her core, and his cock of a smile back at her seemed to know it.

"I bet he was usually late to class."

Ashley nodded at Lisa. "He was late for everything until the time he was late for a date with your mom. She called a friend." Ashley turned to Jason. "You remember Bill Pierce, don't you?" She winked at Lisa. "Susan called Bill, and he took her to the concert instead." She grinned at Jason. "I think that was the last time you were late for anything." Laughter filled the dining room.

"A lesson learned." Jason took a bite of roast.

"I haven't seen Curtis for a while. Did he get accepted to Yale?" Lisa asked out of nowhere before explaining to Ashley. "Curtis is a friend and lives on a neighboring ranch. He's Sam's grandson."

"I ran into Sam at the Black Dog a week or so back." Jason buttered his second roll. "He said everything was all right. I don't know about Curtis. He's a bright kid and should do fine."

"Yeah, he did get accepted to Yale." Gabe took a sip of his wine before he spoke to Lisa. "He'll be there for graduate school. I heard from him a couple of weeks ago. He's a nice kid. Always keeps in touch."

"Lisa has a crush on him." Cody grinned. "I think she's in l-o-v-e with him."

Lisa straightened in her chair. "Shut up. Nobody wants to know what you think. You're a soccer player. Focus on your own balls and failing to score."

"*Dad.* Have a word."

"Okay, you two. Knock it off." Jason was trying to bury a laugh and pointed at Lisa. "You especially."

Gabe leaned over a little closer to Ashley as Lisa did a little victory dance. "Sam Frasier owns High Mountain, the ranch adjacent to ours. Curtis is his oldest grandson."

"Oh," she mouthed, liking the closeness and chaos of family talk. "Did we fly over his ranch on our way here?"

"No, it's a little northeast of us." He smiled back, seeming to like the exchange too as Jason and Cody spoke over them.

Listening to the easy talk and laughter reminded her of how much she missed Abby, and of all the evenings Ashley had spent alone, so she stayed lost in the family talk going on around the table as they ate.

After dinner, Lisa and Cody said their goodnights and headed to their rooms.

Jason nudged Ashley as they left. "I want to show you a photograph." A soft grin spread across his face. "It's in my office, will you stop in before breakfast in the morning?"

If it meant him getting back into his photography? "Sure." She hid a yawn, then eventually pushed to her feet, wanting to give Gabe the space to discuss business because their quiet over it suggested they needed privacy. "Night, Jason... Gabe." She added Gabe's name a little more shyly. "Thank you again for meeting me at the airport." She pushed her chair to the table.

"My pleasure."

As she headed toward the hall, she turned back and found Gabe still watching her. She gave a wince, feeling like she needed to try and pull in every stomach and butt muscle going.

His look lingered on her, and his cock of smile said he knew exactly what her thoughts were, so he looked anyway. "Enjoy your stay," he said softly, and as she turned away, she kept her smile to herself, and yeah…she pulled in those stomach muscles too.

***

After a long shower, Ashley was tired but not sleepy. Her nap in the sunroom hadn't been long, but it'd been enough to keep her awake. Trying to find something to make her groggy, her gaze went to her backpack, which held several of her paperbacks and a loaded Kindle. But then Ruth had said there was a library.

Ashley wrapped her robe snugly around her and quietly made her way down the stairs. After opening the tall, double doors at the end of the hallway behind the stairs, she slipped inside.

Soft light from a lamp and low flames from the fireplace welcomed her. Enjoying the cozy feel, Ashley hummed softly as she walked alongside shelf after shelf of books and slid her fingers over the cool spines.

"Couldn't sleep?"

Startled, she turned to find Gabe in the doorway, watching her, and she flushed as that familiar warmth spread through her body.

"I must've slept too long this afternoon." His blue gaze stayed with her, and she wondered what he was thinking. "This library could best the one on campus."

He flashed her a grin as he came over. "You want a nightcap?" He nodded toward two chairs by the fireplace. "By the fire?"

She needed something to calm her nerves. "White wine, please."

Gabe went to the small bar next to the fireplace and pulled out a bottle. He held it toward her. "Washington Riesling—how does this sound?"

"Sounds good." She took a chair, wrapping her robe around her legs.

Gabe poured the wine and moved to the chair next to her. "Here." He handed her a glass. "So, Ash, tell me about yourself."

She took a sip from her glass as he took a seat. "Well..." She started slowly, not quite sure how to make this sound interesting, because it really wasn't. "I've lived in Cincinnati most of my life. I'm an educator—mathematics—and have a daughter, Abby, in her second year at the University of Ohio." She took in the flames darkening the wood in the fireplace. "There's not much else to tell."

Gabe drank from the glass and gazed at her. "I don't believe that. I think there's much more to you."

Several beats of silence passed. She didn't know what else to say. She couldn't tell him that she was lonely and couldn't move on with her life since her own divorce. Maybe he knew all that because he didn't push her on the details.

"A different question, then." He took another drink. "You're beautiful, so why hasn't some professor swept you off your feet?"

A blush hit Ashley's cheeks and she tried not to smile. She couldn't remember when, if ever, anyone had called her beautiful. "Oh no. What about you? Why isn't there a Mrs. Coulter?" Shadows from the dying flames danced across his face, making his features broody and dark, reminding her of an outlaw from an old western. A shiver ran down her spine.

Gabe crossed one knee over the other. "I've been busy since I came back to the ranch—with taking over the everyday running of Coulter Creek and now working to pass a Land Use Bill to restrict commercial building on ranch land."

"Jason told me about the legislation you've been working on. He said Montana had a similar Bill."

Gabe nodded. "They do. Governor Riley is a big supporter of the law."

"Your governor isn't?"

"Nope. She's from Cheyenne and her family is in medicine. Land-use legislation isn't high on her list of priorities."

"Do you have someone at the capitol willing to push it forward?"

Gabe shook his head. "I thought we did."

"What happened?"

He emptied his glass then gave a long sigh before tilting his head toward the bar. "Another?"

"Yes, thanks." Ashley handed him her glass, but the drop of conversation on politics was more than clear this time. She could understand a little more on why he'd backed away from it all, especially if he'd had his fill of underhand politics from some of his peers.

He returned and gave Ashley her drink before taking his chair again. "I'm not sure what happened. He seems to be pulling back. If nothing's done, we could be dealing with a resort close to the ranch's northern border."

Talking…this was something new. He hadn't shut down on her completely. Deep lines appeared between his brows, and Ashley wanted to reach for his hand, to run her fingers over the creases between his eyes and soothe his furrowed brow. Without thinking, she leaned forward and placed her hand over his. "I'm sorry. I'm sure you're dealing with a lot now along with helping Jason and the kids since they lost Susan."

Gabe spread his fingers and hers slipped between them. He gazed down at their hands. "You asked me why there's no Mrs. Coulter. Not many women care for this type of life. Living on a ranch in a small town. Right from the start, Alicia wasn't happy here. She liked shopping, lunches out, entertainment, and living on the ranch wasn't what she bargained for, that and politics kept getting in the way. It got in the way of me and my son."

Lucas. Ashley frowned. She hadn't gotten used to being away from her own daughter, so God knows how Gabe felt having his kid walk away with his mother.

Gabe gave her a sideways glance. "What are you looking for, though? With life? Mine's here, on the land."

She shrugged and took another sip of wine, savoring the cool, fruity flavor. "Someone who loves the reality of who I am, not the concept of what I should be." It was such a simple statement, but never more true. Her husband had walked away wanting everything she wasn't.

"Yeah?" He took her wine glass and placed it next to his on the coffee table, then pulled her to her feet. As he eased her back against the bookcase, he stepped in close, and she lifted her gaze to his. He ran his fingers through her hair, removing the shell clip she'd worn.

"Everyone deserves to be loved for who they are, not the concept," he said, his voice deep and husky. "I'm gonna kiss you now, is that okay?" He ran a thumb along her cheek to her mouth, and she let her silence be her consent before he brushed his warm, firm lips across hers.

Heat soared through Ashley, radiating from her chest to her toes, erasing all thoughts.

When he deepened the kiss, she wrapped her arms around his neck, praying he'd never stop, maybe just move his touch a little lower, to her breasts. Their tongues met briefly, then he swore and pulled back, taking a deep breath.

"Don't stop," she whispered and offered her mouth again.

He took the offering, deepening the kiss as he slipped his touch beneath her robe, brushing her bare skin. She moaned into his mouth, then heated the kiss as he traced his touch up under the robe and cupped her breasts. His thumb brushed a nipple that more than rose to call out...more, and she groaned into how it played down over the flat of her stomach to heat between her thighs.

Breathless, she pulled away, not sure what to say. What she wanted to say was "let's take this to my room" but all that came out was, "What are we doing?"

"Kissing." Gabe sighed heavily, his breath brushing her cheek. "But I think I need to get you to your room, right?" He took her hand.

Yeah, she needed...something, and she let him guide her as she fought a blush. "The wine...it must have gone straight to my head," she said as they climbed the stairs.

He gave her a sexy smile. "You sure it was the wine?" He walked her to the guestroom and backed her to the door before stealing another kiss. "Y'know, the men in Cincinnati must be damn blind letting you go."

He looked set to take his kiss lower, but, giving a slow smile, he opened the door behind her. "I think I'd better get to my own room, don't you?"

No. She shook her tumbling thoughts away. "Night, Gabe," she whispered instead, seeing he needed to go and slow the heat down. Hard and fast they'd both probably been too used to over the past. Gabe…he was worth taking time with. Although she really wouldn't have minded the hard and fast with him.

He looked her up and down and swiped a hand across his mouth, no doubt questioning his sanity over walking away. He knew she wanted him to stay. She knew *he* wanted to stay, yet...

Chapter 4

Fighting off an early morning yawn. Ashley headed downstairs, only stopping when Jason met her halfway.

"You're up early. Did you sleep well?" He drew up close.

"Yeah, I did actually."

"Good." He took her arm. "Remember I said I had something to show you?"

Now she did. "Your photographs, right?"

"Yep, come on."

He took her downstairs, and Ashley stepped into Jason's office where rows of photos lined the walls. From one end of the spectrum to the other, snaps of people lined the walls, some hugging and smiling on wedding days, others crying fear and confusion as crowds were caught scrambling away from collapsing buildings. Slums, tsunami ruined villages, rugged mountains, deep valleys, green jungles... The effect was like being in several places at once, with all the changing seasons and emotions that came with those experiences.

"Sort of hits you, doesn't it?" Jason watched every ounce of her reaction, but then he was a photographer, where every detail mattered.

"You certainly have talent, but then you both always did." Jason and Susan had been voted as two of the world's top photographers a few years back.

He opened the door to a small storage closet and took out a picture of her and Susan. Her breath caught seeing how huge their smiles were as they hugged each other.

"Do you remember when I took this one? Susan had told you she was pregnant with Lisa."

She did. Every moment of it. "She was so happy." Susan had told Ashley then she was hoping for a girl even though she thought Jason wanted a boy to carry on the Coulter name.

"She was beautiful." Jason's voice was soft as he leaned the unframed photograph against his desk. He'd brought Ashley in here to remember, and she choked a little smile, needing to remember her with him, maybe get lost *in* remembering with him. She'd only had silence at home.

Eventually the sun peeked over the land, and she rested against the patio door, looking out. "I never thought we'd both end up here, like this," she said quietly.

"Alone, you mean? Me either." He ran a hand over his face as he rested next to her.

"When we got married, I thought Rob and I would be together until the end." She took a deep breath. "But it didn't work out that way. I've been alone long before we split up."

Jason placed his arm around her, and she rested her head on his shoulder.

"He didn't deserve you. And just for the record, I hated the guy." Jason gave her a light squeeze as she laughed softly. "What do you think will happen to us?" he asked eventually. "You think we'll marry again?"

She lifted her head and smiled. "I don't know." Giving a sigh, she eased away and headed for the door. "You're a good man." She turned back for a moment. "I know Susan would want you to find someone." He came over and she kissed his cheek. "Thank you for inviting me to visit. I'm so happy to be here with you, Lisa, and Cody." She squeezed his hand then let go.

"Yeah, I'd better go. Gabe and I have a meeting this morning." He opened the door for her, but as she headed out, she collided with Gabe.

"Sorry." Gabe caught her arm, and she eased into a smile to let him know it was okay. Only he didn't look okay as he shifted his look between them, then rested on Jason. "You ready?" It sounded more like an order.

"Yeah, hang on." Jason made sure she was okay, then his annoyance was on Gabe after she nodded. "Yeah, let's go. And try not to rough up my guest next time, yeah?"

***

The sun still crept over the horizon as Gabe and Jason drove toward the Lower Fork Ranch for their rancher s' meeting. Jason held a thermos of coffee in his hand, and except for a few words of greetings, remained quiet.

"Is everything all right?" Gabe kept his gaze on the road, his grip tight on the steering wheel. *He* wasn't all right. Jason had mentioned something about marriage to Ashley—he'd caught that. His kiss and touch in the library forced its way in too, and now he wondered if Ashley had told him about their kiss and this was Jason, stone cold pissed off because Gabe had moved in on his girlfriend despite neither one of them having the goddamn decency to mention they were hooked up.

That kiss…it had kept him awake for hours, and Gabe wanted more of them. But at the price of Jason? If he'd known, he'd have never flirted. He'd have never touched.

Jason had already lost enough. They all had.

What the hell was Ashley playing at?

Jason took a sip of coffee. "Thinking about my conversation with Ash." He looked at Gabe. "It's good she's here." The softness in his eyes called that out more.

It threw Gabe, spinning his head and fists in another direction. Ashley *hadn't* told him about the kiss. That meant what about her? She didn't give a damn about coming between two brothers, where one had lost a wife and the other was still spinning in circles over how to help out?

Gabe's grip tightened on the wheel again.

He hadn't taken Ashley as a player. "Are you two making any special plans?" He kept that so careful. Maybe Jason hadn't mentioned it because he worried how Gabe would react to seeing the kids deal with having Ashley around as anything else but a friend to their mom.

"Not yet. Our lives seem to be at a crossroad. A place neither of us ever imagined." Jason took another drink from the thermos.

Gabe's heart fell. That confirmed it.

"Do you think Sam Frasier will be there today?" Jason flicked him a look.

Gabe turned onto the road leading to the ranch. He needed Ashley burning out of his head for a while. "I hope so. It'd be good to know what Sam's thinking and if he's gotten his drinking and gambling under control. We had a talk a while back and he promised to get help. He hired a foreman, but I haven't spoken to him since. I don't know anything about the new man."

As they walked into the large barn, Gabe looked around for Sam, but he didn't see him amongst the ranchers. He checked the time. Sam had a few minutes yet.

Ray Tanner, owner of the Lower Fork, made his way to them. "Hey, boys. There's coffee over there by the office. Go grab a cup, we need everyone awake." Ray and Bert Coulter had worked together for many years and had been good friends. Now in his midseventies, Ray was slowing down. His son, Charles, had taken over the ranch, but Ray still offered valuable input.

Sam still wasn't there, but his new foreman, Max Banks, arrived and introduced himself. Ray called the meeting to order. He talked about how Evans Development was looking for land near the base of the Bighorns to build a resort. He also talked of the importance of keeping the valley as ranch land and how a resort to the north would change all that. "Now, how many of you have been contacted by this development company looking for a piece of land?"

Two ranchers raised their hands, but they assured they weren't interested in selling any part of their lands.

"Well, then." Ray's voice bellowed through the barn. "If we—" He waved his hand to the eleven ranch owners. "—stand firm and do whatever we can to help each other out, we should be safe." He moved toward Gabe. "What's happening with that Land Use Bill?"

"I'm still looking for legislative support."

"Y'hear that? We need all the support we can get to push that bill through the senate." There were mumblings and nodding throughout the group over what Ray said. "And let's give a welcome to Max Banks, Sam's new man. Max if you need any help, just give one of us a call. Sam's ranch and Coulter Creek are the two largest spreads in the valley, so have Sam check in with Gabe if he's approached by a land buyer."

"Oh. I think we'll manage." Max eased into a smile as he folded his arms.

Jason threw Gabe a cocked brow.

Ray called for any more business, and Gabe stayed around long enough to hear the meeting draw to a close before he headed out with Jason and started back for home.

"We should be back at the ranch in time for breakfast." Jason slipped on his belt. "I want to see the kids before they leave for school."

Gabe nodded. "What did you think of Sam's new foreman?"

"Max? Seemed to be proud of running a large ranch, arrogant too from what he said. He spoke to Ray after the meeting, and I don't think he was listening."

"It's hard not to hear Ray."

"It wasn't that. He didn't appear interested in what Ray advised."

"I got that same impression. Will need to keep an eye on him. Think I'll have Clay check out High Mountain's finances and Max."

"Say, thought I'd take Ashley to Jake's tonight for a burger and beer. Why don't you and Marilyn join us?"

Gabe stiffened at the mention of Ashley's name. "Marilyn and I broke up several months ago, I told you th—" He bit it back. He'd told Jason a lot of things since Susan's death, and he didn't hold it against him for forgetting this one. "She moved to Colorado."

"Yeah, sorry. I forgot." Jason sighed as they pulled up to the ranch. "Come along anyway. You'll get to know Ashley better."

He'd already gotten to know Ashley well enough, he wanted to say that. But at the price of losing his brother, Gabe bit it all down.

***

At the breakfast table, Lisa chatted nonstop about her upcoming shopping trip. Gabe finally relaxed. He loved the energy she brought to the house. Except for Cody, everyone was caught up in her mood, even Ruth, who'd come in to inform Jason he had an important call. Life was moving on without Susan, and it brought a sadness of its own knowing time didn't grieve with them, but Lisa, seeing her take this trip and find her heart pushed Gabe out of his own mood, for her sake.

"I'm so happy you're coming with us." Lisa grinned at Ashley. "It'll be the two of us against Dad." She chuckled before taking a bite of toast.

Gabe narrowed his eyes at Ashley, but said nothing. She looked gorgeous this morning, with her hair pulled back away from her face and her eyes twinkling as she laughed at Lisa. Tightness hit his chest. How could she sit there and fit so snug into their family life? She'd kiss him. Gabe grumbled internally. Okay, *he'd* kissed her, done a little more than just kiss, but she'd damn well reciprocated, and she was involved with Jason. The trip for the prom dress and time out as a family drove that home.

Ashley picked up a glass of freshly squeezed juice. "We'll have fun."

Lisa nodded. "I have my list ready."

"I really liked a couple of the dresses we looked at online this morning, but maybe we should search for a few more?"

Yeah, Gabe had had enough of this. "Do you have plans for the weekend, Cody?"

Cody shrugged as Jason returned to the table.

"That was our publisher in Chicago." Jason picked up his fork but hesitated before continuing. "They need me there late tomorrow to help with the cover of our book." His gaze landed on Lisa.

The kitchen fell silent, and Lisa's smile faded. "Dad...I...I really need a dress for this dance. It's my senior year." She stared down at her plate. "You promised," she whispered.

"I'm sorry, honey, but this trip is necessary if I want to get our photos published. When I sent our pictures in, I figured it would take a month or more before I heard back."

"You could be home by Saturday?" A touch of hope filled Lisa's voice.

"It's important to check in on your Grandma Rose." He smiled sadly. "She's missing your mom too."

"These are Mom's photos, right?" Cody asked, reaching for the bacon.

Jason sighed as he kept an eye on Lisa. "Yes. The ones of Brazil I've spent the winter organizing and labeling."

A tear slipped Lisa's cheeks, and she swiped it quickly away as she looked over at Gabe. "Could you fly us down to Cheyenne, Uncle Gabe?"

After all she'd been through... He took a drink of his coffee. He'd spoken to Senator Stanton and their appointment had been re-schedule to late next week, so... "You bet."

"Really?" Lisa smiled, and she turned to Ashley. "Uncle Gabe's all right. He's a lot of fun."

Ah. He'd forgotten Ashley would be going, but he still threw his head back and found a laugh. "Spending the day shopping with two beautiful women makes it easy." He hadn't meant to say that, or maybe he had. Ashley's cheeks burned, and her smile carried an innocence she damn well shouldn't have, not after that kiss with him, not with how Jason sat three feet away from them both. Maybe she *was* a player and he had a right to make her feel uncomfortable.

"I would appreciate it." Jason patted his shoulder. "If you have time before I get back, could you show Ashley around the ranch?" He paused and turned to Ashley. "I wish you could go with me. We could check out a couple good restaurants."

"Sorry. Lisa and I have plans." She grinned. "Shopping takes precedence."

"Uncle Gabe has good taste. Much better than Dad's," Lisa told Ashley.

"Anything to spend time with you, sweetheart," Gabe said. "Would you like to help me out, Cody?" This was family here, and he wanted to ram it home how no one was missed out here when it came to Ashley. Cody's quiet was always a concern.

"Whoa, not me," Cody picked up the bacon from his plate. "I don't want to go shopping for dresses. Thomas and I thought we'd saddle up and ride out to that Boy Scout Camp our troop master wants to use this year." He glanced at his dad. "Our camp-out is soon."

Jason nodded and swallowed a mouthful of food. "The camp-out's not for another month."

"I know, but we want to ride out to see what shape the camp is in. It's on the ranch," he said as if that explained everything.

When it was clear Jason wasn't going to respond, Gabe said, "That's a long ride, and it's still spring. We could get a few storms yet and—"

"I think they'll be all right." Jason looked over at Gabe.

"Well, then." Gabe reached for his coffee, not overstepping the mark here. Not with Jason. "You and Thomas be careful out there," he said to Cody. "This weather is likely to change."

"Will do," Cody said as Jason scooted his chair back from the table.

Jason glanced to Ashley as Cody left. "I'm sorry to leave you for a few days but let me take you to Jake's tonight for a burger and beer. Just like college." He glanced at Gabe. "Except this time, Gabe's agreed to join us."

I have? Gabe cocked a brow at Jason, and Jason held his look with a shake of head that said *yeah, you did.*

"It's a date." Again Ashley wore a shy blush that came Gabe's way. "How long do you think you'll be gone?" she said back to Jason in a lower, more distracted tone.

Oh she was good.

"I'm not exactly sure." Jason finished his coffee.

Gabe had had enough and he excused himself, uncomfortable with how this was going. He couldn't figure her out. How close she seemed to Jason, but how her look lingered longer Gabe's way.

Yeah, he'd go tonight. He needed Jason to come to his senses and realize, after eight months, he was still grieving the loss of his wife, and Ashley was playing him. Playing them both.

"Damnit," Gabe muttered as he headed into the hall. He'd caught Ashley's gentle touch to Jason's hand as he'd left, how she eased the line on Jason's brow by saying she'd keep an eye on Lisa. But it wasn't that. Ashley brough out a part of him he didn't like. He tried to make this about protecting Jason, but it dug deep how much he wanted that touch of hers to be his.

He needed distance to straighten out his head and heart, and a hard ride on Midnight across the ranch was just the thing.

After his ride, Gabe headed for his office. The ride had done him no good. He'd enjoyed the firelight playing over Ashley's soft skin last night too much and he needed cooling down. That kiss they'd share left his body humming.

***

Gabe swore to himself. Jason always spoke about how close he and Ashley were, and Gabe assumed they were just good friends. He never imagined their feelings for each other had grown into something more and it was no doubt why she he'd come here.

Any other time, any other place, she would be good for Jason—help him move forward, but knowing she went into that kiss with Gabe…?

Caught in the light of the flickering flames, her blonde hair pulled back, her dainty ears and a long neck with smooth skin had been exposed last night. When she'd smiled, those incredible green eyes had lit up her face. He sighed, exhaling a long, trapped breath. Why the hell did he care? He rubbed the back of his neck. Okay, he knew exactly why he cared. Jason was vulnerable right now, and Gabe didn't want his brother played by her simply because he was grieving.

But there was a part of him that saw the lie there. He couldn't forget the feel of holding her and having her mouth against his, and it drove him into dark places because he knew if she offered a taste of her again, he might not turn her down.

And that made him what to Jason?

They'd all lost so much, and there he was, losing himself to kissing his brother's fiancée.

Again.

Damn, what was wrong with him? What was wrong with Ashley? She'd been Susan's best friend. Now she wanted to play both him and Jason. Why?

Gabe frowned, that last question burning so deep, and he picked up his phone a moment later and put a call through to his foreman. "Clay?"

"Yeah."

"Could you start a full background check on someone for me?" He wanted to know exactly how men Ashley had played around with and just how financially sound they'd been. Jason might have thought he knew her, but Gabe didn't. Yesterday had proven that.

Chapter 5

Ashley pulled on her favorite boots. Wearing jeans and a green sweater, she headed downstairs, ready to join Jason and Gabe for a night at Jake's. She found Jason in his office, working on his computer. "I'm ready for a beer." She took in Jason's green sweater and laughed. "You've got to be kidding. That?" She pointed at it.

Jason looked down. "This is my lucky sweater. I thought I should wear it in case we play pool." He glanced up at her and winked. "I'll win."

"You won't, cowboy. Come on." She headed to the door.

"Gabe'll meet us there." Jason shut his computer down and joined her.

"He hasn't offered to drive in case you want more than one beer?" Ashley grinned. She'd gotten a good sense of just how protective Gabe was of him.

"Hmm." Jason scratched at his head as they headed out. "I think he's taking this big brother thing a little too seriously lately. He's watching how many times I disappear with a bottle."

"Good." Ashley offered a soft smile. "Not such a bad thing, right?"

Jason grinned. "Nah, kind of love him for it, that he's here, you know."

Walking to the Tahoe, Ashley gave a long sigh. "I haven't been out for a burger and beer for a while. I'm looking forward to this." She gave him a sideway glance. "You know, I can still beat you at pool, lucky sweater or not."

"We may put that to the test if Jake's isn't full tonight." He opened the door for her then walked around to the driver's side.

As they drove through the valley, Jason glanced her way. "Thanks for stepping in with Lisa over finding a dress for the school dance."

"I enjoy spending time with her. And shopping's no hardship. I'm looking forward to seeing Cheyenne."

They pulled in front of a one-story building with a large cowboy statue at the front and a flashing light that said "Jake's" next to it. "This must be a popular place. The lot looks full." She helped Jason look for a parking space.

"They have great burgers and beer." Jason found a spot behind the building, and they walked in and joined a crowd looking for tables. Country music blared from speakers. "Let's hope Gabe got here first and found us a place to sit. This way." He grabbed her hand and led the way through the crowd, but she ran into Jason as he came to an abrupt stop.

"Sorry," she mumbled as she peered around him.

Gabe stood at a table with a beautiful brunette in his arms, a blonde standing nearby.

For a moment Ashley couldn't move, she couldn't breathe. She was back to watching her ex-husband shove clothes into a case as a car horn blared from their driveway. Throwaway lives, throwaway old brides for younger, slimmer models, ones parked out on her driveway and looking to stake a claim on her home as well as her husband.

Jason pulled her forward, startling her with the jolt. "Hi, Marilyn," he said to the brunette, then he turned briefly to Gabe, lifting his brows. "Gabe told me you moved to Colorado?" he said back to Marilyn.

Marilyn looked up at Gabe, giving him a sexy smile. "I did, for a while."

Gabe stepped back and gave Ashley a nod as he starred down at how she held Jason's hand. "Marilyn," he finally said, introducing the brunette before turning to the blonde. "Debra. This is Ashley Roberts. Ashley, Marilyn Daniel and Debra Cramer."

Shaking, trying to not let ghosts creep in, Ashley stepped forward and offered her hand. Both Marilyn and Debra smiled and shook it. "Nice to meet you both." Ashley nodded their way.

Marilyn seemed to watch her every move as Jason pulled out a chair for her. She took it, not understanding Gabe's whisper in Marilyn's ear as he pulled out a chair for her. The talk looked… intimate. Maybe she just read it wrong, but then she'd spent the end of her marriage questioning if it really was just her reading things…wrong. "Are you guys ready for burgers?" She worked at sounding upbeat.

Marilyn asked for a refill, holding her beer glass up to the server.

"Yeah, okay." Debra took keys from her bag. "That's me out, I'm afraid." She glanced at Marilyn. "Give me a call later."

"Sure." Marilyn settled as Debra left.

Jason ordered two beers as the server put one down in front of Marilyn.

"This is good beer." Marilyn lifted her glass toward Gabe in a toast, and in answer, Gabe picked up his beer and took a drink.

"Have you two already eaten?" Jason looked between them.

"No. I came in for a beer with Debra and ran into Gabe. He arrived a little before you did." Marilyn covered one of Gabe's hands with hers. "He invited me to stay for a while."

Okay, right. Ashley knew she'd not read that wrong. They were friends. Good friends.

Squeezing Marilyn's hand, Gabe gave her a sexy grin—right after looking at Ashley.

More than friends. She stiffened as Jason relaxed back in his chair, lifting his brows again, he seemed to give a gave Gabe a *what the hell?* glance before asking Marilyn, "So you're not living in Colorado?"

"Not anymore." Marilyn took another drink of her beer but still seemed too lost on Gabe.

"Where in Colorado did you live?" She didn't want to, but Ashley tried to keep it nice and so polite as the server approached with their drinks. But her head pounded with just which role Gabe had thrown her into. For years she'd hated the other woman hidden behind her husband's smile, yet here she was, sitting across from Marilyn as just that. Sickness raced her stomach.

Marilyn ignored her and quickly emptied her glass. "I'll take another." She passed the glass to the server.

"We should order food." Gabe tore his look off Ashley and glanced at Marilyn. "You ready to eat?"

"Sure, honey." She gave him a big smile before turning to Ashley.

Ashley wanted to point out her false nails and badly matched shoes for it. Petty, she knew, but she didn't understand what was going on here.

"I was in Denver," she said to Ashley, forcing her to remember she'd asked for the details. "Gabe helped me find a job there, but I didn't like it. I'm thinking of moving back to Sheridan." She leaned toward Gabe, offering everyone a view of her cleavage.

As they placed their burger orders, Ashley glanced at Gabe. He gave her a small smile and placed his arm around Marilyn's shoulders.

Jerk. She'd been nothing but a balm to ease his missing Marilyn.

She'd been stupid enough to fall for it too.

Not in this lifetime. "What kind of work do you do?" Ashley levelled a look on Marilyn, denying Gabe and his games.

Marilyn took another drink. "I manage an art studio."

"What type of art?"

"Contemporary." Marilyn gave Ashley a curt nod. "How did you two meet?"

Her question caught Ashley off guard. "Me and Jason? We went to school together."

"No." Marilyn scowled. "You and Gabe."

Ashley frowned at the aggressiveness. Then—*Oh God... boyfriend and girlfriend.* It really hit her. Marilyn had every right to be pissed off. Either he'd told her or she picked up how Gabe kept looking her way. Ashley glanced away for a moment, her heart fighting rounds of guilt versus anger versus *what the hell, Gabe*? "He's Jason's brother. Jason is husband to my late best friend," she said eventually. "It's called being family, which we are. *Close* family," She failed to stop her bite.

"Yeah? Gabe's never mentioned you beyond tonight."

Gabe snorted, and Ashley threw him a hard look as Jason placed his glass on the table.

"A friend. A damn good one to me and Susan." Jason kept his look on Marilyn, then shifted it to Gabe. "I mention her, and that's all that counts around here."

Gabe eased his hold off Marilyn and swiped at his nose before looking away. He didn't look too comfortable, and Ashley rubbed under the table at Jason's thigh, telling him it was okay. Jason stepped up to any fight, more so lately. But he didn't need this bullshit.

"You think we can eat without the attitude?" he added as the burgers were brought over.

Ashley and Marilyn ate in awkward silence despite the music, and Gabe and Jason seemed unable to settle as the occasional glance was thrown her way off Gabe. As Ashley wiped her lips and tossed her napkin on the table, wanting out and refusing to play whatever bit-on-the-side game Gabe thought he could get away with, Gabe pushed back his chair.

"Yeah, I've had enough too. I'm taking Marilyn home."

Marilyn waved him off. "I could use another beer. One for the road."

Gabe helped her from the chair. "I think you've had enough."

As she stood, she grabbed hold of his arm and fell into him with a smile. "Oh." She giggled. "Y'know, I think I prefer home now."

Ashley eased back on the anger. Marilyn had said nothing about the kiss or caused a scene beyond seeming to have the same trouble reading the awkwardness around the table. Maybe she was the innocent one in this despite how she rubbed her breast against Gabe's arm, flashing him a smile. "It was nice to meet you, Marilyn."

"Yeah, you, too." That sounded forced. "Good to see you again, Jason." That wasn't, and she reach over and roughed up his hair. "Little brother."

Jason eased the cowlicks she left behind and finally found a smile, "Yeah, yeah. Good to see you again, Marilyn. Not."

They headed off and Jason offered an awkward sigh as Gabe helped Marilyn stagger away. "Well, that was…Marilyn for you. She gets a touch possessive. Sorry."

Ashley couldn't watch them for too long. "Yeah. They seem…close."

"Never good news." Jason scowled. "Can't be a good sign she's back and slipping in his bed. She always brings out the worst in him."

Ashley snorted as Jason ran a hand through his hair. He emptied his glass. "Come on. Let's check the back, see if there's a pool table we can grab." As he stood, Jason called a greeting over to a young man who'd entered.

The man waved to Jason, then headed behind the bar where he grabbed the pretty blonde server and gave her a kiss before tying an apron around his waist. Ashley didn't move.

"You okay?" Jason touched her arm.

"Hm? I'm fine." Only she wasn't. It had just been a kiss, a fumble, but Gabe had used her until Marilyn slipped into his lap again. She hadn't recognized him tonight, which only hurt more because she'd wanted to know *more* about Gabe. Maybe it was the best her heart was tossed to the wayside now. She had the feeling the Gabe she'd met tonight would have shredded her completely somewhere down the line.

Chapter 6

The sun broke through the high clouds as the plane flew south. Ashley sat next to Gabe in the Cessna, Lisa behind her. The conversation had been minimum, and Ashley had pushed thoughts on Gabe as far away as possible for Lisa's sake. Relaxed, enjoying the flight, she leaned against the plane and peered down at the wide river. "This is a great way to travel."

For a moment Gabe didn't reply, then—"Private jets, they spoil lot of people." He turned a knob on the instrument panel then glanced at her. "You know what you need before you go home?"

That would be him trying to get rid of her all ready. Of course it would be. Ashley gave him a look. *Yeah, you come and tell me* exactly *what I need before I go, Gabe.*

He eased off, mostly as Lisa coughed from behind them, and he flicked her a look. "Sorry," Gabe murmured. "What I mean is learning to fly's a good way to see this part of the country."

Ashley shook her head at him. "I'll be sure to take lessons when I get home."

"Oh, go with Uncle Gabe." Lisa put a hand on her shoulder. "I'm learning. He's a good teacher."

Gabe winced and turned his head slightly. "That's because you're an excellent student, sweetheart."

"I love it." She leaned forward. "How much farther?"

"We're almost there." The plane banked to the left.

"This is gonna be great." She kissed at Gabe's cheek. "Thank you for taking us."

"My pleasure." He looked at Ashley. "How long are you here?" He asked, but the question seemed more of a complaint.

Ashley focused back outside. "I don't return to classes until fall quarter, but I plan to leave on the twentieth. It's Nathan and Kathryn's twenty-fifth anniversary and they're having a large celebration."

"No time for lessons, then. I wish you could stay longer," Lisa said.

Ashley reached up and squeezed her hand. "Me too, hon. But I'm just a call away."

The conversation stalled, and they continued in silence. She hadn't said anything about Marilyn in the car. Her place in this had been made clear. Gabe had kept to the same silence. But then when it came to talk on Gabe and Marilyn, she didn't want in on the glories Gabe had been parading last night. Some men were jerks, she just had a habit of bumpin into the worst of them.

Lisa leaned forward, breaking into her thoughts. "Look, we're almost there?" She pointed to the small airport straight ahead.

"Is that the runway?" Ashley gripped her seat. "It looks short."

Gabe frowned and he briefly brushed a touch to her arm before he pulled it away in the next breath. "It'll be okay." His tone was back to a more professional *I'm the pilot, you passenger*, but it only unsettled her more with his constant change that match the drops of turbulence that turned her stomach.

Ashley couldn't hide her shaking. "That's not where I flew into."

"No, this one is a private airstrip closer to downtown. Perfect size for the Cessna."

The plane slowed, and Gabe maneuvered the Cessna down onto the landing strip and pulled up along-side a metal building. She breathed a sigh of relief when he shut the engine down.

As he did the post-flight checklist, an airport worker came to them. Gabe opened his door once he was done and stepped onto the tarmac.

"Good to see you, Governor," said the man whilst Gabe did a final check around the smaller plane. "You got company this trip."

Ashley opened her door and got out, waiting for Lisa to follow.

"Yeah. How you doing, Bill?" Gabe shook the man's hand as Ashley and Lisa joined him. "We're here to do a little shopping. And you know I'm no longer governor, right?"

Bill tipped his cap. "Somethings just stick, sir." He turned and pointed to a sedan next to the small hangar. "Your vehicle's over there."

"Thanks." Gabe guided Ashley and Lisa to the car.

***

Lisa had added another shop to her list, which now made three dress shops and two shoe stores she wanted to visit, and Ashley buried a groan.

"Okay." As they headed downtown, Gabe seemed to bury one too. "Seems I'm chauffeur today. Where to, ladies?"

Lisa leaned over the seatback and punched his shoulder. "You're more than a chauffeur. You get to pay."

Gabe laughed. "Lucky me."

"In that case, let's try the dress shop on Ramsey and twelfth first."

Ashley eased into a grin, mostly for Lisa's sake, but then Gabe's glance at her made it pretty clear that's all he was doing: tolerating her too. There seemed a warning in there as well, one that warned her off hurting Lisa. She wasn't quite sure. But why would he think she'd hurt her?

His dark hair touched his collar, his square jaw formed an impeccably sculptured face, and his lips were full and sensuous, and all that played against his core, that *don't date the devil* side of him he'd exposed last night.

"We're almost there," he said, losing his smile.

She sighed.

This was going to be a very long day.

***

Lisa's excitement faded when she saw marketing at its worst: how lighting and a good photographer could make anything look good online, but see it on hanging in a shop? The dresses she'd sorted through weren't as good as they'd seemed. In the third shop, she looked through racks of formal wear, and Ashley tried to bring some of her fire back.

"What about one of these?" She held up a strapless simple black chiffon gown with a split on the left side of the straight, floor-length skirt. In the other hand, she held a taupe silk dress with a sweetheart bodice, empire waist, and a full, fluid skirt.

"Okay, let's try them," Lisa said less enthusiastic than when they began.

The sales lady had shown them to a large dressing room earlier, leaving Gabe seated by the mirrors, flipping through a magazine, attempting not to look bored.

Lisa tried the black gown first. Even though it was a beautiful dress, extensive alterations would be needed to fit her slim figure.

"Let's see how this one looks on you instead." Lisa stepped out of the gown and handed it to Ashley, then opened the dressing room door. The saleswoman came over from finishing with another customer, and Lisa turned to Ashley. "What size are you?"

"I haven't been invited to the dance," Ashley teased but gave the woman her size. She returned quickly and handed the dress to Ashley.

"Put it on while I try this silk one. I want to see what it looks like on someone else," Lisa said, her smile returning as she started to dress.

"All right." As Lisa undressed, Ashley stripped down and stepped into the gown, pulling it over her hips, which had widened over the years.

"Oh, honey" She caught Lisa in the mirror. "You look stunning." She adjusted the thin straps on Lisa's shoulders. "What do you think of it?"

Lisa turned from side to side, checking herself out in the mirror as she chewed on her bottom lip. It looked like a win. "Do you think Curtis will like it? I mean Michael."

Ashley placed a hand on her shoulder and laughed. "I'm positive both of them will love it."

Lisa turned back and forth several more times. "Maybe we should test out Dad's reaction on Uncle Gabe. Do you think he'll think it's okay?" she asked nervously, staring down at the scooped neckline.

Ashley tucked a strand of Lisa's long, auburn hair behind her ears. "Go out and show him what a gorgeous young woman you are."

While Ashley waited in the dressing room, Lisa rushed out. Ashley heard Gabe showering her with all the right compliments, and hearing his care when it came to Lisa had Ashley resting her head against the wall of the dressing room. For a while last night, it had felt good between her and Gabe. It had been too long since she'd let go and allowed herself to miss a man's touch, too long since she'd needed touching, and when she did…

Shaking her head, she reached for the zipper to remove the black gown before stopping to study the woman in the mirror.

Was she really only good enough nowadays for a one-night fumble away from the girlfriend?

"Ashley?" Gabe stood outside the dressing room, and his awkward tone shook her from her self-assessment. "Lisa is waiting to see your dress."

Lisa stuck her head around the door. "Come on. Show us. We'll wait for you in the back by the mirrors."

Ashley looked herself up and down in the mirror, then grabbed the brush from her purse and ran it through her hair before piling it high on her head and fastening it with an old clip she carried.

Gabe had taken her kiss. He wouldn't take her self-respect.

After adding fresh lipstick, she stood back from the mirror, then headed out.

Wearing her taupe dress, Lisa sat with Gabe in overstuffed chairs as the saleswoman stood next to him, staring down as he smiled at something she'd said. He chatted up someone else? Ashley stiffened and was ready to hide back in the changing room.

"Wow. You look great." Lisa got to her feet and started over, but Gabe was to his, holding her back.

"Yeah, that's..." Gabe scratched at his head as a soft smile touched his lips. "You look...stunning."

His look was far too intimate, and for a moment she was back in the library, his touch tracing her skin, her stomach fluttering in the low light as his breath brushed her neck. Maybe he was caught there too because he skimmed his fingers over her shoulder, pushing back the hair that had fallen from the clip.

Get out from under his touch. She needed to. It carried poison, and she swore she'd never be the other woman. A run of anger in Gabe's gaze didn't seem to ask her to be. He seemed as confused as her, and a shiver raced down to the small of her back.

"Yeah, you look good." A lot of sadness carried on his voice as he pulled away.

Lisa hugged her. "You're beautiful. Wish Dad could see you. He'd be speechless seeing her in this dress, wouldn't he, Uncle Gabe?

Gabe stepped away, seeming to want a wall between them. "I'm sure he would."

Anger bit into her. She hadn't known about Marilyn. She wasn't the cheat here, yet his fold of arms as he rested against the door called out otherwise. She wanted to bite back, call him out on it, but frowned and looked away in the next breath. Like it or not, he'd made her the other woman, just good for touching. Easy to leave after sex and get back to real family.

Only they hadn't had sex. He'd been a gentleman, backed away with just a kiss, just a....

She shook it off.

Cheating. It was still all cheating.

"Thanks, but I don't have a dance to attend," Ashley replied. One thing was for certain, she hadn't been the only one affected by that kiss. Gabe had too. That was fine by her. She could walk away knowing she'd gotten under his skin, that she irritated him enough to make him want to show off Marilyn in front of her. Gabe could make this all about him, but Ashley wasn't playing along.

"I think she should get it anyway, don't you, Uncle Gabe?"

Gabe shrugged. "It's up to her, sweetheart."

Ashley sighed and swiped at Lisa's cheek. "It's all about you today, hon." She flicked a look at Gabe. "Right?"

Gabe went to say something, then dug his hands in his pockets and nodded. "Yeah," he said gently to Lisa. "All about you."

***

On the way to the café, Lisa stopped on the sidewalk in front of a drug store, nearly bumping into Gabe and forcing him to bite back a curse. "Why don't you and Ashley go ahead and get a table. I want to run in here and get nail polish. I'll meet you there." She opened the door and headed on in, leaving Gabe standing there on the sidewalk.

"All right." He watched her go, then looked over at the restaurant, then at Ashley. "That's us two then." He pointed the way, wanting today over with.

Ashley turned away and pushed on through to the restaurant as if it was the quickest way out for her too.

As they reached the table, he eased a chair out for her more through routine over dining with a woman, and she sat, offering him a curt smile that called out she wasn't a…routine, she wasn't Marilyn, and like fining her own way into a restaurant, she didn't need her chair pulling out for her.

He'd been an asshole at Jake's. He knew that. There was nothing between him and Marilyn, but he'd wanted there to be last night, just to drive some of the hurt back into Ashley.

Ashley seemed to pick up on it. "Look, Gabe—"

"Not here." He took a seat opposite, his body language stiff and his grab of the menu rough, but he kept a hold on the anger with Lisa not being here. "Let's keep today about Lisa. We kissed, nothing more. Drop it. I have."

Ashley's slight frown called her hurt out. Well that sorted that, then. Kissed… nothing more. She picked up her menu, almost hiding behind it, and Gabe felt more of an asshole for how she forced him into a corner to get defensive.

"You should have told me about Marilyn." It came so quietly, and Gabe lowered his menu so slowly.

"*I* should have told *you* about—"

"Hey." Lisa came over and took her chair, tossing water on Gabe's fire on her, Jason, and the whole not telling him bullshit. "They didn't have the shade I wanted. I'll have to try another store."

God damn it. More shops? Gabe buried his look behind the menu but caught Ashley's eye. Brow raised, she bit at her lip, and for the first she held back a laugh that called out his "so today is all about Lisa, huh?" Gabe sighed softly, his stroke on the menu lost to the feel of her skin as she'd stood wearing that dress. "No doubt there'll be other stores, right?" he asked Lisa. "Better eat, then, build on stamina."

They placed their orders and handed over the menus as Ashley rubbed at her ankles. "It's good to slip my shoes off for a moment."

"Well, there are only two more shops to visit," said Lisa, thumbing through her phone. "I need perfume. That should save your feet."

Gabe hoped the service here was good. He was hungry, but he loved to see Lisa enjoying the normal things in life again. Losing her mom had been difficult. A young woman needed her mom at this time in her life. "All right, then. Cloe's next," he said.

"Are you still seeing Marilyn? Dad said she was at the bar with you guys." Lisa looked at the dish the server placed in front of her. She turned to Ashley as Ashley stilled in her seat. "She always smelled so nice."

Lisa wasn't Ashley. He wouldn't lie and dig into her over a kiss. Truth was his relationship with Marilyn had ended several months ago, and he wasn't interested in starting anything with her again. But Lisa liked Marilyn, they got on well, and Lisa had lost enough in her life. Her eyes seemed a little more alive at the thought she was back on the scene. And there he was, caught by the lie. He couldn't take Marilyn away from her, not with how she frowned at how long it was taking him to answer.

"She's around for a while," he said gently. "Why don't you meet up and ask her for tips on perfume?"

Lisa brightened at the idea, and Ashley lowered her gaze, which got under Gabe's skin more. Had she needed to hear something different? What right had she to expect something different? She was the cheat. No matter how Gabe wished he'd been the one holding Ashley's hand at Jake's, she was Jason's. Her reactions, the jealousy he'd forced out of her, it said she didn't love Jason, and Jason had been through enough. They all had, and for her to step into Susan's high heels and find she wasn't happy with the fit no matter how pretty she looked… Gabe shook his head and finished up his meal.

Lisa took a sip of her iced tea. "We having dessert?" she asked, looking from Ashley to him. Before they could respond, Lisa said, "That's a yes." She swallowed her last bite of sandwich and leaned over to Ashley. "We'll have dessert, then go on to Victoria's Secret. I saw online last night they're having a sale." She checked out the dessert menu and ordered a chocolate lava cake. "We might find some good buys there, and I need a new bra to wear with my new dress."

"I can never turn down a sale." Ashley ordered cheesecake, then offered alook at Gabe.

"Cheesecake," he said over to her. When dessert arrived, Gabe concentrated on the table and eating. This morning, he'd seen Jason leave Ashley's room looking like he'd spent the night apologizing over and over again for not being able to be with them today. That meant they'd spent the night together. A small part of him hated how he wished he'd been the one walking out her door, and the whole implications of that made him lose his appetite. If Jason found out he'd kissed Ashley... Gabe wiped a hand over his face. He felt wrung out and forced a smile. "Are we fortified for the afternoon?"

"I need to hit the restroom." Lisa stood and reached for her purse, then helped pull Ashley's chair back.

As Gabe watched them go, he took a sip of his coffee. He wanted someone to share his life, but had never found a woman who wanted to live on a ranch in northern Wyoming. Or a woman who wanted *him*, and not the Coulter name or money.

After he'd left Jake's with Marilyn, they'd stood outside her apartment and he'd made it clear to her there was nothing between them and suggested she give Denver a few more months. The job he'd helped her get was an excellent start if she was serious about art. He should tell Ashley, stop the digs under her skin, but...

But?

He shifted uncomfortably and his foot caught something under the table. A small paper bag lay on the floor between Lisa and Ashley's chairs. Frowning as he tried to pick it up, the bag slipped away, revealing what had his inside.

A *pregnancy test?*

He turned the small box over and over in his hand as his mind rushed through several possibilities until he quickly replaced the test in the bag as Ashley and Lisa came back to the table.

He stared at them, wondering which one to address. "This must have fallen from your purse." He held the bag out between them.

Lisa's face reddened, and Ashley reached for the bag. "Thank you," she said, dropping it into her purse.

Gabe didn't react. With all of his soul, he tried so hard not to react.

***

The small town of Willow River and the Coulter Creek Ranch were approximately three-hundred miles northwest of Cheyenne. During the flight home, an early spring storm blew in, and even avoiding it as pilots were trained to do, Gabe felt the edge of the storm wind lift the Cessna, twisting and releasing it as crosswinds whipped at the small plane. Gabe held it steady as they touched down on the ranch's narrow runway, conscious of Ashley's fear of flying. He wouldn't play games over her natural fears Once they pulled into the hangar, Ashley breathed a sigh of relief and Gabe gently brushed his hand over hers, grounding her.

"Planes have radar for a reason," he said gently as they unbuckled, anxious to plant his feet on solid ground. "You were safe. It was just a tailwind."

"We just beat the rain too." Lisa muttered, waiting for him to gather their purchases from the aircraft.

As they headed for the Tahoe, large drops of water splashed the ground around them.

"This could turn to snow, especially higher up." He glanced at the darkened sky as he shifted the SUV into gear and pulled out on to the main road. Keep it mind when you go to the cabin. As they were driving back, a call came through and he clicked Answer on the steering wheel.

"Gabe?" Jason covered his cellphone. Muffled voices drifted over from his end, then—"I'm in Chicago with Susan's mother. Remember I said I'd catch up with her?"

Gabe went to speak but Jason beat him to it.

"I'm gonna stay here a few days more, She needs help. Can you let the kids know, and tell Ashley sorry?"

Gabe flicked her a look. "Will do," he managed before Jason cut the call. The tension running Ashley's shoulders had eased since being on the road, but considering she'd just heard Jason was going to be gone a few more days, she offered over nothing but a tired smile that said she understood.

She carried the same look of his wife in the later stages: listening, yet not.

Maybe it was tiredness from the trip that she didn't seem bothered Jason had called him and not her, or maybe she really didn't care about Jason beyond friends and had forgotten to send Jason the memo.

Gabe shook his head, keeping his attention fixed firmly on the road ahead.

***

Ashley tossed her purse and the bag from Victoria's Secret on her bed, then walked to the balcony door. Rain pounded the roof and a mood swept over her as she wondered what the weather was like in Cincinnati.

A light tap on her door brought her out of her head. "Come in."

Lisa entered, her gaze avoiding Ashley's. "I didn't know how to tell you," she said before sitting on the bed. "I picked up the test on the way to lunch and didn't realize it fell from my purse. Thank you for not saying anything to Uncle Gabe."

Ashley took the test from her purse. "Here you go." She wondered what the hell Gabe was thinking and if he wondered if *she* was pregnant. And what about Lisa? If she'd hidden this from Gabe, did that mean Jason didn't know as well?

Lisa buried her head in her arms. "What if I'm having a baby?"

Tears. They were so unusual from Lisa, and Ashley went and sat by her and tugged her in close. "Is this your first test?"

She nodded and wiped at her eyes.

"How late are you?" Ashley brushed her hand over Lisa's hair.

"About a week," she whispered.

"Could it be all the excitement surrounding the spring dance and the rest of your senior year? Stress?" Grief?

Lisa shrugged and stared down at the test. "I'll take it later."

"I'm here if you feel like talking, you know that, right?"

Lisa gave Ashley hold a squeeze. "I know. I'm so glad you're here."

"Have you told anyone? Michael? Cody?"

She shook her head. "I think Cody suspects something's up, but he's being a Coulter: watching Michael a little too closely."

Ashley sighed and nodded. "Where's your brother anyway?"

Lisa gave a sniff. "Off riding with Thomas, I think."

Best place for him, all things considered.

Chapter 7

Ashley sat on her bed, looking out at the gray sky as Abby talked about her history class. They'd been on the phone for about half an hour. Listening to her chatter, Ashley wondered if it was because the professor was a young man. "Is he good looking?" she asked.

"Professor Wilson? Yeah, very. He's meeting us tonight at that little pub I told you about."

A knock came on her door, and Lisa shot it a look, thinking Lisa needed to talk. "I need to go. I'll call you tomorrow. Don't forget to make time for studying."

"Okay, Mom. Bye."

Ashley went over and opened the door. "Oh… Gabe."

He stood there, wiping at his jaw.

"Is something wrong?" Something must have been because he seemed to have forgotten he'd been giving her the coldshoulder all day. She stumbled for a moment, not wanting to ask him in, but whatever was wring had him dropping any arrogance and glancing uneasily down the hall.

He pushed past her, not waiting for an invitation, and Ashley shrugged. "Well come in."

"What?" He glanced back at her, but didn't really see her. "Jason's not here. I need your help." He stopped by the French doors and stared out at the rain, then turned and ran his hand through his hair. "Cody's friend, Thomas. He called. They were on horseback, Cody's colt got spooked, and Cody slid down a hillside and landed on a ledge."

"*What?*" Ashley went over. "Is he hurt?"

"No, just stranded. But the hillside's muddy and he can't get a foothold. Thomas's parents are gone for the day, and with this storm, the threat of snow, I can get out there faster than anyone else. Once we have the boys safe, could you drive them to the cabin? It's close to where they are. Cody can show you the way while I bring the horses back." Gabe ran a hand through his hair again. "I… I think Cody would respond better to you than he would to a ranch hand pulling him out. The kid gets embarrassed, and the ranch hands are, well… ranch hands. They'll rib him enough for it."

Ashley eased into a soft smile. Yeah, this what she'd liked about Gabe. "Of course."

"Did you bring a coat?"

Ashley's gaze went to the closet of lightweight sweaters and the one thin jacket. "No."

His gaze swept over her head to toe. "Check with Lisa. She might be able to find something."

His frown deepened as he looked out the balcony door. "Storm's worsening. We should get a move on." He hurried back to the hallway.

"Go, do what you need to do." She followed him out the door and headed toward Lisa's room. "I'll be down in a minute,"

"Meet me in my office," Gabe said as he went downstairs.

***

Wearing one of Lisa's wool sweaters, a pair of her fleece-lined boots, and carrying a coat, gloves, and stocking cap, Ashley walked into Gabe's office with Lisa behind her.

"No, no, Clay. There's no need for you to rush up. I know where they are and neither one is hurt. Ashley's driving them to the cabin while I get the horses back." Gabe looked up, lifting a hand, indicating he'd be only a minute. "The men have a full day tomorrow. I want that west pasture readied." He paused. "I appreciate your offer."

As soon as Gabe cradled the receiver, Lisa went over. "I could drive the Tahoe."

He gave her a strained smile as he stood. "I know you could, sweetheart, but I want you to call your dad. Let him know what's going on. If we get cell service, I'll have Cody call him from the cabin and Thomas can call his parents. Meanwhile, you call and tell them what happened, that Thomas is fine and will be home tomorrow."

Ruth came in behind Ashley and handed them a bag of sandwiches and two thermoses, one filled with coffee, the other with hot cocoa for the boys. "Let me know if I need to put anything else on for when you get home tomorrow." Ruth brushed a hand at Ashley's arm, but her concern stayed with Gabe.

"Will do." Gabe slipped on his coat and came over. "We'll keep in touch." He kissed at Lisa's head, then Ashley followed him out.

The wind and rain hammered the Tahoe as Gabe drove north on the dark county road. "You mentioned the cabin. Were the boys riding there after checking out the campground?" Ashley searched the landscape through the heavy rain.

His attention on the road, Gabe shook his head. "I thought they were riding back tonight. There's a small canyon that's a favorite camping spot for the scouts. But from there, it's a nice ride on horseback to the cabin." His shoulders stiffened.

She wondered what he'd do if she reached over and took his hand like he always seemed to do with her and her stress and fears, but she closed her eyes and his hold on Marilyn was all she could see.

A gust of wind caused the car to swerve, and Ashley jerked.

"Damn." Gabe handled the jolt to the car. "The wind is getting stronger. It's not much farther to the turnoff."

"Easy. We'll get there."

Gabe leaned back into his seat, forcing calm. The rain had turned to snow, and he took a deep breath, his concern with Cody and the drop in temperature. "I don't know this Thomas well, but Cody's been goofing off at school. Thomas said they were playing around."

"And? That's what young people do. Take risks."

The car slowed as the wind whirled the snow, making it difficult to see.

"I told Jason he shouldn't have let them ride out there alone. They should have waited for their entire troop." He leaned forward. "At times I've been giving him more leeway but..."

"But you love him," she said. "You're doing fine. You know that, right? You're going to struggle with how best to help him and Lisa, not to mention Jason, but you're still grieving too. Susan was a big part of all your lives."

Gabe kept his gaze on the falling snow, which covered the hood of the Tahoe. "Lisa has her own worries, doesn't she?" He sighed. "That pregnancy test was hers."

Ashley shot him a look.

Gabe snorted. "She went into the drug store, not you." He gave her a quick glance.

She nodded. "I'm sure she didn't want you to know."

"Has she talked to you since? Did you know?"

Ashley didn't answer right away. This was dangerous territory. "Not until you did. She'll talk to everyone when she's ready. Just give her space, okay?"

The Tahoe slowed and made a right turn onto a dirt road heading into the trees. The wind eased somewhat, but the snow was still falling. Covered in snow, the landscape presented an eerie ghostlike appearance. Moments later, the road ended.

"We'll have to hike from here." Gabe pulled to the side of the road. "Let's take what we can. We'll have to stay at the campsite for the night." He surveyed their surroundings, but the snow made visibility almost impossible.

"Sorry. I didn't think the snow would be this bad when we left. I thought you could drive the boys to the cabin, and I could bring the horses along. The cabin would be a much better place to wait out this storm." He placed two bags on the ground. "I thought we could drive closer to the campsite," he said as he threw a rope over his shoulder. "We better move fast."

***

Covered in white, the picturesque campsite sitting in the middle of rough country could've been a picture postcard. A circle of rocks for a fire sat in a small clearing on the shore of a wide stream and tucked back from the clearing near an overhang stood a woodshed.

As two horses whinnied from by a tree, Thomas ran over, stopping Ashley in her tracks. "Cody's not hurt, but I can't get him up." Breathing hard, heavy, Thomas blew warmth into his hands. "I couldn't find anything for him to hold on to so I could pull him up the hillside." He looked at the rope Gabe had over his shoulder. "That'll do it."

They dropped the bags by the horses and headed to Cody. Gabe took the rope and wrapped it around a large boulder, then lay on his stomach. "Hey, buddy. How you doing?"

"Gabe?" Thomas's voice drifted up. "I'm okay, but I'm freezing."

Gabe tossed the rope down. "Grab it and tie it tight around your waist, then hang on. Be careful." He glanced over his shoulder at Ashley and Thomas.

She nodded and wrapped her arms around Thomas, trying to get warmth into him too. "We'll get you back soon."

He nodded, seeming unable to move.

"Hey, I think Gabe may need a hand, though," she said softly. Keeping Thomas moving was better than anything she could do. "Go help, okay? Stay away from the edge."

Thomas jerked to life. "Right." He was tired, cold, and losing concentration. She needed to get both boys under some cover.

***

Fighting the swirling snow, Gabe and Thomas pulled Cody up, Gabe needing to grab at the back of his jeans to hurl over the ridge.

"I'm okay." Cody tried to get to his feet. Mud streaked his hands, face, and clothes, and he slipped, snarling as he grabbed at his ankle.

"Easy," Gabe said as he reached to check it out.

"I said I'm good." Cody shoved him away and got to his feet. "You're not my dad. Back off."

Gabe stood and eased off with all the hurt pride coming his way. God, he'd been right to bring Ashley and not any of the ranch hands. "Take it easy, kid."

Cody stood with his hands stuffed under his arms, and Ashley came over with a blanket. She'd already wrapped Thomas up. After unfolding it, Gabe went swung it over Cody's shoulders.

"I said I'm good." Cody went to shove it off, but Gabe pulled it tight around him, then tugged him in.

"Yeah, you're good, tough kid." Gabe rubbed at his back. "Not the first time you fell from a horse either, it just hurt a little more this time, huh?"

For a moment Cody fought against him, trying to pull away. Then he dipped his head to Gabe's shoulder.

"I know," Gabe breathed gently. "It's okay, bud." He pulled back and patted Cody's arms and legs, then turned his hands where there were a few bright red scratches. "No major damage, come on. Let's get you in some shelter."

***

They'd brought fresh clothes and a pile of blankets for the shed, and as Cody ate, huddled inside one, Gabe settled the horses beneath the overhang out of the fierce wind as Thomas slept in a sleeping bag at the back.

As Gabe turned his collar up to the wind and reached the shed door, voices drifted out from inside. Ashley's.

"You sure you're all right?"

"Yeah. I'm okay." With the adrenaline fading. Cody sounded as tired as Gabe felt.

"I didn't mean to take it out on Uncle Gabe."

Gabe snorted a smile. He knew that.

"Sometimes we say things we don't mean." Through the cracks in the shed door, Ashley rubbed at Cody's leg. "He loves you."

Cody nodded, his head dipped a little too much. "He's been there for us since Mom…Mom…"

"From what I've seen, he's always going to be there for you," Ashley shifted and Cody looked up. "Especially through the rough. He's a good man when it comes to family."

Gabe frowned. She knew what to say at the right moment, what to leave out, like how he'd flaunted Marilyn in front of her. She could have used that here to get Cody on her side, but she said nothing. She had a heart when it came to the kids. He wished she'd used had the same when it came to him and Jason.

"Get some sleep" she said to Cody. "I'm going nowhere either. If you need to talk about school or anything else, I'm here for you."

Gabe pulled his hat lower. "Damn," he muttered. He took a deep breath and entered the shed, stamping his feet inside the doorway. "The horses are out of the wind."

Cody settled over by Thomas, and Ashley tugged a blanket around her shoulders and took a bite of her sandwich. "Come and get something to eat. The boys have devoured almost all of them."

With nowhere left to sit but by her, Gabe settled and picked up the other half of her sandwich. The boys used the two sleeping bags Gabe had brought, and he and Ashley were left with a thin bedroll and blanket. He looked down at the bedding spread out on the wooden floor. Wind howled through the cracks between boards put together to protect firewood from the elements, not people.

He didn't like what it signified, but he was too tired to care. "That wind isn't letting up and the temperature's dropping. We're best under there together."

Ashley stopped eating and cocked a brow.

"You keep to your side. I'll keep to mine." He held her look. "You can manage that, right?"

Holding his look, Ashley got up and wrapped the blanket around her more tightly, then she went and lay down, her back to him saying *you do that. Manage.*

***

Silence played around them too heavily as Ashley stared at the shed wall. The cold seeped through it, and giving a rough sigh, she turned over, trying to put it behind her. Gabe sat next to her holding the thermos, his half-eaten sandwich on the edge of the makeshift bed.

He glanced down before taking a sip of hot coffee. "I'm sure this isn't what you bargained for, huh? Being stuck out here."

"Not exactly what I had in mind, no."

"Spring's a better time to visit." He sounded as awkward as Ashley felt. "This year winter doesn't want to let go."

"No worries. I wanted to get away to work on the grant proposal and spend time with Jason and the kids."

Gabe put down the thermos and took the last bite of his sandwich. "Whatever." And there, he was back to being an asshole. "Get some rest."

She scooted farther beneath the blanket and shivered. The cold from outside matched Gabe's, and she was caught in the middle of both. Sleep seemed impossible, but She closed her eyes.

"You really should have told me about Marilyn," she murmured softly.

Gabe tugged the covers up over his shoulder, and she stiffened when he stretched out beside her.

"We both have our secrets, right?" Sadness played his voice. "Might be best to keep them that way. Jason's gonna be mad enough that I dragged you out here."

His warmth soaked into her, and she forced her body to relax into it. Secrets. That was his warning for him not to say anything to

Marilyn. He hadn't told her. So there she was, his…secret. Didn't all politicians have them, locked deep in their closet? Maybe she was one in a long list of others.

Screw that came to mind, but sleep pulled her under.

Chapter 8

As daylight broke through the cracks in the doorframe, Gabe woke and wiped a hand over his face.

A soft breath brushed his neck, and he shivered into it. The hold across his chest felt just as light, as war and—he stiffened.

Ashley huddled close at his side, her arm across him, and his return hold keeping her close as he lay on his back. His first instinct was to shove her off, his second to take a moment to stare at her without all the complications. Long lashes, a small turned-up nose, parted lips, and as she shifted slightly in sleep, the scent of lavender and winter invaded his whole body. Her skin was soft and warm, and he brushed a strand of hair from her lips even though anger still burned deep. She always seemed to be fighting to tame it.

Ashley stretched into him, her soft mumble catlike in comfort, then she opened her eyes. Stilled.

"What the hell are you doing?" She pushed back and her eyes widened as she caught her own touch to Gabe's chest. "What the hell am I doing?" She tugged the blanket up, keeping a divide between them, but it was her look that told him to back off.

"Pity you didn't react the same that night I kissed you, huh?" Gabe raised his hands, needing that divide as well.

She lowered her look at him. "What's that supposed to mean?"

"I dunno, you tell me what's it supposed to mean? What's going on with you, Ashley?"

"*Me?*" She looked him up and down. "You're the one hooked up with one woman yet needing to charge your battery with another.

That's cheating. You made me a cheat right along with you. Marilyn doesn't know, does she?"

"*Marilyn*?" Gabe laughed, hard, then groaned and got to his feet. "I kissed you, that was my mistake. But you, kissing me back? letting me touch you…?"

"What?" Ashley threw his hat at him. "So you touching me is *my* fault all of a sudden?"

"No, it's both of ours, but it seems I'm the only one feeling any damn guilt over it." Cody groaned from under his covers, and Gabe cut all the animosity dead. "For his sake, Lisa's—Jason's, you drop whatever you're playing at." He shook his head at her. "They've lost enough. We all have."

She went to say something, but he left, slamming the shed door behind him. He needed to get away from her. He needed to stay away. He needed the cold wind to chill his head and maybe, just maybe take away the feel of how damn good Ashley had felt up against him, all her fire and ability to get at… under his skin. Again.

Christ. He took off his hat and ran a hand through his hair.

The last time he hadn't known she was Jason's. But back there, under the covers—he had. He'd still touched, if only to get that damn strand of hair away from her lips.

He didn't like where she was taking him when it came to Jason.

***

Ashley closed her eyes and dropped back into the covers. She felt like an idiot. No, she felt like she'd found something good in life, but it came with big-ass teeth and a vicious smile to boot for being stupid enough for *thinking* she could find some good to hold on to. Why did she always choose the assholes?

She curled farther into the bedroll and immediately regretted it. Evergreen and Gabe's musk scented her skin, and a tear slipped down her cheek over how she tried to see if she could catch Marilyn's scent hidden beneath it. Is this what she'd been reduced too? Hating…liking him being near? Catching stray moments before he found Marilyn again? Hating Marilyn. Hating herself?

The wind continued to howl around the shed, and as the air rushed between the boards at her feet, she groaned and shook it all away. She needed to check on the boys on the other side, but the shed was too cold to get out from under the blanket. She forced her mind to focus on something else. Lisa crept in. Ashley hoped she could be a loving sounding board while Lisa navigated the possibility of a pregnancy without her mother by her side.

The door opened, and she turned, raising her head as Gabe entered. Snow covered him from head to toe, with heavy droplet soaking his hair. "You must be frozen," she said before she realized how softly she'd spoken.

He didn't look over. "It's letting up. The snow'll stop soon. We'll be able to go home."

Back to short, blunt statements. It sounded like he was at a meeting, reading out the minutes and counting down the time. Perhaps it was the best way forward. "How are the horses?" Ashley groaned inwardly.

He shrugged. "They'll be all right." He removed his hat and gloves and shook off the snow.

"Here." She offered over the thermos. "There's a little coffee left."

"Thanks." He took it and poured the coffee into the lid. "I'll check the boys." He drained the cup, then made his way between the stacks of wood, then came back a moment later. "They're asleep. Best to let them stay that way for a while." He didn't sound so mechanical, but then it was talk on Cody. Family. "It's not so drafty back there."

He looked down at her as if wondering what to do.

"Take the blanket, Gabe." She didn't give him much room to refuse. "You're froze."

He didn't move for a moment, his look going to the door, to her, back to the door. Then he shook the snow off, dried himself down with a shirt, then sat opposite her, no blanket taken.

Stubborn ass. Ashley eased back down, her look on the rafters to the shed. They didn't talk as the sun rose higher, warming the shed. But that was okay with her. She really wasn't in the mood for much when it came to Gabe.

***

The cold bit into Ashley as Gabe saddled one of the horses. Sunlight glistened off the snow, turning the landscape into a glistening wonderland, and Ashley left Gabe to it as she drove off toward the ranch.

When she pulled the SUV up to the ranch house, Lisa and Ruth were already standing on the porch, waiting.

"Everything okay?" Lisa skidded to a stop by the car. "Where's Uncle Gabe?"

"He's bringing the horses." Cody crawled out of the back seat, and Ashley got out to join them.

"You sure you're okay?" Lisa looked Cody over. A scratch ran across his left cheek.

"He will be." Ruth placed her arm around Cody's shoulders. "Come inside. Let me make sure that's clean, then I'll fix you a nice breakfast." She smiled at Ashley. "I bet you're hungry? I know Gabe will be when he gets back."

"Not for me. I need to get home." Thomas spoke softly from the rear seat.

"It's not much farther. I'll go with you," Lisa said, climbing in the front as Ashley slipped back into the driver's seat.

Cody turned to the car and leaned over. "Call you later."

Thomas nodded. "Make sure you do."

They pulled up in front of Thomas's home, and his mother was beside the Tahoe before Thomas got out. She wrapped her arms around him, then looked down at Ashley. "Thank you for getting him back safely. I hope Cody's okay."

"He is." Ashley gave her a warm smile, glad to see Thomas back in safe hands as well.

"C'mon, you." Thomas's mother tugged at his arm. "In."

Ashley sent them a wave as she backed out. She got a feeling Lisa had come with her for a reason.

"You okay?" she asked softly.

Watching Thomas and his mom disappear inside, Lisa shook her head. Even with the chill, she looked pale. "The test was positive. I'm scared but made a doctor's appointment for next week. Will you go with me?"

"Of course." Ashley stopped the car and reached for Lisa, tugging her in close.

"I'm so scared. I'm not saying anything to anyone until after the appointment."

"It might be a good time to tell your dad."

"No." She shook her head quickly. "I don't want to add any more to his worries. I'll tell him if the doctor confirms I'm pregnant, but please don't say anything to him yet."

"All right." Ashley squeezed her shoulders. "Your decision, sweetheart. It has to be."

Chapter 9

Fog hung low over the valley as Gabe worked in his office, preparing for his trip to Cheyenne. Jason had returned the evening before and gave a light knock on the office door before coming in and offering over a forced smile. "You checking in with Senator Stanton today?"

Gabe nodded. "I hope to see him, yep."

"Good, because I wanted a chat, mostly to say thanks for being there for Cody and getting him back safely."

Jason sat down opposite, and Gabe tensed. Mostly? What else was there? Had Ashley finally come clean and told him about their kiss? "No chat or thanks needed when it comes to Cody and getting him back safely. You know that."

Jason nodded. "So what's going on with you and Marilyn?" He gave Gabe a long look over. "I was surprised to see her at Jake's. Is she moving back to Wyoming?"

Gabe leaned back in his chair, trying to ease the tension in his shoulders. "Marilyn wants to come back. But I made it clear I'm not interested."

"Didn't look like it at Jake's."

Gabe winced. "I'd had a rough few days with…flying. This was afterwards." He shrugged. "She'll stick with the job in Colorado. She's serious about art." He ran a hand through his hair. "But she's sworn off the beer. She had too much to drink."

Jason laughed. "So did Ashley. After you two left, she and I played a couple games of pool, and she had a few more beers. That's so unlike her." He crossed one knee over the other. "Something's bothering her. I tried to get her to talk about it the next morning, but she kept saying everything was fine."

Gabe needed to distract. "Could it be her ex-husband? her daughter?"

"I don't think so."

"So why not ask her?" Gabe brushed a thumb at his lip, needing to test a few things out here. "You're close, right? Doesn't she usually talk to you?"

"Yeah. We talk about everything. She's great." His smile was a private one. "I don't know what I would've done without her when Susan died. She's just not talking over this."

When it cane to cheating, not many did. "So someone like her would be a good match for you, then?" *Just tell him you kissed her, Gabe. Go on.*

"Yeah, the best of."

Christ. Gabe briefly closed his eyes. He needed to back off, leave it alone. Let Jason find some peace even if Ashley would break his heart down the lone with someone else. He just couldn't let it be him who destroyed Jason.

Jason looked at his watch. "Gotta go and get back to sorting accounts for our accountant. Let me know what happens in Cheyenne." He rose and left him alone.

Heaving a rough sigh, Gabe walked to the window. The fog was lifting, and by the time Clay got to the hangar, it should be clear enough for take-off.

He needed the break away from here.

***

Clay weaved the car through the capitol, and Gabe eventually entered the building to find the senators arguing their way through several bills before they'd vote on any of them.

He headed for a lounge as a young woman brought in a carafe of coffee and placed it in the center of a small table. His mind bounced from the senators to Jason and Ashley. He needed a stiff drink along with his time away as he reached for the hot coffee.

"Ex-Governor Coulter, what are you doing in town?"

Gabe looked up as Valerie Hinton waved his way as she weaved her way through the diners. She worked as a congressional aide to one of the junior senators, and Gabe remembered her from a museum fundraiser he'd attended a few months back.

"Val, good to see you again." Gabe stood as she reached the table. She grabbed a cup from a nearby tray, and then sat opposite him as Gabe retook his seat. "Are you waiting for the vote too?"

"Yes, but it may be some time. We don't expect a vote on the Land-Use Bill until tomorrow at the earliest." She gave Gabe a sexy smile. "I presume that's the one you're interested in."

"It is. I'd like to get a feel for how things are going, so how are you up for some dinner tonight? You look rushed." Since he and Marilyn had broken up, he hadn't gone out with anyone, and it seemed he needed the company along with a stiff drink and time away. "I hate to dine alone."

Valerie laughed before taking a sip from her cup. "When did Gabe Coulter ever have to dine alone? And I am rushed. It'll be good to catch up one a few things." After scooting her chair away from the table, she reached into her handbag, took out a card, and placed it next to his cup. "Pick me up at eight," she said as her phone rang. "I gotta take this, sorry." She walked away, almost lost to the crowd again.

Gabe watched her walk away. Nice body, and from what he'd heard, she had a solid reputation as an excellent aide. Normally, the idea of dining with a pretty woman would've put him in a better mood, but it wasn't working this time. He felt lousy over how he'd treated Ashley when it came to Marilyn. He felt even worse for using Marilyn. But Jason was his brother, and that just brought the whole shit storm back on how he felt lousy over Jason too. He more than needed Val's distraction.

***

It didn't work. Dinner with Valerie had been good, but not enough to take Gabe's mind out of the mess. They talked politics and little else, and Gabe knew he was the reason the evening was flat.

The next morning, he was back in the senate chambers, no happier than he'd been the day before. Senator Stanton had been called away on a family emergency, delaying the vote on the Land-Use Bill for at least another week. As people came and went, Gabe paced the senate chamber's marble floor, wondering why Stanton hadn't called him personally. Was something going on with Bob he didn't know about?

Otis Cummings, Stanton's right-hand man, hadn't given Gabe any more information than what was in the message to the committee, which left Gabe wondering if there was something more going on with his old friend than what Otis was willing to say.

As for senators who made up the committee, he considered where they stood. He knew most politicians put their careers first and their constituency second. The longer they were in power, the more blurred the line became between personal ambition and representing the people in their districts.

As he left the capitol building, heavy raindrops patted his face. He looked up into a dark sky thick with clouds ready to light the city with a storm. Then something else caught his eye.

In the parking lot across the street, two men in dark suits shook hands before one of them got into the back of a long gray sedan that sped away as the rain poured down. Gabe had gotten a good look at the two men, and his heart sank a little.

As he reached the sidewalk, Clay pulled up alongside him. "Looks like you got a little wet." Clay, an ex-military intelligence officer, had been with Gabe for six years. He'd come aboard as an assistant when Gabe was in the Governor's mansion and had proven to be a loyal friend. He worked exclusively for the Coulters as ranch manager and as Gabe's right-hand man.

Gabe didn't bother to respond. He buckled up, then opened his briefcase and pulled out paper and pen. "We have work to do, my friend."

Clay lifted his brows. "Something's going on in connection with Land Bill Four-Eighty-Two?"

"Yeah. I think so." Gabe pulled out his phone. "I just saw Sam Frasier's foreman with a man who I think is from Evans Development." He snapped his briefcase closed. "Let's head for the airport. We're going home if this storm isn't too bad." Gabe punched in Valerie's number and looked across at Clay while the phone rang. "I want to meet with the ranch's attorney."

Last night, Gabe had learned Valerie was a congressional aide to Senator Earl Gilbert. It'd never occurred to him to question how a junior senator had gotten on the Land Development Committee. Given the current climate, he figured Gilbert must have important backers.

"Valerie, it's Gabe. I'm wondering if Senator Gilbert heard why the committee meetings have been postponed."

"The only information we have is the chairman, Senator Stanton, had been called away for a family emergency and meetings would resume next week." She paused. "Did you hear differently?"

"No, Otis said the same. Didn't get to speak with Bob."

"Sorry. That's all the information we got."

"Thanks." He hung up.

Clay narrowed his eyes. "Something bothering you? You were awfully quiet on the flight down. Hell, you've been acting strange for over a week."

"A lot on my mind lately." He left it at that.

Clay laughed. "That's it?" He glanced at Gabe as he pulled up to the private air terminal.

Gabe nodded. "Need to work through a few things. Let's run a background check on Max Banks, High Mountain's foreman."

"Will do. I'm almost done with Miss Roberts."

Gabe nodded. "This one first, okay?"

***

After arriving at the ranch, Gabe and Clay drove into Willow River and sat across a rosewood desk from Albert Gallagher. Gallagher managed land issues for many of the ranchers in the valley and Gabe's father had chosen him for Coulter Creek more than thirty years ago. Today Al Gallagher no longer resembled the man of his youth. He leaned back in his chair after a quick review of the file Gabe had presented.

"Well, son, it looks like you have a problem." Al's voice boomed, the one part of him that hadn't diminished with the rest of his body.

"So, we're correct?" Gabe asked.

Al leaned forward and placed his forearms on the desk. "I'd say you boys hit it right on the head. Sam Frasier is in real financial trouble, and with the gambling debts he's piled up lately, it looks like the situation might get worse." The old attorney shook his head. "Poor Sam. Got himself a bad habit. You boys think that foreman of his is seeing to things on Sam's behalf?"

"Could be. Is there any chance Sam could lose High Mountain?" The Frasiers had been in the valley as long as the Coulters, but Gabe's dad used to talk about Sam's inability to manage his land and had hoped his only child, Megan, would grow up to be the cattlewoman her mother had been, thus keeping the ranch. But Megan had never been interested in working the ranch. She'd taken off with some cowboy when she turned eighteen and gotten married, later divorced.

Al closed the file, his focus moving from Clay to Gabe. "There's a good chance if this information is accurate—" He tapped his forefinger on the manila folder. "—he might have to sell some land to cover these losses." Al picked up the folder and tossed it back to Gabe. "Where'd you boys get this material?"

"Rumors were floating. I was concerned about High Mountain," Gabe said. "I called on Sam a while back, and he assured me the ranch was fine. Nothing he couldn't handle. But I had a feeling he was keeping something from me. I asked Clay to check it out when Sam didn't show up for the meeting at Ray's and the new foreman came instead." He nodded to Clay.

"I hired a guy I know from our time in military intelligence." Clay pointed to the file. "He's good, damn good, and he doesn't make mistakes. If he gives you information, you can depend on its accuracy."

"Well, then, I'd say Sam has a serious problem." The lawyer scooted his chair back and leaned forward, getting slowly to his feet. "Let me know what you boys want to do here."

"Will do." Gabe said his goodbyes and headed out of the small office into a bright, cold afternoon, Clay close behind.

This business with Sam added another dimension to the Land-Use Bill. Now that Gabe knew Sam might need to sell off a section of the High Mountain, likely Alpine Ridge, Gabe wanted to find out more about the interested buyer, Evans Development, and Sam's foreman, Max. They couldn't afford to have developers buying up land. "After the flight, drop me off at the main house. I want to give Sam a call, then I may take a drive up to the ridge. Maybe get an idea of how to handle this situation."

Maybe he was still trying to find ways to distract, but he needed it.

Chapter 10

Ashley sat in Jason's office, pleased to hear about his soon-to-be published book. This was the first time they'd had to catch up since he'd gotten back. "Susan would be over the moon you're getting back behind the lens."

"Yeah." Jason leaned forward, his arms on his desk. "I still have more photos to go through, so the book won't be published until next spring." He gave her a wide grin. "Let's go tell Gabe. He's been in his office since he got home."

Ashley's smile fell. "I've...I've got to get ready for the cabin trip."

Jason came over and gave a sigh as he offered his hand her way. "Gabe's a shock to the system at the best of times, especially around Marilyn, but he's harmless, I swear. C'mon. Just think Pitbull and how they only roll over and offer you their belly after small, frequent *How you doing there, lad* visits. Just keep your hands behind your back and he won't bite."

Ashley rolled her gaze and gave a smile, but she took Jason's hand anyway. It was hard not to.

As Jason led the way in, Ashley paused in Gabe's office doorway when she saw he was on the phone. That...awkwardness crept back in with him seeing him back at the ranch, and distance seemed the safer bet. Jason had already taken a seat and waved her over as Gabe caught her by the door and tossed the file he'd been studying on the desk. He cut the call a moment later but didn't say anything.

"You into hiding now?" Jason took a seat opposite and Ashley joined him. "Accounts are up to date with the accountant, and I wanted to tell you something else."

Gabe gave him a slight nod but didn't look Ashley's way as she took a seat. "A lot on my mind, that's all." He scribbled something on the pad before him. "I've been trying to get in touch with Sam to figure a way to approach the situation at High Mountain and his foreman meeting with Evans Development. He hasn't returned my calls."

"Yeah, I thought there was something odd about him. You think Sam hired him to set up the deal?"

"Or the foreman works for Evans and started whispering in his ear." His gaze caught Ashley's, but again it didn't rest for long. "So what's the other news?" He looked sick.

Jason took him through the details of the upcoming book, and the lines on his face started to ease, but moments later, Ruth knocked on the open door, then glanced around the office. "Gabe, you've got a visitor. Should I bring her in here?"

He furrowed his brows. "Her?"

"Megan Frasier."

Ashley frowned at Jason. "Sam Fraser's daughter."

"Oh," mouthed Ashley.

"We'll see her in the main room. Give us a minute." Gabe turned to Jason. "I'd like you in on this."

Jason nodded. "What's going on?"

"How should I know?" Gabe got to his feet.

Jason touched Ashley's arm. "Come on, 'bout time you met our neighbor."

Something about that had Gabe lowering his look back at her, and Ashley read the warning over getting too comfortable.

When they reached the main room, a young woman ran to Gabe and threw her arms around him. "Gabe, I'm so glad you're home," she said before turning to Jason, "and you, too." She planted a kiss on Jason's cheek then returned to Gabe's side.

"This is Ashley Roberts." Jason nodded her way as Gabe took a seat next to Megan.

Ashley smiled. "Nice to meet you."

Megan offered a smile but she barely seemed to see her. "You, too," She looked back at Gabe. "Something's happened to Daddy."

Gabe frowned. "I've been trying to get in touch with him. What makes you think that?"

She wiped her eyes with the back of her hand and took a deep breath. "He hasn't been home for two nights, and we haven't heard from him. I found this by the gate this morning." With shaky hands, she pulled an envelope from her purse and handed it to Gabe.

He read the note inside then let out a harsh breath before looking at Jason. "A ransom note. Sam's been kidnapped. It warns about involving the law and asks Megan to get together two hundred and fifty thousand dollars. She'll be contacted for the drop site."

Ashley's breath caught. Megan's dad had been kidnapped? In who's reality did that happen? Not hers. "I'm so sorry."

Megan slumped her shoulders. "I can't get my hands on that kind of money."

Gabe nodded. "We know Sam has gambling debts. A lot of markers out there. Could be one of the people he owes money to is trying to collect."

"I don't know anything about Daddy's finances. I knew he was gambling, but I didn't know he was losing this kind of money."

"Does Sam have someone he sees on a regular basis?" Jason brushed at his jaw.

Megan swiped hair from her face as it caught in her tears. "A woman, you mean?"

"Yeah. Someone he spends the nights with occasionally."

Megan's gaze shifted from Jason to Gabe. "Daddy's seeing Martha Ellis. But I called her this morning, and she hasn't seen him for over a week."

"Would you know if he were seeing someone else?" Jason asked.

"Probably."

Gabe leaned back. "Rumor is he's out several nights a week." Gabe held up his hand when Megan started to speak. "Who's running High Mountain?"

"Daddy," she said in a whisper. "Him and the new foreman."

Jason glanced at Gabe. "How much trouble is the ranch in?"

"I don't *know*. What makes you think I do?"

"Okay, okay, take easy," said Gabe. "We can help you get the money, but have you contacted the sheriff?"

"No." She looked at him sharply. "I'm afraid they'll hurt Daddy."

"They could hurt him anyway." Gabe placed his arm around her shoulders as tears streamed down her cheeks. "He needs to be told."

"*No*." And she took the letter back off Gabe.

"Could I get you a glass of water?" Ashley started to stand.

Megan shook her head, and a moment later, she leaned against Gabe. "I'm so scared."

He gave a rough sigh. "What do you want us to do?"

She pulled back and looked at him. "Use Clay and find Daddy. You've always been there for me, for all of us."

"This isn't our area, Megan. The sheriff needs to be contacted."

"The note said not to."

"Megan," warned Gabe, but she shook her head.

"No police. *Please*. Clay's the next best thing."

He took a moment, then nodded, but Ashley read it in his look. She got a feeling the sheriff would be called in behind the scene. "We'll do it your way, for now," he said getting to his feet, then he placed a hand on Megan's shoulder when she joined him. "We'll get back to you in a couple of hours. You need to let us know if you hear anything else and call us as soon as they contact you again, or if you think of anything that could help us find Sam."

"I will." She held on to Gabe. "I don't know what I'd do if I lost Daddy."

Gabe wrapped his arms around her. "We'll do whatever we can to find him."

"I hope your dad is safe and home soon," Ashley said gently, not really knowing what else to say, but it was there with Gabe, how away from politics, from her, he had such a gentle way of handling family and friends.

"Thank you." Megan's smiled her way before returning to Gabe. "Will you come by later?"

"I need to get the search started." Gabe opened the door for her.

"I'll drop by later to check in with you and let you know what we've learned." Jason rubbed at her arm before she left.

"Damn," Gabe muttered as he closed the door. "Sam's in real trouble." He rubbed the back of his neck. "There's no way they can pay that off, I'll call Clay and see what he can do about bringing the sheriff in on the quiet. He's got be involved, but we might be able to work friends and family a little better than he can without scaring the kidnappers. While I do that, why don't you check with a few of our men? They might know something." Gabe looked at Ashley for a long moment, then turned away and headed out.

She sighed and stayed by the door with Jason. "You and Gabe have a lot to focus on right now, and since I promised Lisa I'd be here later in the week, I thought I'd drive up to the lake tomorrow for a couple of days. Ruth said the cabin is stocked and ready for use." She'd hoped Gabe's trip would have been enough space for both of them, but it hadn't. She needed out, just for a few days until things calmed down.

"I'm sorry, Ash. I really thought we'd have more time together. I wanted to take you around the ranch and show off Willow River." He shifted his feet. "I'll get the keys to the SUV we arranged for you."

"I'll tell everyone I'm leaving. Go ahead. I hope you find Sam quickly." She turned toward the kitchen. "Think I'll drive out to Sally Talltree's place. Ruth told me about her. My sister-in-law would love one of Sally's quilts for their anniversary."

"Why don't you wait on heading out to Sally's and stay close to the cabin this week. Like Gabe said, the weather's changing. Spring storms can be bad, and Sally's place is in the mountains." He grabbed her hand and squeezed. "Thanks for helping with Cody. He feels really bad he and Thomas got stuck at the campsite."

"He's a good kid." She smiled. "The accident wasn't his fault."

"Yeh, I know." He offered her a smile. "But you need a break, huh? Okay. I'll give the cabin's caretaker a call and tell him you're on your way. His name is Ted. He'll meet you there."

Chapter 11

Coldness bit hard into the afternoon but the sun was bright and high in the sky. A sure sign spring was on the way. Ashley grabbed her sunglasses and checked the directions Jason gave her. Then she drove steadily north, allowing her mind to wander.

If she could scrub away the asshole traits, she wouldn't mind a man like Gabe. Good to have around when chaos hit, pushing through her barriers with such a tentative touch one moment, then full-on heat the next. But he came with a poisonous side, one that liked to come back for another shot, then another.

But at least the past week had shown her she was ready for something more in life. But being someone's dirty secret wouldn't ever be it.

She turned her attention back to the road. She hadn't passed another car for miles. Giving a frown, she stayed on the narrow road for another twenty minutes before turning onto state route forty.

On the side of the road, water tumbled from an outcropping of rocks and movement caught her eye. She slowed, glancing repeatedly at the large rocks as she pulled onto the shoulder. With camera in hand, she opened the door and got out.

A whitetail deer ran out and stood for a moment grazing on the fresh green grass before racing to shelter among the trees. She snapped a couple of pictures before getting back into the SUV.

Half an hour later, she exited the paved two land road onto a private well-packed dirt lane, and a large cabin near the shore of

High Peak Lake came into view. The land from the cabin to the lake descended gradually to the water's edge.

The cabin door opened, and a giant of a man moved toward her. She flinched as she parked in the wide drive, then opened her door to get out and pull her bag from the back.

"Been watching for you," the man said as he took the final steps to reach her.

"You must be Ted. I'm Ashley Roberts. Jason said you'd be here."

Ted stretched out a large hand. "Good to meet you, ma'am." Her hand disappeared in his. "Welcome to the lake." He nodded at the cabin. "Anything you need, let me know." He gave her a smile that wrinkled his weathered face but brought light to his dark eyes.

"Ruth sent you something." Ashley took another bag out of the back seat and offered him some of the containers Ruth had packed inside.

He took the containers from her and gave her an even bigger grin. "That woman sure can cook." He laughed as he followed her up the front steps and into the cabin.

A kitchen was to the left of the entry, polished stainless appliances shone in the light and were separated from the rest of the huge room by an oak dining table with ten straight-backed chairs. Brown leather loveseats sat next to a square coffee table, and a rock fireplace dominated one wall while windows and old-style French doors opened to a wide deck overlooking the lake. The deck, furnished with several Adirondack chairs and two small tables, ran the entire length of the cabin, then wrapped around its sides.

The northern pristine forest surrounded by evergreens and snow-capped mountains was definitely cooler than the valley. She'd felt the difference when she stopped to take photos.

Ted showed her around the cabin, which included a small, well-stocked library. This was a place to get away from the outside world, so no television or land line, and cell service was hit or miss, otherwise, the cabin had all conveniences of home. A radio and CD player, along with a stack of CDs sat on shelves behind an oak roll-top desk.

"I live in the smaller cabin about a half mile north, so you aren't really alone." Instead of leaving, Ted hung around to start a fire and to check to see if she needed help with anything. He swept the deck before running water over the chairs and wiping them down.

Ashley stood in the kitchen, making a cup of tea and thinking of lunch since her stomach complained she'd skipped breakfast. Ted filled the inside wood bin by the fireplace before placing a big log on the bright flames.

"Thought I would head home. Anything you need?" He shuffled his feet. "Usually, I come by twice a day to do a little work around here." He raised his brows, giving Ashley a questioning glance.

"That's fine, don't let me get in your way." She poured steaming water over a dark tea bag. "Would you like a cup of hot tea before you leave?"

"Nah, thanks." Ted gazed down at his feet, and Ashley smiled at his awkwardness. She figured someone who chose to live on the mountains would prefer life to be less...social. "I'll be back to tend to the fire. Those are the instructions: a fire at the main cabin everyday this time of year when there's visitors." He looked at the massive rock fireplace. "It's a pretty sight." He stood by the decorative wrought-iron screen in front of the wide opening.

"I can build a morning fire, you know? Save you coming over."

"No, ma'am. That's my chore. I come down on cold days to start a fire to warm the place and keep things from freezing." He paused. "When you leave the cabin, make sure the screen is placed in front of the fire." He pointed to the containers he'd set by the door earlier. "I want to see what Ruth sent. I'll come by later."

The aroma from the containers had filled the cabin and was causing her stomach to rumble.

Standing by the window, she watched Ted disappear around the north shore of the lake. After he was gone, she wandered through the cabin, walking from room to room, familiarizing herself with her home for the next few days.

Eventually, she dumped her bag on the king-sized oak bed. A dresser stood against the wall, and two nightstands flanked the bed, each had a tall lamp. She'd be able to read at night once she was tucked in. The bathroom was off to the right and another bedroom and bath were located at the end of the hall.

The perfect place to forget about it all or face personal demons.

***

Sitting at the long dining table with Ruth's chicken salad sandwich, and a cup of hot tea, Ashley closed her eyes and listened to the silence. This place really *was* perfect. After a moment, she put away the rest of Ruth's food and stood by the French door, looking out at the serene lake. Maybe she'd get back to normal and lose this feeling of malaise that's been swamping for a while. Giving a sigh, she went to find her cell phone and it took only one try to reach Abby.

"Hey, Mom, how's it going?"

"I wish you could see the cabin and lake. It's beautiful."

"You didn't tell me what happened when you had to cut our call short? How's the family and what is the ranch like? What's Jason's brother like?"

Ashley's ease dissappeared. "First, is everything okay?"

"It's great. I found a part-time job on campus processing registrations for next quarter, so I've been busy. What's going on there?"

"Jason is fine, and Lisa and Cody love living at the ranch. They miss Susan. Cody and a friend rode out to check on a campsite and Cody slipped down a hillside and couldn't get back up. Gabe and I drove out in a snowstorm to get them. Cody wasn't hurt except for a couple of scratches." She curled up on the sofa, leaving out the bad. "Lisa's dealing with a personal issue. When you speak with her, get her to talk. They miss their mom so much."

"I'll try to call her tonight. Tell me about the big ranch."

"It's bigger and more impressive than Susan or Jason said. Even though I visited them several times in Cheyenne, I never got up to Willow River or Coulter Creek. The ranch is huge. I don't know about livestock, but the homestead, as Jason calls it, resembles a big lodge. I hope you'll be able to visit for a few days. Does that still look likely?"

"I'm not sure. It's up in the air. But I'll let you know as soon as I figure it out. Don't forget Jason's brother. What's his name?"

"Gabe." She fell quiet. "He's tall like Jason and has—" *gorgeous?* "—blue eyes. There's certainly a family resemblance." And that's all she wanted to give him.

"He looked good on TV. I can't wait to meet him."

She'd come here to get her head away from him, so opted for…distraction. "Tell me about your summer plans."

***

Dusk came early in the high country, and as the evening settled in, Ashley realized she had been curled up on the large leather sofa reading for too long. She got up to check her email, then took out her camera so she'd remember to take it on a morning walk, unless she woke to a foot of snow.

She zipped her jacket, made a fresh cup of tea, then went out to the deck. This was her favorite time of day. The sky and lake were lighter than the surrounding forest, but a gray film had begun to settle over the water.

She relaxed into the sounds around her—the lake lapping at the shore and the rustle of the gently swaying treetops as a cool breeze blew across the water and played in the branches. As she looked up, a bright star caught her eye. Ashley went into the house for the binoculars she'd seen hanging on a peg on the back of the door when her phone rang, breaking the silence.

She glanced at the screen and answered. "Hello, Jason."

"Hey. How's it going there?" he asked. "Was Ted there to meet you?"

"Yeah. He was waiting for me. This place is gorgeous. I love it."

He was silent for a moment. "Is everything all right? I know you didn't feel like talking after we left Jake's the other night, and I can guess Marilyn made you uncomfortable like she does with most new women close to Gabe, but I felt something more was bothering you. Anyone you need me to sort out? You know I'm here."

Ashley gave a soft smile. "Yeah, I know you are. But I'm good, really. I just have a few personal things to work out. But being up here, I'm feeling good."

"Good. Then you sleep well."

"I will. 'Night, Jason."

Chapter 12

The sun pulled itself out of bed, and Ashley sat eating breakfast when Ted came to replenish the firewood. As he worked, he spotted the camera on the kitchen counter. "Looking to take some pictures?"

She'd been taking pictures more and more lately. "You got any recommendations for a good spot?" She forgot she was drinking, and he wasn't. She lifted her cup. "Care to join me for one?"

He nodded, then stacked the wood neatly in the bin before coming to the table. "I could drive you out to Alpine Ridge. Part of the ridge is on Coulter land and the rest is on High Mountain. Nice views. You might see some wildlife."

She got up and poured a cup of coffee. "Perfect, thank you. Here." She placed it in front of Ted who'd taken a seat across from her. She was surprised by the offer. Ted didn't seem to be much of a talker. "Do you have time?"

He chuckled. "I have a lot of that."

"Good. I'd love to go." She cleaned her plate and cleared the table. "Finish your coffee. I'll get my things together."

"Be sure to grab a warm coat. The sun looks pretty, but you never know. This is unsettled weather."

***

Ted's pickup headed northwest as the sun warmed the inside of the cab. Ashley removed Lisa's borrowed coat and settled back in her seat.

"This place really is beautiful," she said, thinking how good it was to see for miles without a building blocking her view.

Ted rubbed his chin. "You haven't been here before?"

"No," she said as he turned the pickup on to a one-lane road. "I visited Jason and Susan when they lived in Denver and Cheyenne."

The sun climbed higher in the sky and would soon melt the ice that clung to underbrush. She relaxed as Ted mentioned a small ranch he and his wife, Lacy, had bought a few years before she'd passed away.

"I'm sorry. Was it an accident?"

He shook his head. "She'd been sick for a year or so." He adjusted his hat. "She was a good woman. We'd been together close to fifty years."

It was often she heard someone say that. "What brought you to Coulter Creek Ranch?"

"After Lacy passed, I wanted to fish. Bert Coulter, the boys' dad, bought my place and helped me build my cabin on the lake." He smiled. "He actually pounded a few nails himself."

Ted's dark eyes were clear and bright beneath gray brows, and his face was tan from years of working in the sun. His old hands were strong, but she could see arthritis had settled into several joints of his fingers. "Fifty years is a long time. You two must have been a good match." She opened the window, allowing fresh air to whisper across her skin. "Do you have children?"

"Naw, we weren't lucky there. The Coulter boys were lucky, though. Gabe and Jason brought those kids of theirs up for a week last year, and they were fun."

"What about Gabe's son? Do you see him often?" Jason had told her Gabe brought Lucas out to the ranch every summer and she wondered if he was anything like his dad.

Ted slowed the truck and made another turn, this time on to a dirt road. "That's a sad deal. Sure was hard on Gabe when they left. He loves that boy, and the kid seems to like being here well enough on holiday, but I guess the agreement was to let him live with his mother and find his way away from the Ranch."

She'd steered the conversation back to Gabe without realizing, and she kicked herself for it. *Move on, let it go.* He was already taken and, boy, did he like to show it.

Chapter 13

Gabe returned from a ranchers' association meeting and headed straight for his office to call Clay. He wasn't in a good mood. He hadn't been in one when Ashley was here, but to not have her here?

"Have you heard anything more about Sam?" he asked as soon as Clay answered. "I made a call to High Mountain earlier. Spoke to Megan and Max and they say they're still in the dark as to what's going on. Max seemed genuine over the kidnapping. They've had no further contact from the kidnappers." He leaned over and turned on his computer. "They both admitted Sam sold his section of Alpine Ridge."

"No sightings of Sam yet," Clay said. "I've spoken to Sheriff Logan and he's handling things on the quiet his end and asked if we can get him a copy of the ransom note. I recommend bringing in T.J. to look at helping Megan with the farm, get someone in there to keep an eye on Max. This isn't going to be kept quiet for much longer."

"Agreed." Gabe rose and walked to the window overlooking the Bighorns. Thomas Jefferson Brooks was an investigator and friend of Clay and Gabe's. "The ranchers have made it clear we need to figure out a way to stop commercial building on ranch land. Gotta say, I don't trust Max, Sam's new foreman. When will the check on him be ready?"

"I hired a local guy, and he never rushes." Clay chuckled. "Hey, one of the cowboys said he saw several cars up at the northern boundary by the rapids, but he couldn't tell if one of them was Sam's or Evans Development surveyors. Can you drive up and check out that border whilst I chase my guy up? See what you can find."

"Sounds good. Maybe I'll get an idea how to keep all that land for ranching."

Gabe cut the call and headed on in to the kitchen. Ruth stood in front of the stove, stirring a pot. It seemed this was where she spent most of her time, her small frame not much taller than the stove. Gabe took a deep breath, and the spicy aromas tickled his nose, reminding him of her famous chili. "Could you fill a thermos for me? Think I'll take a drive north."

Ruth looked at him and smiled. "You look like your dad." She studied him a bit longer. "He knew how to wear a suit too." She moved to the counter. "It will be ready by the time you change."

"Thanks." Gabe had made it to the top step when Jason appeared at the bottom of the staircase.

"There you are. How was your meeting with the ranchers' association?" Jason came up a few stairs. He'd been showing more interest in the ranch since he and the kids had moved in. Usually, Gabe was glad to keep him informed, but today he was tired and wanted to get to the ridge area while there was still plenty of light.

"The president acknowledged he'd checked." Gabe went down to meet him. "Building could take place on the land Sam sold unless I can somehow get the developer to sell it to me. If he can be convinced to sell, I'm sure he'll want a large profit. I wish Sam had checked with me first. Then again, I heard the rumors Sam needed money. I couldn't believe he'd sell any part of the ranch to me or anyone else." He loosened his tie. "I'm taking a drive north to check on a car Clay mentioned might be his. We'll come up with something to stop the development."

Jason nodded. "You all right? Is there more to the deal?" He scratched at the back of his neck. "You've been in a foul mood lately. You sure there's nothing wrong?"

Gabe tensed. That was his younger brother there, all his shyness and the need to stay behind a camera to boot unless there was trouble, and he'd finally found someone—Ashley—to hold on to after all the hurt. Gabe felt sick, mostly for how he was losing sight of him, how badly he hurt. "I'm fine. Got a lot on my mind, s'all." He cupped his neck, patted it. "I'll let you know if the plan changes." He started to turn, then stopped. "Is there something going on with you I should know about? Anything with the kids or Ashley?" *Something personal like an impending engagement?*

"I dunno." He shrugged. "She's not talking to me, even after my call up to the cabin." Jason seemed to shake it off. "I called Megan last night and told her I'd drop by today after dinner." He exhaled loudly. "Talks damn hard, though."

"Okay, but be careful," Gabe said as he walked down the hallway. "I don't want you disappearing on me too." He hadn't felt this displaced since losing Lucas. He hadn't lost Jason and his kids yet, but it felt like they were starting to slip through his fingers. Back there it had just been a kiss, a fumble with Ashley, and he could have hid behind how he hadn't known, But it was still there. He'd known when he held her in the cabin. When he hadn't moved away when he should have done. He didn't think anything could hurt as much as losing his kid, but the threat of losing his brother was fast coming up close.

At least Marilyn had agreed to fly back to Denver and give the job a few more months. He would help her any way he could, but he didn't love her. She wasn't in love with him either but she had a side to her that matched his, and although he hadn't told her about Ashley, she'd picked up something was off and had run wild with it.

In his bathroom, he leaned over the sink to splash water on his face, as much to slap himself out of this mood. Lifting his head, he looked in the mirror. His eyes looked tired, the lines on his face appeared deeper, and the gray in his hair was taking over. He turned to grab a towel, then threw it on the counter and walked to his bedroom to change.

***

As Gabe finally headed back into the kitchen looking for his thermos, Jason rummaged through the refrigerator, and Ruth hummed while stacking dishes from the dishwasher onto the counter.

Gabe headed over to the fridge, and Jason turned with a beer in hand.

"Would you talk with Sam's girlfriend again, Martha Ellis?" Gabe asked Jason. Clay had sent a text to him upstairs, and her name had come up again from his source. "She might know more than she thinks she does. Clay checked with a few other ranchers, and they haven't seen or heard from Sam. Also, when you have dinner with her, try to convince Megan to contact the sheriff."

"Yes, sir." Jason added a salute to his smile.

"Smartass." Gabe punched his shoulder.

Ruth tutted their way placed a bag on the counter. "You coming back tonight?" She filled the bag with containers of food. "Seems a way to go just to check out a car."

Jason lifted a brow at her.

Gabe shrugged. "I might call on Ted, see if he's seen or heard anything."

Ruth nodded and failed to bury her smile. "I thought you might."

Gabe scowled and ignored her. This was about Sam, not Ashley. He wanted to check in with Ted after he'd checked out what Clay had said about the northern border. See if Ted might have seen anything going on around Alpine Ridge.

Ruth didn't believe him, but that was okay. He didn't pay her for her counsel. She cocked him a brow almost as if she caught that in his look, and Gabe dug his hands in his pockets and looked away. Okay, that had been a little brutal.

"I packed a bag for you and Ted." Ruth busied herself with another container. "Poor man can't boil water." She looked up as Gabe and Jason chuckled. "Now, get out of my kitchen." She handed Clay the bag and thermos and shooed them out.

"I'll call Ashley again tonight and I may drive up to see her tomorrow if I can," Jason said as they were walking. "If you drop in on Ted, check with her. Make sure all's well."

Gabe tightened his jaw. "I'll tell her if I see her."

"You do more than that if someone's gone missing around here, okay?" Jason pulled him to a stop. "You make sure she's okay, right?"

Gabe gave a rough sigh. "Right."

***

Gabe drove fast through Coulter Ranch, trusting the dips and turns in the road a lot more than he trusted most people. *"Never forget your roots,"* his grandfather had said one morning as they sat on the bank of High Peak Lake, waiting for a bite on their lines.

How long since he'd been fishing? As governor, he'd tried to take a few days a year to spend with his dad at the cabin, but life got busy. Hell, politics kept him busy putting out one fire after another. When he'd been the chief executive, he'd thought the citizens might benefit if there were a three-party system instead of two and realized there'd probably be more game playing, not less.

Up ahead, the peaks of the snow-covered Bighorns towered over the lowlands. Ashley was right, the view was breathtaking. This country had always been a part of his soul. It seemed to watch over him. He could no more leave here than he could part with a piece of himself.

He'd been following the river until he turned onto state route forty where he could make a little better time. He had to prevent construction so close to Coulter Creek's northern boundary. He wasn't against progress, but all development needed to be well planned, and certainly didn't fit in the middle of grazing land.

He wondered if Clay had made any headway. Maybe T.J. could help find Sam who was probably kidnapped because of his gambling debts. Gabe made a mental note to give Curtis, Sam's oldest grandson a call to see if after graduating, Curtis would come back to Willow River for a while and give Sam a much-needed hand.

Gabe stopped where the Coulter and Frasier lands met and got out of the SUV, then reached inside for his binoculars and jacket. The cold air funneled through the gorge as he walked to the edge of the cliff where he gazed down at the wide river. White rapids filled this section of the river, especially when the water ran high, as it did now. "The power of nature," he muttered. This land meant more than one man, one family. It reminded anyone who saw it that the land was enduring, and man was but a visitor upon it. He lifted the binoculars and searched across the gorge for signs of recent activity.

He hoped Jason and his kids would stay and put down roots here. As for himself, he'd grown tired of politics and was glad to be back home. But Jason was right when he'd said Gabe hadn't made much of a life for himself since he'd gotten back to the ranch. He enjoyed having his brother and kids around and began to wonder what the ranch would be like if they didn't stay.

His chest tightened, and he pushed the thought away.

***

The sun hung low in the sky by the time Gabe pulled off the road and turned away from the gorge. He hadn't seen evidence of surveyors or Sam's car, but that didn't mean they hadn't been there, so he'd packed up and headed to Ted's cabin.

The log cabin came into view at the same time the eastern tip of the lake became visible through rows of evergreens. Gabe pulled the Tahoe up to the gray wooden steps, grabbed the thermos and food Ruth had packed, and stepped out. The fresh mountain air carrying the aroma of pine filled his lungs, and he hoped it would clear his head too.

The cabin door opened, and Ted stepped onto the porch. "I wondered which of you boys was visiting me."

Gabe nodded over to him. "Ted."

"It's been a while since you were here." Ted waved him in before turning to walk into his small cabin.

Nothing had changed from the last time Gabe had been here. Everything was neat and orderly. "A bag of food from Ruth." He held up the thermos. "She made coffee," he added before going into the kitchen and placing the bags on the rustic stove top.

"That woman send you up here to feed me?" Ted took a deep breath and looked inside the bag at the neatly stacked containers. "Smells great, but I recently got a haul from her."

Gabe moved to stand in front of the window where a Bighorn peak stood out. Ted had chosen well. The small cabin was nicely situated. The lake was at his fingertips, and with a view of the mountains to the west, he could watch the weather move in. "I drove up to the northern ridge. Water's high," he said with his back to Ted.

"That it is. I saw it for myself earlier." Ted checked the thermos. "Want a drink? Got Ruth's coffee here, or something stronger."

"Coffee sounds good." Gabe felt Ted studying him as he took the chair across from Ted's rocker.

"You boys are a lot like your father. I can read trouble on your faces as well as I could Bert's." Ted shook his head. "Your dad used to sit in that same chair where you are now and stare into my fireplace."

Gabe knew Ted missed his dad. The two of them had shared many evenings before this old hearth.

"Got something on your mind?" Ted asked.

"Mulling over a few things." Gabe mentioned about Sam, but Ted shrugged, the whole act saying he'd seen nothing. "Okay. I'll take that coffee now."

Ted poured and handed the cup to Gabe. "Mulling's good."

"Hm?"

"You said you were mulling over a few things." Ted took his seat. "But that means more than one. What's troubling you other than Sam?"

Gabe took a sip of coffee. "Been fishing lately?"

"Yup, too much like your dad." Ted smiled at the avoidance. "Always one that gets away, right?" He added another dry log to the fire. "Still a good stack of this dry wood here and at the cabin. Noticed this morning when I was in the woodshed loading my buckets for the day."

Sly old dog was verbally fishing, but Gabe didn't take the bait. He didn't want to talk about Ashley. The logs crackled in the fire, and Ted recounted fish stories, and by the time he was done, dusk had settled over mountains. They were still holding their empty cups when a soft knock on the door broke their silence.

Ted placed his cup on the table by his rocker and made his way to the door. "Well, what a nice surprise."

Gabe didn't have to turn to know who was standing on the other side of the threshold. His pulse quickened and he couldn't tell if it was anger or...something else.

Chapter 14

"Thought I'd bring dinner to you tonight, but I see you have company." Ashley nodded at the SUV parked in the drive.

Ted stepped back from the door and smiled her way. "Not company exactly. Gabe dropped in with coffee."

Ashley froze. Damn. All hopes on relaxation and quiet time with Ted was shattered. "Well, I'll leave you two…" Her words were lost in her throat as she watched Gabe walked toward her, his long, muscular denim-clad legs covering the distance in a few long strides.

"I brought dinner. Thought Ted would like a casserole tonight," she rushed to say, trying to cover her nervousness. "Ruth stocked the freezer." She held up the dish in her hands.

"Jason told me to check in on you." They both quickly covered bases on why they were here, and it felt painful. "It'll save a drive if you're here," added Gabe. "You better come in."

Ted took the casserole, and Ashley smiled her thanks as he looked out at the dark western sky. "It's getting to be that time, isn't it?" he asked no one in particular. "Why don't we all sit down and have a bite of supper. Not often I get company at mealtime."

Ashley stepped inside and glanced at Gabe. "Any news about Sam?"

Gabe rubbed the back of his neck, avoiding looking at her. "Nothing yet. Got a few people looking into it. I'm confident they'll learn something soon."

They followed Ted into the small kitchen, and while Gabe set the table, he told Ted more about Clay's involvement with the kidnapping.

"You think this has to do with that company wanting to buy ranch land? Ted asked.

Gabe reached for the silverware. "How'd you know about that? I didn't mention it earlier."

Ted held a basket of rolls. "I visit the Black Dog for a beer from time to time. A few ranch hands are always there. From what I hear, nobody's happy with the land deal Sam made."

"Here." Ashley placed the casserole on the table.

Gabe pulled out a chair for her and Ashley gave him a thin smile. "It likely has to do with whatever he's gotten himself wrapped up in. Either the gambling or land deal." He took a seat beside her.

Ashley reached for a roll, then frowned awkwardly as Gabe did too and their hands brushed. "How's Megan?"

Gabe pulled away, indicating she go first. "I talked to her this morning, and she's heard nothing. Odd. You'd think they'd want the ransom paid. I hope to hell Sam's still alive." Gabe dished a serving of casserole onto his plate, but then seemed to shake something off. "This smells good." He passed the dish to Ted, and it relaxed Ashley a little. He was back to wanting to avoid trouble and politics around the table.

That she could handle. She tried to lighten the mood with a smile. "It's delicious."

"Ruth's a great cook," Ted said with a gleam in his eyes.

Gabe glanced at Ashley. "Jason said he'd drop by tomorrow. Did he call and let you know? He's over at Megan's tonight."

"He did, yeah." She rested her roll on her dinner plate. "It's why I came over to Ted's. Does Megan have other family?"

Gabe shook his head. "An only child, but has three boys of her own." He finally took a roll from the basket.

"Shame Sam and Grace didn't have more children." Ted started to eat as a loud pop came from the fireplace.

"That wood you use burns hot and slow," Ashley said. "I enjoy a morning fire, especially with a cup of coffee. Thank you."

Ted nodded. "My pleasure. A morning fire is nice. These mornings are getting pretty cold." He leaned back in his chair. "What brings you to Wyoming this time of year?"

Ashley took a drink, conscious of how Gabe stopped eating for a moment. "Jason convinced me this was beautiful country and a good place to relax. It was also a good time to get away from work and to spend time with him and the kids." She glanced at Gabe. "I feel remiss I haven't spent much time with him, but Lisa and I keep catching up over the phone." She wanted Gabe to know she was still looking after her, but he didn't seem to take it that way for some reason.

"Is your daughter planning to visit?" Gabe asked, his voice harsh.

Ashley placed her cup on the table. "I hope so. I'd like for her to get to know Jason and the kids better. She and Lisa hit it off a few years ago and they talk regularly." She swallowed through a tight throat. She missed her best friend. "Susan was a wonderful person," she said, her voice barely a whisper.

Ted nodded.

"She and Jason were a good match." Gabe added a bite to that, almost like a challenge.

"A great match," Ashley muttered gently.

"Susan spent many a night here at the lake."

Ted's words stopped her eating as it hit her. She saw why Jason might delay coming up here. She really hadn't thought this through.

"She'd bring me warm sugar cookies fresh from the oven from time to time." Ted emptied his cup. "That cancer sure moved fast." He looked down at his empty plate and stared. "Good meal, right?"

He was like Gabe in many ways, trying to avoid upset around the table, but some memories, no matter how sad, would always be welcome. But she saw the hurt was too raw, so changed the topic for him. "Fishing. I hear you do a lot of it, Ted?"

His world brightened as he looked over and nodded. Then they were lost to several fish stories, a couple including Gabe and Jason, which had them laughing, which was obviously Ted's intent.

Gabe told a couple of stories of his fishing misadventures with Jason, and Ashley felt like she was getting to know him better away from any vindictive play. This was the side she liked: talk around the dinner table, a fire crackling along with soft laughter. "Makes me want to go fishing" She put her napkin on the table. "But I need to let you two catch up." She stood, surprised at how good she felt.

"Sit for another cup of coffee," Ted ordered.

Ashley shook her head as she carried her plate to the sink. "One more cup and I won't sleep a wink."

"You having trouble sleeping?" Gabe's voice was so close she could feel his breath on the back of her neck, but she didn't know how to take his comment. It seemed to ask if she had a conscience because of the lack of sleep. He leaned in and placed his empty dish next to hers, and she held her body rigid.

"No, but I've had way too much coffee tonight." She stepped away and headed to the table. "How long are you planning to stay? Are you here to fish?"

Gabe turned to Ted, and Ashley saw the questioning look in the older man's eyes. When Ted lifted his brows, she knew he was waiting for an answer to her question as well.

"Thought I'd take a morning to fish with Ted and give myself time to figure out what's going on with Evans Development."

No rush back to Marilyn? To find out about Sam? Ashley narrowed her eyes. *What are you playing at now, Gabe?* "So, fresh fish for dinner for us tomorrow, huh?" she asked without thinking. Then she froze. She'd invited herself to dine with them, or at least Ted.

"Fresh fish it is for us, then." Ted grinned. "I'll expect you for supper." He pushed back his chair and stood.

"Ted fries a good fish at least." Gabe was back to digging his hands in his pockets, looking as if he wasn't sure what had just happened either. "And dinner's good." He found her gaze. "Has to be, right?"

He'd just called truce, and yeah, for Jason's and the kid's sake, maybe it had to be right. Ashley washed, and Gabe dried. She covered the remaining casserole and placed it in Ted's fridge. Satisfied everything was clean, she wiped her hands and turned to the door. "It's getting late. I should go."

"Stay for a while. I want to show you something." Ted hurried from the room, returning quickly and placing a case on the table. "Now that there's three of us, I dug out my game." He ran his hand lovingly over the top of a dark, wooden antique case the size of a clarinet case. He smiled with a far-away look in his eyes, then turned to Gabe, "You up for a game?"

Gabe folded the towel and put it on the counter before going over. "Absolutely. But it's been a while since I've played."

"It's a game one never forgets." Ted opened the intricately carved lid, lifting out two red felt-lined trays filled with tiles. He turned the trays over, and small, rectangular tiles, looking like tiny bars of soap, scattered across the table. The backs of the tiles were blank, but their faces were covered with strange symbols. "This is a Chinese game. Lacy taught me to play so I could fill in for one of her sick friends." He grinned. "I don't get to play much anymore."

Ashley held her breath as she stared at over a hundred tiles with mysterious Chinese symbols lying on the surface of the table.

"The game is *Mahjong*." Ted waved his hand above the table. "Over the years I've taught the Coulter boys how to give me a good game. But we need three players, and they're rarely here at the same time."

Ted selected four of the tiles, placing them in front of her as she took a seat, and saying the name for each of the symbols shown. "They're magnificent, aren't they?"

Without taking her gaze from them, Ashley nodded. "They're beautiful."

Gabe removed three racks from the case as he sat, placing one in front of each of them. "These are used to build our walls, but first we need to turn the tiles face down on the table and shuffle them. Then we select the tiles for our walls."

Ashley watched as Gabe and Ted mixed up the tiles then began placing them face down against their racks until they had a length of eighteen tiles and a height of two. She followed their lead.

"Lacy once told me this game was played quite a bit in the Midwest." Ted took his seat too. It was the second time he'd mentioned his late wife. Both times with longing.

Ted removed a small pair of dice from the case and seconds melted into minutes as they guided Ashley through the game. Three didn't feel like a crowd here. It felt like a safety net. She felt transported back to days long gone, sitting here in this small cabin with crackling wood in the fireplace playing an ancient game.

She was enjoying herself and was surprised she felt so content and relaxed here with two men she'd known only days. She lifted her gaze and caught Gabe's. She offered him a smile, and for once his came back her way with no gameplay behind it.

Ted won the first game, and in the second, Gabe threw his hands into the air as he called out "*Mahjong.*"

Ashley laughed at the pure pleasure on his face.

Ted shook his head, muttering, "It's about time. I thought maybe you forgot how to play."

Everyone pushed the tiles to the center of the table, and Ted turned to Ashley. "What'd you think?"

"I understood precious little." She laughed and helped Ted stack the tiles in the trays. "But I enjoyed it." She gave a tired stretch. "But I've really got to get going now."

Ted nodded as she got to her feet and headed over for her coat. As Ashley buttoned her jacket, Ted reached for the lantern she'd found by the door of her cabin. When she turned to say goodnight and take it, Gabe had a jacket over his shoulders and another lantern in his hand.

"I'll walk her back," he said to Ted.

"You don't have to. I—"

"No." Gabe stared down at her. "For once you let me be a gentleman and get you back safely like Jason said."

***

The sounds of night surrounded them as they walked down the steps onto the gravel drive. The crunch of the rocks under their feet and the moonlight peeking through the evergreen branches made for a fairytale scene.

Neither spoke until they'd left the drive behind and turned to follow the dirt path along the lake. A breeze blew Ashley's loose hair across her face, and she tugged it behind her ears.

"Is Ted keeping you busy?" Gabe asked in a low voice, sending a chill through her.

Her throat was dry, and he walked too close. She had a hard time concentrating on more than putting one foot in front of the other. "He drove me up to Alpine Ridge. I took a few pictures." She described their trip to the ridge, then asked, "How was your trip to Cheyenne?"

Gabe didn't answer, and she began to think he hadn't heard the question. "Didn't go as planned, but all in all, I learned a few things," he finally said.

"A few good things, I hope." She moved the lantern to her other hand to keep something between them. When the path narrowed, she felt the heat from his body, and too often his arm brushed against hers. She wanted to ask if Marilyn had gone with him, but didn't need the aggression tonight.

It wasn't until they took the left turn from the lake to the cabin he said, "Yeah, a few good things. I need to find a way to stop commercial construction on grazing land."

"I can see why you want to preserve it around here. Does part of that land belong to Sam's ranch and that's why you're so concerned over it being sold off to developers?"

"Yeah. The section across the river is part of High Mountain." He sighed. "Or it used to be."

They'd reached the lake side of the cabin. Before leaving the path, she stopped and turned to look back the way they'd came. A panoramic view of dark water shimmered in the moonlight, and the long shadows cast by the trees looked like shady figures lurking in the forest. Loneliness swept over her.

Gabe sat on the top step of the cabin's deck, looking out over the lake. "I'd hate to lose any of this. I grew up here." He paused. "I wish Alicia had seen it like I do."

Feeling a little awkward with being left standing close to her door, Ashley sat beside him and took a deep breath as she looked at Gabe. "Marriages end despite our best efforts, don't they?"

Gabe looked her way, smiled. "Yeah, they do," he said gently. "What went wrong with yours?"

She shrugged. "Does there need to be a reason nowadays?" She couldn't get into the whys with Gabe now. Not when she didn't trust him, not with what he'd pulled with Marilyn. "We were young. Rob didn't like responsibility. A wife and child prevented him from being…him." She took a deep breath. "Abby and I have been on our own for several years."

He watched her for long moments. "So you're after stability? Someone with a proven track record of staying around kids."

"What?" She knitted her brows. "I'm not *after* anything. Most women aren't. Falling for someone either happens or doesn't it."

"So you play by chance?"

Ashley stared at him. "This isn't politics, Gabe. Love's not the next bigger, better deal." She tried to kick herself from saying it, but Gabe was pressing little buttons here. "Maybe to you and Marilyn, but not the rest of us."

He went to snap something, but Ashley denied him the snide comeback and headed into the cabin, closing the door behind her.

Chapter 15

Moonlight lit the path around the lake as Gabe headed back to Ted's, and he kicked a branch to get it out of his way. This wasn't him. He wasn't a jerk, but Ashley brought out the worst in him.

His father used to say, *"It's not about doing what we want, it's about doing what's right,"* and he was trying to, so badly. He'd took a moment to see if Ashley would be all right with Jason despite what had gone on because, damn his head, he liked her. He damn well loved his brother, so he'd wanted to sound her out on her feelings for Jason. Only she'd taken the high ground when they'd both rolled around the mud behind his back.

So maybe now he'd tell her about Marilyn, how they weren't even dating when he pulled the stunt he had, let her see just how she'd been played. At least that would bring her back down to his level and all the fears over losing Jason and the kids.

He'd spent all night trying not to push it, just see her in the cabin light: how she played her hand at Mahjong, if her poker face was as carefree over kicks as it seemed, how firelight flickered across her face, highlighting lips he'd kill to taste again...

"Christ." Gabe groaned.

She and Ted seemed to get along well. Hell, Jason and the kids treated her as if she were already family. But he understood why Jason wouldn't want to rush to be with her here. This had been his and Susan's place, but beyond that, he didn't seem to push to spend more time with her either. Maybe they were caught in grief, second thoughts, and missed moments. Gabe was, and could he really blame

Ashley for screwing up and faltering with someone else with everything in the mix? She hadn't been here, so everything around cried Susan and Jason or Susan, Jason, and the kids, even Gabe came with her memories, everything a reminder on how Ashley couldn't haunt their thoughts like Susan did. Was that why she'd given into him and kissed him? She was feeling the strain?

What a mess. Gabe wiped a hand over his face. He hadn't stopped to think just how much of a mess this was for everyone concerned when it came to losing Susan, and that included Ashley.

He needed to ease off and give them both space, maybe allow for a screw up on Ashley's part and stop going in like a wounded bull.

When he entered the cabin, Ted sat in his rocker. "Poured us a nightcap." He raised his glass in salute before taking a sip.

Gabe picked up the second glass. "Thanks." He took his seat across from him.

The fire still burned bright, and the cabin felt uncomfortably warm.

"Fine woman," Ted said. "Makes me wish I was years younger." He squinted across at Gabe. "She's right easy on the eyes, and certainly likable."

Gabe finished the last of his drink as he sat down, letting the smooth liquid slide down his throat. "Everyone at the ranch seems to think so." The conversational tone he'd hope to use didn't come through, and he peered down at his empty glass.

Ted frowned over at him. "You don't?"

"Dunno. They seem like an odd couple." Gabe twirled the glass in his hand. Ted had been the Coulters' confidant for years. First Gabe's grandfather, then his father's, Jason's... Each of them had made his way to this chair.

"They? Who are we talking about?"

Gabe raised his head. "Jason and Ashley. They're talking marriage, but I don't think I'm supposed to know yet."

Ted widened his eyes a little. "That's a surprise. She's more than a mite different from Jason. And Susan, for that matter."

Gabe crossed one leg over the other. "Yeah, she is."

"She might be exactly what Jason and those kids need, though," Ted stated, rubbing his chin. "But you don't think so, hm?"

"What?"

Ted stood and took the empty glass from Gabe before heading to the kitchen. "Fishing," he said quietly. "I know which bait you set to test out what's beneath the waters." He looked back. "But you know the rules as well as most: don't fish from a reserved spot that doesn't hold your name. Things get ugly at the water's edge when you're caught baiting from a friend's fishing chair."

Gabe nodded and Ted turned back to him. "But you know, son," he said quietly. "Jason, he's no fisherman. He always was one to stand back and catch the competition in a camera lens. Make sure you're working the same angle and are sitting in his reserved seat when it comes to finery like Ashley."

Gabe gave a sigh, then plucked out his phone when he got a call. Jason's named flickered up, and he frowned down before thumbing Answer. "What's wrong?" Something had to be for him to call this late.

Chapter 16

Gabe put the Tahoe into gear and slowly drove away from Ted's. Stars along with a full moon lit up the high plateau and the road before him as he swore under his breath. This wasn't the way he wanted to leave things with Ashley. Jason's call had taken his feet from underneath him. He never called that late. The only time he had was when Susan had died, and for a moment, Gabe had held back answering.

"What's wrong?"

"Gabe, sorry. Senator Robert Stanton's had a heart attack. Jean needs you over there."

His grip tightened on the steering wheel. He'd been right. Although why Stanton's wife needed him over there didn't register. He wasn't immediate family. Bob had been a friend, but nothing more. Gabe contacted Clay, who'd have the plane fueled and ready by the time he got there, then Gabe let Ted know and quietly slipped from the small cabin. Clay had let him know he'd also found a witness who'd seen Sam leave the Eagle Casino the night he went missing.

But then Clay had pulled the trump card and mentioned that the condo in Hawaii that Senator Stanton and Jean had accepted was a gift from Evans Development. The paperwork had been handled by someone accustomed to doing these type of deals. The transaction and the parties involved were buried deep.

Gabe now knew why Bob had backpedaled on the Land-Use Bill, and as he was now "out of the way", the bill would probably die in committee. It might be too late to find another senator willing to bring the bill to the floor for a vote. There had to be another way to stop Evans Development from building a resort on Alpine Ridge.

As he drove east, his phone rang. "Clay? What now?"

"Sam's been found. Just got a call from one of T.J.'s men who said he's been taken to Memorial Hospital in Sheridan. It looked like he was running from someone and fell down an embankment. We don't know his condition yet."

"What the hell? I'll stop by to see Megan after we've been to Cheyenne."

"Something else that might get you going. That new foreman, Max Banks? He's nowhere to be found. Seems he's disappeared."

This whole mess got stranger and stranger by the minute.

Chapter 17

After he landed in Cheyenne, Gabe made it to the hospital and pushed through people to find Jean sitting alone in a small family waiting lounge.

"How's Bob?" He crouched down by her.

She looked up and a tear streaked her makeup. "Gabe? He didn't make it."

Jesus. He took her hand and rubbed warmth into it. "I'm so sorry. Bob was a good friend." He glanced around. "How long have you been here alone?" He couldn't believe no one was with her.

"Not long. I sent my friends home, but I wanted to wait for you." She glanced around but didn't really see anything. She echoed Jason, how he hadn't wanted to leave the hospital, leave Susan behind, alone.

"C'mon, let's get you home." He kissed at her head, then helped her to her feet. As she looked back down a corridor, no doubt the way she'd come, it took a lot of coaxing to get her to move away from it.

He made the drive quick, but as smooth as possible, and wasn't surprised to find reporters and the flash of camera light blinding and blocking the view of the driveway. He eased through them and pulled the car to a stop.

"Wait here." He got out the car and headed over. "Not now, guys. Seriously." He made one or two back off with a gentle touch. "I know you've heard the news, but respect the family's privacy. I'll arrange for a spokesman to talk to you soon."

A few questions were thrown his way, but Gabe dismissed them now the jostling for space eased. He helped Jean into the house, and the housekeeper met them in the entry. "They've been there for hours." She nodded toward the media at the end of the drive. "Should I make some coffee?"

"Get a call through to family first," Gabe said quietly to her. "She needs someone here, and that isn't me."

"I'm not an invalid," said Jean, pushing away. "I've lost my husband, not my sanity." Her face creased. "Not yet anyway."

She led Gabe into the den and he took a seat next to her on the couch, her hand in his.

"You sure you're up for talking?" he said gently. "This can wait." Whatever *it* was.

"No." She patted his hand. "Bob made me promise to do this right away."

"Do what?"

"To ask you to take over Bob's senate seat. Bob needed you to."

Gabe rose and walked to the fireplace where a picture of himself and Bob rested on the mantle. Politics wasn't in his future. Not anymore. He didn't want to go back into all the double-dealing, today proved that. "I'm sorry, Jean. No. I'm out of it." He shook his head, and Jean fell quiet.

"Bob knew how important stopping the land development was for you and the ranchers. He wanted to make it right by putting you forward."

"*Then maybe he should've started by putting it forward himself and not taking backhand deals.*" Jean jolted a touch, and Gabe instantly regretted raising his voice.

"You know about 'the gift?'" It came as a flat statement.

Gabe nodded. "Yeah. What the hell happened?" This was what he hated, how everyone could be bought for a price, or condo in this instance.

She stood and came over, face pale. "Bob told me a man named James Harris from Evans Development was putting pressure on him to make sure the Land-Use Bill didn't get passed." She rubbed at Gabe's arm. "I don't know how many conversations they had, but Bob recently began talking about 'the gift.'" She looked away. "That wasn't who he was, Gabe. You know that. Bob was a good man. They put him under so much pressure."

"They threatened him?" He lowered his look. "You?"

Jean snorted. "Not that you'd get proof on paper."

"Goddamn it." Gabe ran a hand through his hair.

"I'm returning the condo. We both knew it wasn't right. But Bob said that if you said no, that I was to give the name of the contact in Evans Development. He said you'd know how to handle it where he couldn't."

"Thanks, Jean. I appreciate you telling me. I'll look into James Harris. Find out exactly who he is, just what he's been up to, then notify the sheriff."

***

The bright sun did nothing to ameliorate the cold temperature in Cheyenne. According to the calendar, spring had arrived. Before he left the city, Gabe spoke to Valerie in Senator Gilbert's office and learned the Land-Use Bill was stalled. Then tired, almost down and out with little sleep, he met Clay for a late lunch at Marty's Grill, close to the private airstrip.

The lunch crowd had thinned, and they were seated in a booth near a back window. The smells from the kitchen made Gabe's stomach growl. He looked over the menu, and after they ordered, he leaned back into the booth's padding.

"Jean talked about the condo and Evans Development. A guy named James Harris was putting pressure on Bob to keep the bill stalled. I wonder if that foreman, Max, was working with Harris. I'll passed it all on to Sheriff Logan when we get back, along with a copy of the ransom note Megan received that I managed to get hold of." He nodded his thanks as the waiter placed cold beers in front of them. "She also said Bob wanted me to take his senate seat."

Clay took a long drink. "You thinking about it?"

"No. I'm through with politics."

"You were a natural, but you've changed," Clay said as their food arrived.

Gabe began to cut into his steak. "You don't think I'm electable now?"

"Oh, you'd win the election. I'm not saying you wouldn't." Clay took a sip of his beer.

"Well, what the hell are you saying?"

"You don't want it anymore. It's not your focus."

Clay was right. "The party's still looking for someone they can back. More so now."

Clay placed his fork on his plate and looked him in the eye. "The Coulter name carries a lot of weight, so what about Jason? He may want to follow in your footsteps. The kid can charm the pants off the men as well as the women voters."

Gabe's fork was halfway to his mouth when he shook his head. "He's never shown an interest in running for office or politics beyond the ranch."

"That's because he was always overshadowed by his you." Clay raised a brow.

"*Overshadowed*?" Gabe's voice was hard. "Jason knows how to speak his mind, He keeps me in check most times."

Clay wiped his mouth with his napkin. "Not when it comes to politics. You always had the voice there."

"Because it was my choice to. His was photography and Susan."

"Jason stood in your shadow and looked your way when you helped increase the state's economy while giving taxes cuts to small businesses." Clay took another drink. "Tourism also increased when you were in office, which helped all business as well as increased the state's reserves. He's been watching you on the quiet. His also back with you and still watching and learning."

"That wasn't all me. I had a good team behind me."

Clay tightened his jaw. "With you as the front man, calling the shots. You shout, Jason always had this smile going on as he watched people jump and move around you. It's what he does: steps back, takes in the whole picture, but never misses the finer detail either." He dipped his chin. "I'm saying Jason's got some kick like you and could do a good job filling your shoes if you help him."

Gabe thought it over. "Not my decision. But you think he has a chance and would want to run?"

"He's a shoo-in. Almost as good as you'd be."

Gabe frowned. "I'll sound him out, nothing more."

"He'll need to get his name added to the list early. See what type of reaction it generates."

Gabe winced. "Not my place to add him to anything. That's his. But we need someone on our side in there."

Clay's phone rang, and he pulled it from his pocket to check the display. "Got to take this." He stood and headed to the restaurant's exit.

Gabe mulled over what Clay had said. Jason would have the backing of the ranchers if he ran for senate, and he was a Coulter. But would he want it? Would he need something like that when he had Ashley?

When he got home, he'd have a talk with Jason.

Gabe finished his beer as Clay headed back inside. He was as solid as he'd been when he'd left military intelligence several years ago. "Short conversation," he said as Clay slid into the booth. From the scowl on his face, it hadn't been a pleasant call.

"It's done. The deal's closed. Evans Development won. We knew how desperate Sam was with those gambling debts hanging over his head."

Yeah, they needed someone there in the senate on their side.

Gabe suddenly felt exhausted. All those trips here to Cheyenne for nothing. "Damn, I never thought Sam would sell a piece of High

Mountain." He leaned forward on the table. "If the deal's closed, why the kidnapping?"

"I don't know, but I'm really looking forward to what Sam has to say."

Chapter 18

As evening crept in on their flight back to the ranch, Clay had the controls. Gabe stared out the window, trying to concentrate on the landscape. He wondered if Jason had managed to meet Ashley at the cabin, then he bit down the pang of jealousy if he had in the next breath. Were they getting ready to go fishing like they'd planned, and if so, did Ashley think about him. He snorted. If she did, he bet none of her thoughts were pretty

He'd been taught to take care of everyone. Over and over his dad reminded him he'd be head of the family. He could've gotten custody of Lucas, but felt it was best for his son to be with his mother if Lucas didn't like the ranch beyond holiday stays. He could've run for a second term as governor but the responsibility of the ranch pulled him home. What he couldn't do was get Ashley out of his damn head. Having her around reminded him of just how alone he was. He wished she'd never come to visit, and he'd never felt the softness of her skin and the suppleness of her body pressed against his. He closed his eyes. "Shit."

"What's wrong with you?" Clay glanced at Gabe.

"You know what's going on: Sam. High Mountain being sold, and Bob's death."

Clay pushed the yoke forward and the small aircraft began its descent. "Yeah? I'd have opted for woman trouble."

Gabe grunted. "Don't. Not when it comes to me. There's no woman in my life , and I intend to keep it that way."

Clay laughed as he brought the plane down on the runway. "Maybe that's the problem. You and your…intentions when it comes to women."

***

Dressed in jeans and riding boots, Ashley returned from the barn with Jason, and headed onto the lit porch as Gabe arrived. They stopped on the steps and waited for him to park as Jason leaned toward Ashley, and whatever he said made her laugh. Gabe watched them for a minute before he got out of the Tahoe, then head down, he made his way over as Clay said his goodbyes.

"I thought you were staying at the cabin. You were going to eat at Ted's after he'd been fishing." His look stayed on Ashley.

"Ashley was going to, but I dragged her back." Jason messed with his phone, then slipped it away. "I offered to go and take Megan over to the hospital to see Sam, but hospitals…" He gave a shrugged and looked lost with it. "Didn't fancy going alone. Now you're back, you wanna come?"

Gabe eased off. Jason couldn't find peace at the cabin or any hospital. Of course he'd ask Ashley to go with him. She glanced back his way before heading over to the ranch.

"I'm going to check on Lisa." Ashley tugged out her phone and headed in.

Gabe looked back at Jason. "Before we go, can I talk to you first?"

"Sure."

"My office?"

He got a nod, and Gabe led the way and poured them both a drink. As Jason took a seat with a sigh, Gabe explained the land sale, the pressure Senator Stanton had been under to keep the bill from the senate floor, and the open seat. He gave Jason a long look, then also told him what Clay had said about needing someone in the senate to give the ranchers a voice. "What do you think? Would you help the ranchers out? Run for office?"

Jason stayed silent as he rubbed the back of his neck. "You were the one with the knack for it. It's never really been my thing." He sat in one of the two brown leather chairs on the other side of the desk, his hands on his thighs, the way their father used to sit. Their dad had been a busy man, and even when he was seated, he appeared on the verge of getting to his feet. "You think I have a good chance of winning?"

"You have an excellent chance of being elected. The party chair would be glad to see your name on the list. Dad was here for me and that helped. It meant a lot. I'm not Dad, but I'm here to help if you decide it's something you want to look in to."

Jason slowly nodded. "That means a lot. How much time do I have to decide?"

Gabe leaned back, his legs stretched under his desk. "Not long. Names will be popping up daily and you'd need to get your name on that list to start being seen. Give it a couple of weeks, then everyone will know you've had time to think it over and you're serious. That's if you decide to go for it. I suppose you want to talk with Ashley over it." Damn, he shouldn't have pushed her out of this.

"Ashley?" Jason frowned. "What's she got to do with this?"

Gabe fidgeted in his chair. "Look, I know you probably wanted this kept under wraps until the kids are ready, but I know how politics screw with family life. I don't want you losing her in the backdrop."

"What the hell are you talking about? Lose who?"

"You and Ashley."

"Oh Christ, me and..." Jason ran a hand through his hair. "Is that why...?" He let out a laugh. "Gabe, there's no me and Ashley. For God's sake, she's a good friend, but that's all she is. What on earth made you think there was anything going on with us?"

"You…" Gabe sat forward in his chair. "I heard you two in your office the other morning, talking about getting hitched. You came out of her bedroom the morning after Jake's."

Jason tried to sober up. "I'd taken her a coffee to say sorry for not being able to go shopping with you guys, nothing more. And talk over getting hitched together? Seriously?" He threw out his hands. "She's Susan's best friend for God's sake."

"So you…?" Gabe gave a rough sigh and slumped back, everything hitting full force. He got to his feet and moved to the window. "You're sure you're nothing *but* friends?"

"Hang on a minute." Jason got up and came over. "This isn't you just being pissed off about me seeing someone new and it upsetting the kids, is it?" He dipped his head as if to get a look inside Gabe's head. "You…like Ashley?"

Gabe downed all of his drink. "Doesn't matter either way," he said flatly. "I've fucked it up."

Jason shrugged. "How, you've only known her properly for a few days. You—" He widened his eyes. "You make a move on her?"

"We kissed, nothing more." There was more, but he didn't play kiss and tell, not the full details, not over Ashley. "The night she got here."

Jason searched his look and seemed to connect some dots. "You heard us talking the next morning, you…" His look softened. "You thought you'd messed about with her when she was mine."

Gabe put his glass on his desk. "No. I thought she was a cold-hearted bitch away from the heat who didn't give a damn she'd slipped between two brothers and it could cost me you."

"Dammit, Gabe. She's grieving over Susan with the rest of us. She came here to get her head clear, and you…." Jason screwed his face, then stepped back. "Marilyn—at Jake's. Don't tell me you—"

Gabe looked away, briefly screwing his eyes shut. "Yeah, like I said. I fucked it up." He knew what was coming.

"You *utter* asshole." Jason jammed a finger into his shoulder. "What the hell is wrong with you? No wonder Ashley fought anger, mostly hurt after you left. She finally let someone in—and you went all butthurt bull on her with another woman. One you're not even interested in anymore. Christ. Did *Marilyn* even know?"

Gabe rubbed at his head. "Like I said," and it was all he had left, "I *really* fucked this up."

Jason headed back around his chair, pointing at him all the way. "Fix your shit." He reached the door. "I don't care how, but you damn well make it better when it comes to her, to Marilyn too. And don't make it any more than that, an apology to Ash." He tugged the door open. "You know her ex-husband cheated on her, right? Did you take time enough to think beyond your dick and ask her about that? Because what you did with Marilyn, in front of her, I'm surprised she didn't smack you one, or at least talk to me so I could have saved her the effort."

Gabe swore under his breath. He'd asked, but it had been to dig into her each time. He'd put her on the defensive. She wouldn't have opened up.

And that last one made him sick to the stomach.

Jason snorted. "Yep, I'm pretty much thinking that's how sick Ashley's been feeling over the past few days." He shook his head. "I'm getting the cars pulled around to pick Megan up and to head to the hospital. You think you can get your head back in the game and call Sheriff Logan and let him know about the pressure Evans put on the senator, give him the name Jean gave you?"

The door shut and Gabe kicked at his chair, then tugged out his mobile. At least he could do that, maybe also look at arranging some help for Megan on her ranch to keep an eye on her foreman.

He hadn't got a clue how to fix it with Ashley.

After one ring, someone answered. "Matt Logan."

"Hey, sheriff. It's Gabe."

Matt laughed, then gave a long sigh. "Well, damn. When you call me sheriff, I know it isn't good news."

Chapter 19

"Any word on how Sam's doing?" Gabe rubbed tiredly at his eyes as they entered the lounge in Sam's large, sprawling High Mountain Ranch house. He'd made a call to Ashley, asking if she wanted him to handle getting Megan over to the hospital, and her breath had carried so much relief. She was rightly caught up in memories of hospitals and late-night calls, they all were, but he'd lost sight of her grief along the way. She'd said a quiet thinks, and he'd left it at that. He couldn't talk to her over the phone. He owed her so much more than that, but he needed sleep before he could handle anything with a clear head as the evening crept in.

Standing near the sofa by the window, Megan looked his way. "No, I called earlier, and he still isn't awake. He should be by the time we get there."

They sat in chairs across from her when she took a seat on the sofa. Gabe had to give her credit for putting up a strong front. "Where are the boys?"

Megan curled her legs under her. "Curtis is still at university. I haven't told him about his grandfather yet. Sean and Brad have been with Molly." She looked at Jason. "You remember Molly Forrester, don't you? She's Molly Green now."

"Yeah. I remember Moll." Jason gave her a soft grin. "We had some fun times."

Megan went to speak, looking to share memories, but fell quiet a moment later as it all seemed to ghost too close to her dad.

"Sam will be all right. Don't worry." Jason shifted in his seat as Gabe let his gaze roam the lounge, taking in the furnishings Grace Frasier had selected. Grace had been a beautiful woman with a head for business, but she'd also had expensive tastes. Megan got her mother's looks but not an ounce of her business smarts.

"Do you know where your foreman, Max Banks, has gone?" Gabe rested his look back on her. Sheriff Logan had asked him to try and get a little more out of her, but he wanted to know too for the call he'd had to make after speaking to him.

Megan wiped her hand over her face. "I don't know. I've been trying to reach him since he didn't show up yesterday."

"I figured as much." Gabe frowned. "I've asked a friend to come over and help out, if that's okay? He should be here in a minute."

"Help?" Megan looked at him sharply. "Why? Who?"

Loretta, Megan's housekeeper, came through carrying a tray. She set the tea on the table as Gabe moved to the French doors overlooking the pool. In their teens, he and Jason had almost drowned in there as they'd tried to show off for Megan. The doorbell rang a moment later, dragging him back into the lounge.

Loretta disappeared, then escorted the man in. "Gabe, your guest's here. Mr. Brooks."

Stocky, in his early forties, and with dark hair streaked with a touch of gray, T.J. was the kind of man who commanded attention when he walked into a room. He did now as he sized up everyone in the lounge.

"Megan, this is T.J. Brooks." He didn't yet mention he was Clay's contact when it came to security and running checks. "He can run the ranch for you until Sam's back on his feet if that's what you want."

Jason threw him a "that's better" smile as T.J. stepped forward and offered his hand. "Yes, ma'am. I run a spread in Montana, but when Gabe said you might need some help, well, I'm here to see what I can do."

With a sigh, Megan came over and shook his hand. "Maybe Gabe's right. I do need help with the ranch." She offered a thin smile, not looking happy, and Gabe offered a sigh. She had a lot of her dad's stubbornness, but unlike her dad, she knew how to shake a hand when it was offered. "Let's all go to Dad's office and sort the legalities before we head over to the hospital."

"Don't rush with the paperwork." Gabe rubbed at her arm. "Not when it comes to the legal side, okay?" He looked over at Jason. "We'll make sure this is sorted first, then head over to the hospital in the morning." He glanced at his watch. "It's getting late."

"Yeah." Jason came over. "Gabe's right. Take time to work the paperwork, make sure you're happy."

Megan let out an unsteady breath. "Okay. Thank you."

"We want to know what happened to Sam too, so we'll check out where he gambled the night he was last seen and talk to anyone we can find who was at the casino," Gabe said. "Maybe with a lot of liquor, Sam told someone about the money for the land sale and this kidnapping and ransom was an opportunity someone couldn't pass up." Now Megan seemed a little more focused, it was a good time to let her know just why T.J. was here. "T.J. has a few men looking for Sam since you didn't want to notify the sheriff."

"You're into security like Clay? Don't you live in Montana?" Megan asked.

T.J. nodded. "Southeast of Billings. Not that far." He grinned. "But always glad to give Gabe a hand."

T.J. not only ran one of the largest conglomerates in the Midwest, which included his ranch, but several other enterprises with top-notch investigators.

"Do you know if Dad's car's been found?" she said to T.J., then to Gabe—"Do you think this is over and Dad is safe? What do you think happened to Max?"

Questions rightly tumbled from her, and Gabe stepped back and left this to T.J.

"Those are things we can't answer right now, but we will. Are you happy for me to look after a few things around here and continue to check things out in the mean time?"

Megan looked at Gabe. "I think so, don't you?"

"You need to know this is over," Gabe said. "I'm hoping Sam is able to tell us what's going on. I have a bad feeling about Max and the land sale, how it ties into the Land Use Bill."

Chapter 20

Ashley sat next to a large plant in Dr. Joyce Thompson's bright reception room, flipping through a Health magazine as she waited for Lisa. She wondered if Gabe had said anything to Jason about seeing the pregnancy test, and she took a deep breath and sighed. He'd seemed so different on the phone last night when he said he'd take Jason over to get Megan. Gone was the Aggression from his tone, and he'd just sounded so tired. He'd had a tough day flying and come away having lost a friend, so Ashley had backed off as well, maybe let out more of a sigh relief. Death lingered, dragging so many down with it.

She'd kill for a coffee, something to bleed out the stress.

Lisa pushed through the doctor's door, and not even looking Ashley's way, she slipped outside. Giving a frown, Ashley put her magazine down and followed.

"Lisa?" The clinic door closed behind her as she went over.

Lisa was already in the car, and Ashley climbed into the passenger seat without speaking. Lisa started the car and pulled onto the road.

"Honey, you all right?" Ashley touched her shoulder.

Lisa shook her head, and after a few blocks, she drove into a lot and parked in front of Jan's Salon and unbuckled her seatbelt. "I want to confirm my appointment with Sandra. She's doing my hair for the dance. Do you need a trim or something?"

What? She reached out and took her hand. "Slow it down, hon. Talk."

Lisa took a deep breath and gave a shaky exhale. "I'm not pregnant." She shrugged. "I know it's for the best, but..." A tear sipped free. "But it feels strange to be told I'm not."

"Oh, hell, honey." Ashley pulled Lisa into a hug and rubbed at her back. She felt guilty for the breath of relief she felt, but—"You need to know it's okay to feel like that. And for what it's worth, you're your mother's daughter, so I know you'd make a wicked mom. You still will."

Lisa pulled back before offering Ashley a shaky smile. "Do you have a tissue?"

Ashley dug through her purse. "Here," She handed a small packet over.

"I know it's silly. I'm lucky that the home test was wrong." She blew her nose. "Still hurts, though."

"Did Dr. Thompson talk to you about precautions?" Ashley wasn't sure this was the time to discuss birth control.

"Yeah. I went through it all with Mom. It was Michael's and my fault. We were careless. We both knew better."

"Is there anything I can do?"

Lisa leaned forward and gave Ashley another hug. "I'm just glad you're here. I never really realized the full weight behind that."

Ashley nearly strangled her in her hold. "Going nowhere, not for a while, sweetheart." Out of the corner of her eye, Ashley caught a small stand advertising smoothies to go. She pulled back. "I think it's smoothie time while you check your appointment, right?"

Lisa grinned. "Okay, strawberry for me."

They got out of the car and went their separate ways.

Ashley arrived back at the car to find Lisa talking with a pretty woman in black jeans, red sweater, and perfect makeup. "Hi," Ashley said as she reached them.

"Ashley, this is Jodi Williams. Her family owns a ranch north of town." Lisa moved closer to Ashley's side. "Jodi, Ashley went to school with Mom and Dad."

"Are you here for long?" Jodi asked.

"Only visiting."

"You staying in town?"

"Oh, no. She's staying with us." Lisa opened the car door as Ashley handed her a smoothie.

"Oh, right." Jodi looked between them. "How is your dad doing? I haven't seen him in town for a while."

"We really like being at the ranch. I think Dad's thinking of staying in Willow River." She took a long drink of her smoothie.

"Well, tell everyone hi for me." Jodi smiled at Ashley. "I hope to see you again."

"I'd like that. It was nice meeting you."

"You, too. Bye, Lisa." Jodi stepped back as Ashley and Lisa got into the car.

As Lisa pulled out onto the road, Ashley asked, "Did Jody go to school here with your dad?"

"She and dad dated in high school. And I think she still likes him. She's always asking about him."

Ashley kept quiet for a moment. "She seems…nice."

Lisa finally found a small laugh. "You're as bad as Uncle Gabe, you know that?"

"What?"

"All that she seems—huge pause, I hate her getting close to Jason—nice. You'll be running back to Clay for a background check on her like Gabe when we get back."

Ashley chuckled. "I'm not that bad… am I?"

Lisa nodded, then measured a "just a little" between finger and thumb. "She's okay, to be honest. I like her a lot, but Dad isn't interested. He misses Mom something fierce."

Ashley placed her half empty cup in the cupholder. "It'll take time."

Lisa tapped the brakes, slowing the car. "I thought maybe someday you and dad…" she said softly.

Ashley brushed her hand over Lisa's, "Your dad and I are good friends. But he's like a brother, nothing else."

Lisa laughed. "Yeah. I heard Dad call you a bossy sister."

"See? We're not meant to be together. Not like that. He's so madly in love with Susan. Always will be. Rightly so too. Sometimes you need space to live and love with the memories. Life shouldn't have to move on, not after love like that."

She'd tasted the bad kind, where she'd been forced to move on without knowing it was bad. But Jason, Susan…they'd had something special.

Ashley gave a sigh and looked over at Lisa. "How about I take you out for lunch later, huh? A little retail therapy shopping? My treat in order to get you those last few things you need for the spring dance." They both needed the break. "We can fit it in before you meet your mates for your hair appointment for later."

Lisa grinned over. "Who in their right mind says no to that?"

***

As Lisa headed up to the ranch to get changed, Ashley finished locking up the car as Cody jogged over.

"Hey," she said, giving him a smile as he turned to watch Lisa.

"She okay?"

"Lisa?" Ashley watched her too. "Yeah. I think she will be. I'm taking her out for lunch in a bit, do some shopping. You want to come along?"

"Hell no." She got a big grin. "I want to show you something, though." Cody tugged her over to the barn and opened the door to flip on the light.

"Wow, Cody." Ashley went in. "This…this is some music studio." She'd forgotten about how he'd grown up with a guitar never far away, although it had been locked away in a case lately. Ashley gazed around at the posters covering the walls and the electronic equipment set up in one corner.

He glanced over at the guitar resting against some speakers. "Been tough getting back into it all. I wanted it to be a secret until it was finished. Dad and I laid the carpet and painted the walls." He went over and turned some knobs on a sound system. "Thomas and Ed said they would come over sometimes to practice. We're hoping to start a rock band." He shrugged. "Maybe we'll get to play locally."

"Okay. Let's hear what you've got." She got comfortable on a guitar seat.

"You sure? I'm rusty." He picked up his guitar and ran his fingers over a couple of strings.

"Oh yes." She needed the distraction.

Giving a grin, he played a song she didn't recognize, but his skill had come on since last time she'd heard him.

"Not that rusty, I see."

He laughed. "Maybe not." He pulled his phone from his pocket and checked the time. "Sorry, I've gotta get my homework done before dinner."

"What you doing?"

"Math."

Ashley got to her feet. "Well, let me know if you need any help. It's kind of my area."

"Oh yeah," he said with a wide grin, and Ashley rolled her gaze at all the cheek that came out with maybe get out of doing it himself.

She levelled a finger his way. "Professor of," she said, adding a narrow of eye. "One who knows how to make you work it out yourself."

"No mates rates?" He looked so much like Susan in that moment.

"Okay, maybe one, but only one, mind."

His laugh played around her as Ashley pulled up the collar of her coat against the cool breeze blowing down from the north while Cody closed the barn door. They walked back to the house and Cody rushed upstairs no doubt to tug Lisa down to his studio, so Ashley headed to the library to grab a book. As she pulled a novel from the library shelf, voices echoed in the hallway then entered the library. She turned to greet them, but Gabe and Lisa hadn't seen her and went to stand by the fireplace. She looked around for another way to leave unseen, let Cody know Lisa was in here, but there wasn't a way out behind her. Feeling like an intruder, she stayed where she was.

Gabe took Lisa's hand in his and looked awkward, as if holding it would break her too somehow. "You all right?" He always had this quiet calm around family.

Lisa gave a hard sigh and hugged him. "I'm trying to be."

"Yeah, I know, kid. How'd it go at the docs?"

Lisa had told him she was going? That she was pregnant?

"Scared me." She buried her head in his chest. "Relieved…made me want to throw up, then not at the same time." A few tears streaked her cheeks. "You disappointed in me?"

"*What?*" Gabe placed his chin on the top of her head. "Commit murder and I'd still blame the cop for catching you." He eased into a smile. "No, never disappointed. Just worried." He pulled back and looked at her. "Love you, kid."

She nodded. "Dr. Thompson said the test was a false positive. Said it happens sometimes."

"You went alone?" Gabe eased her over to one of the chairs in front of the fireplace, and Ashley tried to shrink further into the corner.

"No." Lisa rubbed roughly at her cheeks. "Ashley went with me. She's taking me out for a few hours."

A soft smile crept up on Gabe's lips. "Yeah, I thought she might." He searched her look. "Not your dad?"

"No." Lisa stiffened. "He doesn't know. Don't tell him, okay? Me and Michael had a long talk. We're not ready for something like this. I mean, I like him but..."

"Yeah." Gabe sighed and pulled her in. "You need time to grow into who you are without me telling your dad."

"How'd you find out?"

Ashley turned her ear. So Lisa *hadn't* told him about the appointment and pregnancy.

Gabe looked down. "I was the one who found your test, remember? But when it came to the doctor's, Ruth heard you make the appointment and was concerned."

"She didn't say anything to Dad, did she?" She brushed hair from her face.

"No. I asked her to leave that to you." He winked. "I pay her for her counsel, it seems."

Lisa grinned, but it soon fell. "Do I have to tell him?"

"That's up to you." Gabe stroked at her cheek. "Lord knows I could never force your mother to do anything when it came to Jason, so there's no way I'm pushing her daughter."

"In that case...thank you for being...you." She got up, leaned over to kiss his cheek, then turned and left. As she did, Gabe stood and his gaze met Ashley's.

"So sorry," she said quickly, going over. "I didn't know how to slip out without Lisa seeing me, and I didn't want to interrupt." She didn't know what else to say, and she turned to leave.

"Hey." He gently caught her arm. Always that touching and breaching personal space despite the sting that came with it sometimes. "Thanks for being there for her today."

She turned back. "I always will be." Sadness rushed the blue in his eyes, and she frowned. "I'm sorry to hear about the death of your friend—the senator."

He offered a shrug. "I've got a lot more to be sorry for. I..." He struggled, so badly. "I had a word with Jason yesterday and—"

"Ashley?" Cody came over, a textbook in his hand, not looking where he was going until Gabe stopped him bumping into him. "Sorry." He always had been naturally accident prone. "So, it seems I have a question about this trig problem," he said distractedly to Ashley. "It has to do with cosine and calling in mate's rates." He smiled at Gabe. "Hey."

"Hey back." Gabe let go of his shoulders and turned him toward Ashley. "You're getting out of homework again, huh? That something else I don't tell your dad?" Gabe gave a heavy sigh. "I'm out of here and over to the hospital with Sam." He moved to the door, then stopped and scratched at his head, a blush brushed his cheek and the change confused the hell out of her.

"Can we try and catch a few minutes later?" He frowned over at her. "Talk? Mostly for me to try and say sorry."

Ashley raised a brow. Now that did take her back a little. It didn't let him off the hook, but apologies, when it came to focusing on these kids without the emotional jousting…yeah, she could maybe handle that. "Sure," she said gently, and he nodded before turning away. "Come find me later.

Chapter 21

Gabe stood in Sam's hospital room as the machines beeped around his bed. He hadn't come around yet, and Gabe lowered his head before leaving him in peace. Dr. Mathis and Megan were waiting for him in the corridor, and he gave them a nod. He'd made sure Jason took some time away from here today. Jason was still barely talking to him, but he'd gotten a relieved smile his way when Gabe had offered.

"Let's go to my office, shall we?" Dr. Mathis led the way before she took a seat behind a large desk littered with papers and folders. "Have a seat."

Gabe pulled out a chair for Megan, then took a seat across from her, surprised the doctor would speak to someone outside of family. Perhaps Megan had pushed for it.

"As I was telling Megan earlier, Sam's neurological tests came back, and I'm glad to say we didn't find any brain damage. He does have a little swelling, but it should subside in a few more days. We're keeping him in an induced coma because he was fighting the medications." Dr. Mathis adjusted her computer screen. "He has a broken tibia and a few cuts and bruises, but I believe he's going to be fine."

Gabe frowned. Megan had been under the impression her dad would be awake, and Gabe hadn't realized his assault had left in such bad ways. Megan struggled more, and he realized he was here more for her reaction as everything tried to sink in. He helped her to her feet. "Okay, no questions yet. Let's get you back." He nodded his thanks to the doctor. It had been a mistake to push everything so quickly. But then he was screwing things up a lot along the way lately.

As they made it back, Gabe pulled the Tahoe to a stop in front of the High Mountain garage, and T.J. came out to meet them and opened the door for Megan before looking Gabe's way. "I was thinking we—" He pointed to Megan and himself. "—could stop by for an hour later." He checked his watch. "A *couple* of hours later?" Looked like he had something to say, but caught that Megan needed a break.

Gabe nodded. "That's fine." He didn't linger, and once Megan had gotten out, he turned back to the main road. He was anxious to get back to the ranch to see Ashley, apologize, or try to at least. It hadn't been the right time this morning, not with the state Lisa had been in.

A call came through a moment later, and he stared at the dust on the road, letting it ring for a long time. "What now?" he mumbled under his breath as he eventually thumbed Answer.

***

Frustrated, Gabe rubbed at his head as he headed for his office. Ashley was still out at lunch with Lisa, leaving a note that she'd be back around three. That gave him half an hour of trying to fill time before he could try and sort this mess out and settle into the news he'd just received.

"How's Megan doing?" Jason came in, working on his iPad tablet as Gabe sat at his desk and wrestled the paper trail Clay had uncovered. "You get chance to talk to Sam?"

"Not yet, he's still out of it." Gabe caught sight of something and tugged the note over.

"Yeah?" Gabe got a serious eyebrow raised in his direction as Jason sat down. "You get chance to talk to Ashley yet, then?"

Gabe stopped messing with the file and flicked a look up. Jason had been sorting the ranch roster. With Clay having his nose shifted away from the ranch, they'd needed to shuffle staff around here too.

"I'm working on it, I swear. Just been so swamped with everything." He rubbed at his head. "Jean called on the way back with details over Bob's funeral, also the official coroner's report."

Jason eased off and gave a sigh. "You know, this is why I'm here, Gabe: to help out. You keep trying to steer the horse away from me and the kids when we've tamed it already. Stop thinking of us and take time out to deal with your grief. It's taking you bad places. You're not usually this...self-destructive. An asshole sometimes, but not to the point you sabotage someone like Ashley. She's one of the good guys."

Gabe gave a rough sigh and slumped back in his seat. "I know. Sorry," he said softly. "I'm saying that so much lately. Or need too." Then he held up Clay's memo. "I now know why Sam took the deal, though. Evans paid him above the odds for the land." He read off the number to Jason. "And from Clay's uncovered, Max, High Mountain's foreman, is up to his neck in this mess. He's worked with James Harris of Evans Development before."

Jason cocked a brow. "Okay, you let me deal with that. I'll fax it over to the sheriff."

Gabe nodded. "Megan needs to know he's got to handle if from here. It's out of Clay's hands."

A knock came on the door, and Ashley eased through the gap a moment later but didn't come over.

"Hey..." Gabe started to get to his feet, felt awkward with it, then stood anyhow. He ran a hand through his hair. "Did... did you enjoy shopping?"

Jason winced at him, even shook his head as Ashley frowned his way.

"Erm, yeah...?" She didn't look like she knew how to really answer that one. "Sorry." She thumbed behind her. "Just wanted to let you know Megan and another gentleman's here. You want Ruth to send them through?"

Christ. He'd forgotten T.J. said he needed to come over. "Thanks, yeah."

She went to head out but a kick at Gabe's desk off Jason had Gabe jolting, then—"I'll be done as soon as I can, then..." What? He needed to talk, but not here. "Go grab a coffee with Ruth and I'll find you, yeah?"

Ashley threw Jason a look, another frown, then nodded Gabe's way. "Okay, sure." She still looked like she didn't know how to answer that, and Gabe kicked himself for forcing that "you gonna bark or bite?" look into her.

After she left and Jason coughed "goofball" a few times, a knock came.

"Come in," called Gabe, and T.J. and Megan filed in. "Take a seat." Gabe waved to his desk, and Jadon got up and let Megan take his.

Gabe went back behind his desk. "You said you needed to talk, T.J.?"

T.J. pulled out his phone and started flicking through something, then handed it over to Gabe. "Since Max took over, there are errors in High Mountain's accounts. Along with helping Evans to seal the deal with Sam, he's been skimming off decreasing profits."

Gabe ran a look over the figures as Jason came over. "Okay." He went and crouched by Megan. "I know you didn't want this because of what might come out, but this all has to be handed over to Sheriff Logan for an official investigation now. Do you understand?" Although most of it had already been handed over, but Megan didn't need to know that. "Even if Max and Evans wasn't responsible for his kidnapping, which something's telling me they wouldn't be that obvious, there's too much going on over the deal and with other sources I've spoken to not warrant Logan's involvement."

Megan nodded, but the look in her eyes said she'd been expecting it.

Chapter 22

Tired of all the driving to and from the doctors and town, Ashley headed to the kitchen for a cup of tea. They'd hunted out shoes, more makeup and jewelry, and anything else Lisa needed to match her new dress, and with Lisa gone for her hair appointment with her friends, Ashley had placed them on her bed so they would all be in one place when she got back.

For once Ruth didn't haunt the kitchen, and she took her drink and sat at the kitchen table, wondering what was going on with Gabe. He'd looked…petrified, and it bit at her inside. He was guilty over something, and pictures of him letting her know he was going to come clean to Marilyn over their kiss had her feeling sick. That had to be it, right? His time away over the death of his friend snapped him out of the game he played. Now she had to stand at his side and come clean to Marilyn.

"Like hell," she mumbled over her tea.

"What was that, love?" Ruth came in, removing her jacket.

Ashley waved her off. "Just talking to myself." She frowned at her. "You okay? You look harassed."

"Me? I'm running late." Ruth turned the oven knob and removed two homemade pies from the fridge and placed them on the counter. "I'll stick these in the oven and join you for a cup of tea." She glanced down the hallway. "They still busy with Megan?"

"Yeah." Ashley rose from her chair and tugged another mug out of the cupboard. "I'll get you a drink."

"Thanks. I was at church earlier. We're planning a gathering for the new assistant pastor. I think he'll fit in nicely..."

Ashley sat and hugged her tea to her, a little too lost to pay attention until someone called her name. "What?"

Gabe sat down by her, and Ruth looked between them before giving them some space. "We lost you there for a while, huh?"

Ashley snorted a slight smile. "Had my Loading sign going on there, right?"

Gabe smiled as he rested an elbow on the table. "Just a little." He went to say something else, then wiped a hand over his mouth. "Listen, I'm taking a drive up to a summer pasture just to clear my head and check out some fencing that's been reported. Can you take a ride with me?"

"Gabe." Ashley rested her cup down. "I don't think that's a good idea, do you? Marilyn—"

"Yeah, I know." Gabe frowned. "You have my word it's just to talk, but I..." He offered such a boyish half smile. "I might just need you away from sharp knives in order to do this."

Unease didn't bite into her stomach, it dug deeper into lungs, heart, and most vital organs. "For clarity here..." She searched his gaze, trying to find signs of any spoilers. "I don't carry a knife either, nor gun. Just in case you were wondering."

He gave a soft laugh, but his look strayed to her bag, and she choked a laugh, nearly spilling her tea. "Joke, Gabe. Joke."

"City girls," he said to her. "Can't be too careful." Then he winced. "Nor with country girls when they've been hurt either." He eased out of his seat and dug his hands in his pockets. "Five minutes, yeah? Outside."

She took a sip of tea and made it slow. "When I'm done." She winked up at him. "City girl here." She'd make him work for this talk, no gun needed.

***

Ashley grabbed her favorite wool sweater, pulling it down over her shoulders as she met Gabe outside. On their way to the Tahoe, she took a deep breath of fresh air and glanced up at the wide sky darkening with clouds, not wanting to take this drive now she was out here. "It's cool today."

Gabe opened the door for her. "You may want to run in for a jacket. It'll be even colder up there. We're heading up to one of the high pastures used for summer grazing.."

"I'll be all right." She shivered. She wasn't, but she wasn't about to admit it either or help prove him right. She got in and buckled her seatbelt, wanting to get this talk over with. "What are you checking?"

He started the engine. "Fencing and if we can take the cattle up soon. I don't want them to have to dig beneath snow for food."

"You're moving them to high ground for the summer, then?" She peered at the mountains ahead.

He nodded. "Make the best use of the land."

"I never realized all the responsibilities of owning a ranch. Jason filled me in on some of them." Small talk was safe ground.

"You mean like rotating the herd through the pastures, keeping the land and herd healthy, running the breeding program, plus all repairs to fences and outbuildings?"

She laughed a little. "Yes, all those."

Gabe turned onto a dirt road that led them higher onto a flat plateau. The mountains seemed closer as they towered over the wide valley. "Okay, talk," she said quietly. "Open the window if you really need that fresh air, but you tell me why we're here."

Gabe threw her a look, then his hands tightened on the steering wheel. "I got it wrong. I got you wrong." He kept pure focus on the road ahead. "After I kissed you, I thought you and Jason were an item. That you were getting married."

"*What*?" Ashley went to say something else, failed, then—"What the hell, Gabe?"

"I know, I know, all right." Gabe shifted gear, more forced it into position. "I misheard you both back outside his office."

"And you thought..." Ashley couldn't finish it. "Goddamn it. Susan." She gripped onto her seat. "You think I'd screw with your family like that? That as soon as she was dead, I'd jump into bed with Jason, insist Lisa and Cody run around calling me mom as I tear down her pictures off the wall? What's *wrong* with you? This isn't politics, where backhand deals between the sheets get further than integrity these days. She was—still is—my best friend. That makes Jason my best friend by default. It makes their goddamn kids my priority *as* best friend to their mom, you idiot."

Gabe's look didn't stray from the road. "Not the worst of it, Ash." He gave such a hard sigh. "Marilyn..."

He started to talk, but nothing seemed to register after he said there was...nothing between them.

"Stop the car."

"What?" Gabe flicked her a look.

"*Stop the goddamn car, Gabe.*" She started to open the door even before he slammed the brakes on. Only her seatbelt stopped her from getting out. She hit the clasp to it a moment later, and with burnt rubber and smoke hitting her, she pushed out and slammed the door.

"Hey... *hey.*" Gabe was by her, trying to twist her around, so Ashley shoved him off.

"You weren't even *seeing* her." She threw out her hands, laughed, but it left her shaking. "You...you." She shoved him again. "Who does that? I mean, seriously?" She held out her arms. "Who in their right mind *behaves* like that, Gabe?"

Gabe wiped a hand over his mouth. "We lost Susan." He shrugged. "I nearly lost Jason with it. You never saw him like I did, not in the early days. Then you—"

"I *what*?"

All the tensions seemed to drain out of his body. "I forgot about it all when I kissed you. I slipped so badly *with* you, I didn't want to think beyond us for just few damn moments. Then when I thought you were his, you played us?" He shrugged. "He didn't matter. I still wanted to hold you, and that...?" He fought back anger. "I hated myself so damn much. He's my *brother*. I wanted you even if it cost him and the kids, and I felt so shit for it."

"Not an excuse." Ashley let out a hurt snort. "We're all hurting, Gabe. We're all grieving. Christ knows we all do stupid things because of it, but you...you could have spoken to me at any time. I'm not a player. I wouldn't even know where to start."

Gabe nodded. "I know. I think I knew it back then, I—"

"You don't *know* it. That's the goddamn problem," said Ashley, going over. "Forget that you threw me back into being cheated on— you molded into the other woman. You sat Marilyn down at our table, didn't tell her what you were doing, and you damn well made me sit and look at myself, all my screw ups over not being good enough, over being a chess piece you picked up only when you were in the mood. I didn't get a choice over being cheated on, but I damn well made a choice never to be the one cheating." She eased back, forcing all heat back. "But I had even that choice taken out of my hands. *You* took it out of my hands. I'd have never have kissed you if I'd have known you were seeing her because that's who I am." She shook her head. "But in the end, you weren't even seeing her."

Gabe ran a hand through his hair. "My fault," he said softly. "There's no excuses. I wish to God I knew why I'd gone down that path. I just..." He frowned. "I just wanted to try and put it right. Let you know it's all down to me."

Ashley shrugged. "Doesn't take it away, Gabe. You wanna know why?"

He didn't answer. He was back to looking like he didn't know how best to answer anything for fear of it breaking.

"Because I wanted you too back there, even knowing about Marilyn." She shrugged. "That makes us *both* cheats. And I don't like that side of me you've brought out in me either."

Saying nothing, Ashley got back in the car and closed her eyes as she rested back. Gabe got in a moment later, and the silence between them said it all.

He eventually pulled up into a clearing, and Ashley pushed out. Gabe was right about one thing: she needed the fresh air to clear away all the mud dragging her down.

"C'mon," Gabe said softly. He stood close to a trail, but looked away when she glanced over. "You don't have to stay close, just watch your step. Take the walk with me. Please. I don't want you left here on your own."

She didn't think she'd be any better off with Gabe, but she followed him down a beaten trail through a stand of trees. The sound of flowing water crept through the bush, and moments later, the trail opened up to a stream filled with crystal-clear water tumbling over a bed of rocks worn smooth from years of erosion.

The wind picked up, and Ashley buried a shiver in her sweater. Usually, she'd stop and take a few pictures of hidden gems space like this. She'd been doing it more and more since Susan's death, maybe finding a way to talk to her beyond words. But it came with a bitter-sweet taste today, so she carried on after Gabe up to the pasture and watched from a distance as he made his checks on the fence. It took a while, enough for the sky to darken and shadows fall across the pasture.

"Here, take this." Gabe came over and slipped off his jacket. Ashley eyed him, rubbing at her shoulders, so he slipped it around her and pulled it tight as he looked up. "I thought the rain would hold off until much later."

The first raindrops fell, and Ashley blinked against them. Then the downpour started, and they made a run back for the stream and Tahoe.

In the heavy rain, clothes pasted themselves to Ashley's body, and she clambered in the Tahoe, struggling to pull the wet sweater away from her skin. Gabe was worse off, his shirt sculpting his upper chest. He ran a hand through his hair, and Ashley looked away, more annoyed at his offer of a wet T-shirt competition he unconsciously gave off. He won, hands down.

Gabe's look lingered her way, then he reached behind them and tugged a blanket off the back seat. "Take this as well."

He pushed it at her, more dropped in her lap as if she'd smack his touch away, and she raised a brow at the constant contrasts he brought out. He didn't know what to do, what to say, and that differed so much from how he handled trouble on the whole. He thought hard and over the logistics, over what was needed, what need to be said in public, but get him away from that logical process, take away the equation, he stumbled and faltered with trying to find the answers.

Ashley buried a sigh and looked out her window. Everybody screwed up with grief. Gabe's seemed to run deeper than that. Maybe that was why she'd never read anything about him when it came to settling down with someone since his ex-wife. He'd gotten used to women walking away with his kid or, like Susan, leaving in one form another. So he slept around with Marilyn when he needed and then he'd gone knee-jerk reaction with when it came to Jason and her, unconsciously trying to push her away without realizing it.

And that was her, making excuses for him, and she screwed her eyes tight shut, thrown back into making excuses for everyone, her own ex-husband and why he had nights away. But despite his vicious play, there seemed honest screw ups behind Gabe. She just didn't know if she could trust that instinct anymore to judge safely. "Thank you," she mumbled eventually, not liking she had to say thank you.

Gabe started the engine and turned the SUV around. A sleet had replaced the rain and now streamed down the windshield. Neither spoke as Gabe drove fast down the road back into the valley.

"I really should have worn a jacket," she said eventually, wiping at her eyes as the roll of the car lulled her almost to sleep.

"There's a concert tonight. Harper Johnson asked me for assistance in hosting a classical musical event on his ranch several years ago, and the concerts grown ever since."

Ashley frowned at Gabe. "And?"

"And I was wondering if you'd go with me."

Ashley sat up. "Are you *serious*?"

Gabe looked at her. "Utterly." He offered a tired smile. "We're both stubborn and going nowhere because of Jason and the kids." His confidence fell. "So I'd like to say sorry properly if you'd let me? Maybe try and show you I'm not an asshole at heart?"

"You'll need more than a night for that." She folded her arms. "Think lifetime."

"If you'll have me." He threw her a boyish grin. "For a lifetime, like."

Ashley rarely flipped anyone the bird, but she was really, really tempted to in that moment.

***

In her guest room, Ashley stripped, stepped into the shower, and the hot water hit her skin causing her to shiver until the heat penetrated deep, relaxing the muscles she hadn't realized were tense. She closed her eyes and lifted her head to the flowing water.

She dusted her fingertips against her hips and gentle nips and licks came easily at her skin. Or they did in her head anyway. She needed touching beyond her own and she pushed it away, not liking where her head was going when it came to who she almost let ghost the shower with her.

Giving a sigh, she stepped out, then wrapped a towel around her hair and another around her body as she walked to the closet for her robe. While she was tying the sash, a knock came at the door. Ruth had caught them on their way in and had promised to get her a cup of tea, and she went over and opened the door, expecting to see a friendly smile. "Gabe?" Christ, couldn't he leave this alone?

"Here." Like the blanket, a tray with a hot drink was pushed her way. "Ruth, erm, she asked me to bring it up."

"*Ruth* asked you?" Ashley cocked a brow, and Gabe dug his hands in his pocket as she took it.

"Yeah." Gabe sniffed. "Ruth."

Sure she did. She placed the tray on a small table. He didn't come in, just stood awkwardly on the threshold, and it seemed to mirror everything they were. Always on the threshold. His hair was still shower fresh, and a mix of cologne and deodorant couldn't hide that feel of long walks in the wild.

"Wanted to make sure we were good," he said quietly. "Not for Jason, not for the kids, just for us. The possibility of friends, if nothing else."

"You think I need you as a friend?"

He shrugged. "I'd like to hope so. I've never cheated, Ash, not beyond the screw up with Marilyn, but I know I'm far from perfect. I'm—"

"An asshole? Overbearing, overprotective—more Id than Ego and Superego in Freud terminology?"

"—*Prone* to screwing things up." He blushed through all of that. "But for what it's worth, if it's worth anything, you're ex-husband's the idiot. He didn't even get to stay near you as a friend and see the chance he screwed up."

Ashley watched him for a moment, then narrowed her gaze and gave a rough sigh. "Friends, the possibility of." She measured between thumb and finger. "A small one." It killed her not to offer more, but he burned badly in grief when rejected. And he was still grieving along with the rest of them. He had to see that like she did.

"Friends, the possibility of." He nodded, the lines on his face easing as he measured between thumb and finger. "A small one."

Ashley reached up and closed the gap he'd offered between his fingers. It had been a lot bigger than hers.

He laughed softly, then caught her hand and kissed coyly at her cheek. He pulled back, looking like he really meant nothing by it, but then he paused and lingered so close by, his breath brushed her cheek. He went to say something, then giving a soft blush, he shook his head and pulled back.

She was grown up enough to know she missed the kiss that was almost there, but she thanked him for stepping back, because she would have pulled away if he'd tried.

"Uncle Gabe?" Lisa came down the hall and eyed him up. "What you doing here?" A lot of protection for Ashley came in her look, and Gabe raised his hands and backed away.

"I brought Ashley a cup of tea. From, erm, Ruth." He glanced back at Ashley. "I'll let you two ladies talk." And with one last longing glance at her, he left.

Lisa pushed through and sat at the small table across from Ashley. "You okay?"

"Yeah." Ashley shut the door and hid a small smile with it. "I got caught in the rain today and am not feeling myself at the moment."

"Your cheeks are flushed. You coming down with something?"

Damn. She was mad, not blind, and Gabe always seemed to play with both sides: head and...heat. "Thanks. I'll be fine. Really."

"Good, because—" She framed her face with her hands. "—tah-dah. What do you think of my hair? I really like it.

Ashley picked up her drink. "It's very you. What time does the school dance start tonight?" She'd nearly forgotten that was going down as well.

"Eight, but friends are picking me up early." She narrowed her eyes at the door, then back at Ashley. "What about you? What you doing tonight?"

Chapter 23

Gabe waited in the foyer, shifting from one foot to another. This was Lisa's big moment, what all the shopping had been about, but he couldn't help but want to move it along and get Ashley out of here. Jason stood close by with camera in hand and looking every part the proud dad waiting to see his daughter, Cody moaning close by as Ruth told him to hush. This was why he really didn't want to be here: this was Jason's moment as Dad, and as much as he loved Lisa, he wanted Jason to own this moment with her.

A door upstairs opened, and Ashley came down to join them. Shower-fresh and wearing suit pants and shirt, she looked as professional as ever, but her smile was so relaxed, her move to Gabe's side saying she shared what he did, how this was Lisa's and Jason's moment. "I told her to wait a moment so you could get pictures of her coming down," she said over to Jason.

"Shush, shish," said Ruth, waving at them as noise came from upstairs, and Ashley threw Gabe a smile, almost as if she'd forgotten what he'd done. Maybe she had because she was all Lisa in this moment.

Lisa came to the top step and looked down, knowing this was her moment.

"Slowly slowly, honey," called Jason. "Let me get some good shots."

Gabe hadn't seen her dress, and she owned it with every ounce of her mother's confidence. She looked stunning, but he couldn't help letting his gaze slip to Ashley, all the pride she had there for Lisa as she walked down the stairs.

Jason stopped snapping pictures every now and again to show off a goofy smile. "Stunning. Just stunning, baby." He gave up and gave her a hug along with Ruth.

"Makeup, my makeup. Stop."

He did and she pulled back, grinning. "You like it, then?" Lisa twirled. "You're not mad at the low cut?"

"Your mom would be scowling at me if I did." Jason kissed at her cheek. "You look gorgeous."

"Uncle Gabe?"

He gave her a huge thumbs up, then went over and hugged her as well before looking at Cody. "Hey."

"What?" Cody bit a nail as he looked up from his phone. "She looks nice."

Jason laughed as Lisa hit him.

Ashley came over and gently tugged Gabe away with a pull on his shirt cuff. "I'm gonna go and get change, okay? Then we'll head off."

"You go," he whispered in her ear. "And thank you...for all of this."

She shared his look for a moment, then offered a soft smile. "Wouldn't have missed it."

He watched her go. He couldn't refrain from *not* watching her go.

***

Gabe opened the car door for Ashley as she made her way over. She'd changed from suit pants and shirt in to jeans and a blue jumper, but her hair was loose, and it framed her face.

"You look...gorgeous."

He didn't scrub up too bad himself either and she gave a sigh. This...friend business was going to be tough on them, and he seemed to check himself and threw over a wince, a sorry. She offered a smile before climbing in. "You say the concert's in a barn?" She'd made sure to bring a coat this time.

Gabe got in and fastened his seat belt. "You're real city gal, huh? And, yup, it is. Have you always lived in Cincinnati?"

"Yeah." She fastened her belt as he pulled away. "Jason had a habit of calling me a city girl too, but I've always loved the woods when I was a girl." She glanced around the ranch as it faded into the night. "I love it here." She shook off just how much and glanced at Gabe. "My brother and I built a fort on a forested acre behind our house. That was before the land sold and a housing development was built behind us."

Gabe winced. "Developers…they'd snatch up a snake pit if they could. How long did you get to use your fort?"

"Only a couple of years. I've always wanted a cabin and a few acres on Lake Lorelei. It's not far from Cincinnati."

"Do you go there often?" A car honked as it passed them. They were back to small talk, but no awkwardness came with it, just natural curiosity.

"Not as often as I'd like. Elaine, a colleague, has a place there, and I visit her." Ashley eased back in her seat. "Definitely not often enough."

Gabe turned from the highway onto a hard-packed grass lane lined on both sides by tall evergreens, creating a darkened tunnel. Once they cleared the trees, a young man walked toward the car and Gabe lowered his window.

"Good evening, sir." The man held out his hand. "I'll take care of the car for you."

"Thank you, I appreciate it." Gabe stepped out and handed him the keys.

By the time Ashley had undone her seatbelt, Gabe was around her side, holding the door as her gaze went around the sea of small lights strung throughout the grounds and the throng of people pushing past them. Giving her a smile, he took her hand, then threaded a way through the crowd heading toward a large, newly painted red barn.

Still that touch on skin off him, that offer of care away from his bite. "Stay close," he said softly as they headed for the stage.

Gabe introduced her to Harper Johnson, and pictures of them were taken, then Gabe looked her way. "Sorry, I got roped into doing this, I hope you don't mind."

Ashley went to ask what, but Gabe tugged her farther onto the stage and stepped up to the microphone.

Oh. She clasped her hands together, suddenly conscious of being center stage as everything fell quiet. She got a feeling she knew what Gabe had been roped into.

"I want to thank each of you for coming tonight. Your continued support and efforts have made this concert a continued success. We're especially thankful to the Johnson family for bringing live classical music to their ranch and this area each year." Gabe eased into a less professional smile. "Now go and enjoy yourselves, you lot."

After a cheer and applause for the speech being so...short, Gabe winked Ashley's way. He knew crowds, when to spin something, when to call enough and let them enjoy the night without the politics. He took a hand again, more discreetly this time, but a few whistles came their way as they left the stage.

"You know you could have left me on the sidelines for that."

He shook his head and stopped someone from bumping into her. "You're with family here. We look out for one another, which means no being left on the sidelines." He offered a soft smile. "Friend or...otherwise."

Okay. Maybe that was a small win for him. She measured it between thumb and finger, mentally anyway. Just a small win.

They were given programs and seated in the front row, directly below the wooden platform. Bales of hay, loaded with concert goers tightly squeezed together and deep in conversation, were stacked around the walls. Up above, more bales held dozens more people, and a few gazes and smiles focused her way. She stiffened.

Gabe leaned in close. "You all right?" His warm breath brushed her cheek, and she nodded his way.

She'd not thought a lot of Gabe's prominence as a former governor since she'd been here, but it hit home now, and it took a little of her confidence away with it. Gabe too with how he lost his smile.

"We can leave if you want? I didn't intend to—"

Ashley took his hand and rubbed at the back of it. "Family...friend, we look out for each other, right?"

A frown crossed his brow along with a soft smile. He'd tried to make this about her, and she liked him for it, but this was about them, which meant both sides of the coin, as friends or...otherwise, ones learning to acknowledge insecurities as well as screw ups. Didn't matter how far down the line he'd come, Gabe had seen someone he love walk away from him with his kid because of his career path.

The musicians arrived on stage and Mozart's Sonatina Number Four soon filled the barn. The rich melancholy timbre of the viola and clarinet had the audience silent. Ashley enjoyed the feeling of soaring. The clear tones kept her in that melodic world, suspended in time.

She'd lost track of time, and it surprised her when the musicians stood, and applause rang out loudly just before Mr. Johnson walked across the stage and announced an intermission.

"Is this your first visit here?" The gray-haired woman on Ashley's right asked, and Ashley realized then she'd not being paying attention to anyone close by but Gabe. "We come every year, don't we, Fred?" She smiled at the man seated next to her.

"Yes. The music's wonderful," Fred replied.

"It's my first time." Ashley looked up as Gabe stood to greet a man who'd made his way around the feet of the crowd, his cane hitting the wooden floor with a loud thud each time he took a small step.

Gabe quickly glanced down at her, smiled, then turned his full attention to what the man was saying.

The woman chuckled and leaned in closer to Ashley. "That's George Watson. He owns a large spread just north of here and thinks of himself as an expert on whatever is going on in this valley."

"Do you live in the valley too?"

"Oh my." She put her hand to her chest. "I'm Martha, by the way, and Fred and I have lived here all our lives. Our son runs the small ranch now. He's also a veterinarian."

"You must know most of the ranchers, then?"

"Pretty much," she said. "Say, Fred and I have been wondering if Gabe is going to take Senator Stanton's seat." She gave Ashley a sly grin. "We certainly couldn't get anyone better."

Ashley shook her head. "You know, I honestly don't know." She did. Jason had mentioned something about looking into running for the seat, but…family. She knew when to talk, when not to.

Martha placed a hand on Ashley's arm. "Well, honey, I'm sure you would be the first to know." A wide smile crossed her face as she looked at Gabe.

The lights dimmed and everyone retook their seats, waiting for the musicians to return to the stage. The selections for the second half of the program were as splendid as before, and Ashley relaxed, letting the music touch her. The piece by the German composer, Schumann, was dark and mysterious and at times terrifying and intense, reminding Ashley of a novel she once read of scantily clad women dancing around an open campfire with their long hair flying and their eyes filled with desire. It was a contrast between light and dark, between loathing and desire, and she smiled into how it called her and Gabe out. Gabe seemed just as lost. He wasn't here just out of duty over politics or to win a friend over, and that was another plus in his direction. A huge one. Mostly because he unconsciously gave away a piece of himself now, what he loved no matter the company. By the time it finished, she felt relax and more content with who she took a seat next to.

After a moment as the crowd began to find their feet and filter away, Gabe stood and took her hand. They spoke with Martha and Fred for a minute, then eased into the crowd, with Gabe stopping every now and again to introduce her. An hour later they'd made it back to the young valet.

The long line of cars crawled back down the evergreen tunnel toward the highway, and once they reached the highway and turned left toward the ranch, Ashley's excitement spilled over. "What an amazing concert."

"It is each year. The organizers do an excellent job finding young talent."

Gabe's deep voice sent shivers through her. "Do Jason and the kids usually join you? Did…." She stopped, but Gabe caught on.

"Marilyn when I was seeing her?"

Ashley winced. "Sorry, I didn't mean for it to sound like that."

"It's okay." He flicked her a look. "We both have pasts. And no, she didn't. It wasn't her thing. Susan and Jason came a few times, Lisa too. But Cody is pure rock. You wouldn't catch him here." He fell quiet for a moment. "You're the first…friend I've brought." He winced. "Except Ruth, of course."

Ashley let out a laugh. "That's… that's comforting to know. I think."

He laughed too and it fell into a comfortable silence as he drove through the valley, all nature—not a building in sight. Then he turned off the road and drove through the gates of the ranch. Once he reached the house, he parked, and Ashley kept her smile private as he walked around to open her door for her.

A hand came her way, and she took it, but after he shut the door, she was the one to keep hold of his hand and tug him up to the porch. As they reached the door, she turned and eased him back against the wall, going in close to his body, her breath brushing his.

"Oh-kay," he said, hands going out wide as if caught between wanting to touch, then knowing he shouldn't. "Slightly confusing signs going on here as my…friend."

She searched his look for a moment, then brushed her lips against his, then nipped the bottom one before he had time to respond. "Good, because I wanted to show you something." She ran a touch up his inside thigh, all to drag fingernails over the cut of jeans and thickness of cock. "This is the right kind of confusion we should have been dealing with." She nipped at his lip again, and he instantly slipped a hand through her hair, cupping the back of her neck as the other gripped her hip, tugging her into a gentle bump and grind.

With a last kiss, she pulled away and patted gently at his cheek. "If ever you feel like being an ass to me again, you keep that in focus, okay?"

He didn't answer, looked like he couldn't, and she bit back a smile seeing it.

"'Night, Gabe." She gave him a wink and turned away.

"Christ," she heard him groan—then he tugged her back, pinning her up against the wall.

For a moment he shared her look, searched in it for something else—then his kiss roughed her neck, and she gripped his hair as he freed the clasp to her pants before he was down, stroking roughly at her with only her damp pants as a barrier.

"Jesus…" Ashley threw her head back, her leg wrapping his waist, all heat and friction, loving his hand, but needing the feel of all the thickness in his cock to grind into her.

He denied her, not stopping stroking her until she tugged him close and buried her cry of release in his shoulder.

"Yeah." Gabe started to fasten her trousers and gently tidy her up as she tried to catch her breath. Arms still wrapped around his shoulders, he pulled back and wiped at her cheek. "That's the right kind of confusion. "He kissed her, then reached over to open the door. "Night…Ashley."

Ashley laughed into his shoulder. "Oh gonna be like that, is it?"

He ran his thumb lightly up the side of her neck. "I certainly hope so."

Quiet fell around them, then—"Who left the damn door open?"

Jason came over, and his eyes widened as they both buried soft laughter. "Oh...there you are."

Jason stopped, eyed her up, then Gabe. "Everything—" He waved it off, seeing how they huddled together. "Yeah, I can see everything's all right between you two now."

"He *told* you?" Ashley cocked a brow.

"Eventually. But brother here, I get everything out of him eventually." Jason pointed to Gabe. "Don't screw this up again, we clear?"

"Christ." Gabe stayed hidden in Ashley's shoulder, and Ashley kept him there as he tried to stop chuckling. "Scout's honor."

Jason only narrowed his eyes at him. "Good, because I got a call off Megan."

Gabe looked up.

"Sam's awake and wants to see us. T.J. and Megan will pick us up in the morning." His gaze swept over them. "Sorry."

"No need to be," said Ashley, and she looked at Gabe and stroked at his cheek. "You go talk to Jason. I'm calling it a night. Let me know how you get on with Sam in the morning."

He nodded, then as she went to walk away for a second time, he eased her back. "Night," he said quietly, and his kiss touched hers.

He was still hard, and she searched his look with a bite at her lip. "You can handle things from here alone, can't you?"

He buried a laugh. "Go. Leave me in peace. Please."

Chapter 24

Sam's voice boomed down the hallway of the hospital, his complaint coming loud and clear right through the closed door, or so it seemed to Gabe.

"Dad's back," Megan said before entering his room.

Gabe waited in the hallway with Jason and T.J. as a nurse hurried out, laughing. "He's your friend?" She looked at Gabe first as he stood against the wall.

"Sounds like he's giving you a hard time."

"Some patients think they know best." She shook her head as she walked toward the nurses' station.

Megan opened the door a moment later. "Dad wants to see you."

Gabe headed in first and found Sam sitting up in bed. "Good to see you. Sounds like you're going to make it."

"If I do, it's not because of the food they serve." Sam pushed a bowl of fruit away. "That's all they serve at this hour."

"It's good to see you awake." Gabe went over. "Sam, this is Thomas Jefferson Brooks, T.J. for short. He's been running your ranch since you were in hospital."

"Running? Who the hell hired him? I didn't and—" He seemed think for a minute as he looked past Gabe to T.J. "Hang on. T.J. Brooks, from Montana?"

Megan got up and stuffed a pillow behind his back.

"Yes, sir." T.J. stepped forward and offered a hand. "Nice spread you got."

Sam nodded and took it. "I've heard of you. Sort of like a troubleshooter. Help ranchers get back on their feet."

"Plus other things," Gabe said.

T.J. pulled a chair closer to the bed and took a seat as Megan sat on the other side. Gabe stayed back against the wall with Jason.

"Okay, Sam," T.J. said gently. "I know you'll have been through this with the sheriff, but…" He glanced back at Gabe, at how sometimes family and friends got at the truth a little better. "What do you remember about the kidnapping? If you need to stop to rest, that's all right."

"I'm not that soft, cowboy." Sam cleared his throat. "I had a few drinks, and after several hours of playing poker, I went to my car. Two men were hiding in the back. They put a cloth over my mouth and nose, and when I woke up in a shack somewhere off a logging road, my hands and feet were tied. After a few days, I was able to free myself and headed out." He reached for a drink of water. "And no, the sheriff hasn't been around yet. The doctor said he'll be allowed to come by later, when I'm fit to file a report, that's why I called Megan and had her bring you boys here." Sam looked from Gabe to Jason.

"We'll do what we can to help, Sam. Just let us know what you need," Gabe said. "But, when you feel up to it, we need to talk about Max and the land deal you made."

Sam looked away and clammed shut for a moment. "Look. Sorry I sold that land, but at the time, I didn't know what else to do."

"I know," said Gabe, "but I want to run a name by you." The one Jean had given him. The sheriff had asked him to press Sam to see if they could tie it all together. "See if you recognize it as anything to do with the kidnapping…"

Chapter 25

Finally back home, Gabe headed for the kitchen, needing coffee, but needing more to chase alone time with Ashley. He just didn't want to come over as overstepping the mark as well as overbearing, overprotective, and more Id than superego, whatever the hell those last two were. He snorted to himself at the reminder. Ashley didn't hold back. Rightly so too. He'd been more than an asshole.

"Hey." Jason stuck his head out his office door. "In here. You'll want to see this."

Giving a frown, Gabe went over. "What?"

Jason waved for him to follow. "Ashley's been showing me a photo she took with Ted. Take a look at this." He lifted the camera screen so Gabe could see.

As he did, Ashley came over, and Gabe threw her a smile, not bothered with photos in that moment.

"Pay attention." Jason hit his arm and snorted a grin as Gabe was forced to focus away from Ashley's smile, her lips, face, hair...body, hold of mug and how her hands wrapped around it. "The hawk in the background is clear, but look at the location."

Hawk? Gabe grabbed the camera and looked closer, then shot a glance to Ashley. "You took this with Ted? At Alpine Ridge?"

"It's Alpine Ridge, all right," Jason took the camera for another look.

Christ. This changed everything. "I'll call Pam Dryer." Gabe grabbed Jason's phone on the desk. "Where's her number?"

"Here." Jason turned his computer screen to face Gabe.

"Why?" Ashley came over, her mug of tea held protectively in her hands. "Jason's just seen it and I haven't got a clue what's got him going."

"Pam Dryer is head of Wildlife Conservation in Wyoming." Gabe pinched her mug off her and took a swig of tea. It earned him a "So it's gonna be like that" cock of brow, and damn his soul, he loved her for it. Damn right it was gonna be like this. "The organization has been concerned for years about the lack of sightings of the broad-winged hawk. You got one here." Gabe pointed at the camera. "This might help us put a stop to the Evans Development plan to build adjacent to Coulter Creek at Alpine Ridge. This could be exactly what we need."

"You think it'll work?" Ashley asked.

"Oh I'll make damn sure it does," said Gabe. After he spoke to Pam, he hung up. "Pam wants to know if you have any more pictures."

"Not of the hawk, I don't think." She pinched her mug back. "Sorry."

He nodded. "She wants the picture sent over to her, and make sure you back a copy to cloud storage, so we don't lose it. I'm flying down to Cheyenne for a meeting with her tomorrow."

Jason handed Gabe the camera. "Stored and double stored. Anything else?"

"Yeah." Gabe flicked him a look. "You thought anymore about taking that senate seat, because right about now would really help us out."

Jason dug his hands in his pockets. "You think I'm good enough?"

"You constantly go up against me," said Gabe. "Damn right I do. You also know the ranchers, the land, but most our ranchers know you. When it comes to anything else, I can teach you. I'll also be your ears with the ranchers."

Jason looked at Ashley, and Gabe saw it then. Jason had been so used to making a decision with Susan around, this was his first really big leap alone. They were all learning and re-evaluating shattered lives as best as they could. "I'll be right there, brother."

"Okay." Jason nodded. "Let's do it. Could you give me your contacts?"

"Absolutely, I'll make a list and get it to you."

Jason ran a hand through his hair. "Right, but for god's sake, can someone please tell me what's been wrong with Lisa lately? I haven't got a clue where to start asking."

It fell into quiet, and Gabe and Ashley shared a look.

"I mean, I thought she was doing okay up until last week." Jason shrugged. "I thought it was to do with missing the shopping trip, but I know her. Something like that wouldn't eat into her like this."

Ashley went over and rubbed at his arm. "Go talk to her," she said gently. "But don't push it if she doesn't want to, okay. In fact..." She glanced back at Gabe. "If she doesn't talk, just hug her, and for as long as possible. Sometimes it's the only answer."

Jason frowned at her, then pulled away and headed out.

Ashley gave a sigh and came back over to Gabe. "I'm losing you tomorrow too, huh?"

Gabe tugged her in as he wrapped his arms around her. "You could come with me?"

Ashley looked up and narrowed her eyes. "You're gonna need to work fast and get this sorted. I'll be here when you get back." She let a smile creep in. "It's what friends do, right?"

"Yeah, right." He ran a hand through her hair, gripped the back of it, and kissed her. "Good friends," he managed eventually.

Ashley measured friends up between finger and thumb, then widened it a little, and Gabe laughed.

"I'd actually like to drive up to the cabin today, just to get my head right."

Gabe frowned at her.

"Just take time out to breathe," she said gently, kissing him back. "You're pretty intense no matter how you come at me. From there I want to visit a place Ruth told me about—get a gift for Nathan and Kathryn's anniversary, so it's not all about you and—"

"Friends?"

Ashley measured it up and widened the gap a little more. "Good ones." She rose to her toes and placed a soft kiss on his lips. "Both of us with our heads clear, the best kind of complications, no other baggage?" That was her way with trying to move forward, past the screw ups. "It'll be worth it, I promise. You need some space too."

Gabe stroked at her cheek, maybe seeing it. "Do I at least get to say I can come find you if you're not back before me? Asking for a…friend here." He winced. "Mostly because the asshole will come in too heavy, and I'm talking horses, shotguns, a few tanks."

Ashley grinned up at him. "I'd kind of just like you. Leave the asshole behind."

Gabe laughed and tightened his hold. "Deal."

Chapter 26

Ashley glanced at her watch as she looked for her coat in the cabin. Gabe would be in his meeting now with Pam. She'd spent a quiet night alone, just enjoying a bottle of wine, a book, and trying not to think about Gabe. Despite him leaving today, she'd deliberately left yesterday to cool things down and she'd kept her phone switched off to ensure it. Strange how she kept switching it back on to see if she'd had any messages, and smiled when one or two came through when she did. She didn't reply, though, and Gabe seemed happy to send more texts her way despite knowing she wouldn't.

Although she'd sent him a *stay safe* message this morning when he knew he'd be boarding his plane.

Ted was waiting for outside, and he carried her bag from yesterday into the cabin before setting it by the door. She'd been too tired to unpack fully.

"There's two for you as well. I'll help you get them back to yours." Ashley reached back into the Tahoe and pulled out the bags Ruth had sent. Then she grabbed her camera and walked with Ted to his place. The path along the lake was wild and pristine, and the aroma of evergreens filled the air.

"You up for a day of fishing?" Ted shifted his bag in his arm. As they rounded a clump of thick shrubs, an elk appeared on the trail before them, and with a catch in her throat, they stood quiet, watching.

The elegant animal raised its head to sniff the air, then looked their way. Large, dark eyes stared, and his body quivered. She thought of lifting the camera to capture its beauty but was afraid any movement would break the spell. Instead, she took in every detail from the animal's long legs to the nick in the right ear that now pointed skyward. A breeze rustled through the trees, and the elk turned to its right before another quick glance back. An instant later, it was gone.

"Actually, I was thinking of driving over to the Talltree place later this afternoon to look for an anniversary gift for my brother and his wife. Would you like to come along?"

They'd reached Ted's cabin. "Tell you what," Ted said, "you go, and I'll stay here and catch us a fish we can have for dinner."

"Sounds good."

***

Ashley drove west with a cool bite in the air, but the sky stayed clear and bright until she reached the small town of Dayton. Clouds darkened and thickened in the sky, but the Talltree shop wasn't much farther, so she continued. As she reached the foothills, a fierce wind swept down from the north, and she held tightly to the steering wheel as a crosswind knocked her car about. On windy, rainy days in her childhood, her mother had often baked chocolate chip cookies, and she smiled not remember making cookies in any other weather.

The road turned north, away from the small town, toward the high craggy peaks of the Bighorns. She shivered, barely able to make out the outline of the mountains through the clouds.

It was too late to worry about getting involved with Gabe—she was there, paddle overboard and lost. All that was left now was to make sure he didn't burn her despite the threat of drowning that came with him. Hot and cold seemed to go hand in hand with hard and fast where Gabe was concerned.

Ashley slowed to check the directions she'd copied from the website and kept watch for the gravel road that led to Sally Talltree's place. After turning onto the gravel road, a beautiful, carved sign appeared with *Talltree Quilts* in script lettering in front of a large chalet. The wooden building looked inviting, and Ashley parked next to three other cars in the lot.

Homey was how she'd describe it as she entered. Not only was it a quilter's paradise but attached to the back sat a small coffee shop, and the aroma told her they served homemade pastries.

"Welcome," said someone from behind her. "I'm Sally."

Ashley turned to find a short Native-American woman in her mid-forties with braids, wearing jeans and a plaid shirt. The woman's smile was irresistible as she stocked a shelf. Ashley smiled back. "Thank you. What a beautiful place you have."

Wiping at her apron, the woman came over. "Are you looking for something special?"

"An anniversary gift for my brother and sister-in-law."

"Did you find us on the Internet?"

"A friend told me about you. Then, yes, I found you online."

"Welcome. Our son, Marcus, brought us into the twenty-first century. He takes care of all our online marketing. Did you have any trouble getting here?" Sally gave a sniff.

"The directions on your website were easy to follow."

"Would you like to look around? Over there are the newest creations." Sally pointed to the left section of the building. "On the other side are the cards, tablecloths, kitchen towels, and quilts with designs of our local wildlife and plants."

Sally nodded to two men heading out the door carrying paper cups as a loud commotion came from the back. "Just have a look around and let me know if I can help." She headed off in the direction of the noise.

Ashley narrowed her selection down to two, not sure which Kathryn would like best. Struggling to decide, she jolted when she found Sally stop by her.

"Sorry. Have you found one you like?" Her braid had fallen over her left shoulder, and her round face, high cheek bones, and deep brown eyes made Ashley instinctively reach for the camera she carried in her purse, but then she stopped herself. Permission. She needed Sally's permission before she ran with instinct and snapped the shot.

"Can't decide?" Sally asked again.

"I'm having trouble between these two. They're both beautiful. But I think I'll go with the yellow and blue. The colors are so bright, especially on a day like this."

Sleet had begun to fall, and Sally nodded. "If you'd like, you can go on back and Ray will fix you up with a piece of pie and a hot coffee while I get this wrapped for you. Anniversary, you say?"

"Yes, thank you." Ashley made her way to a small table for two by a window and watched the evergreens sway with the wind. She was glad she'd chosen a wool sweater this morning and scrunched her shoulders, pulling the sweater tighter. She'd left her jacket in the car.

A man who must have been Ray approached. "Sally said you'd like a hot drink and a treat. Coffee and pie?"

"Yes, thanks."

A moment later he was back, and he placed a slice of berry pie and cup of dark steaming coffee in front of her. "Will this do? Cream and sugar there." He pointed to the tray he'd brought.

"It looks wonderful. Thank you." He had shiny black hair, large dark eyes, a straight nose, full lips, and the most beautiful, light-brown skin.

He smiled, and she noticed the twinkle in his eyes. "I'm so sorry, but I would love to take a photograph of you and Sally. Do you think that would be possible?"

"A photograph?" He chuckled, then called out, "Sally, this lady would like a photograph of us. Are you busy?"

***

Ashley said goodbye to Sally and Ray Talltree an hour later. She liked the couple and enjoyed chatting with them while they posed for her. She also had the perfect anniversary gift. Kathryn would go crazy when she saw the quilt—the hand stitching was beautiful, the best Ashley had ever seen.

As she pulled onto the road turning east toward the cabin, wind racing down the Bighorns seemed to push the SUV toward Dayton when it wasn't trying to blow her off the road altogether. She kept both hands on the wheel.

As she rounded a wide curve, a man stood in the roadway, waving his arms. His car, a black Lincoln, was parked by the side of the road.

When she got closer, Ashley recognized him as one of the two men who had been at Sally's earlier. She slowed, not sure what to do. If he was having car trouble, she could call for a tow truck or give him a ride to Dayton.

The man tipped his Red Sox cap as she slowed to a stop next to him. "Ma'am," he said as she rolled down her window.

"Are you having car trouble?"

"Yeah. Would you be so kind as to give me a lift to Dayton since it looks like that's the direction you're heading?" He looked up. "We could get a few inches of snow here."

Ashley hesitated. "I could call someone for you." She pulled her phone from her purse and found there was no cell service. She slipped it back in, conscious of having her phone on display. "Well…"

The man walked around and slid in beside her. "Sorry, ma'am. But we're gonna need a ride."

"What? Wait. We?"

The second man she'd seen at Sally's, a redhead, stepped up and opened her door, and Ashley widened her eyes at the gun her passenger pulled out.

"Like I said." The man in the passenger seat smiled her way. "We're gonna need a ride. Get in the back." The gun shifted from her to the door.

"What…what about my purse?" Ashley made sure to keep a lot of distance from the gun. "Can I please have my purse?"

"You mean your phone. Like you've already seen, there's no service here in the Bighorns, so no need for it, right?" the passenger reminded her as Redhead pulled at her jumper to get her out.

"In there." Redhead took her arm and opened the back door. "Get in."

"Why?" Ashley really didn't want to.

"Like he said, we need the car."

"Then you don't need me."

"Stop messing around." The passenger leaned over. "Get her in and drive."

A shove sent Ashley onto the back seat, then the redhead slammed the door as the gun levelled her way, daring her to make a bolt for it as the lock clicked into place.

She took the hint and didn't as the driver put the car in gear and rolled forward. "What are we going to do with her, Darrell?"

"Stop the damn car." It came to a stop, and Darrell jumped out and rounded the hood. "You idiot. I told you not to use any names. Now out, I'll drive." He opened the rear door. "Get in there with her."

"Are…are we taking her all the way to Arizona?" The redhead slid in next to Ashley.

Names…places. The redhead didn't seem the brightest sparkplug in the engine with giving out details. But sometimes stupid caught holding the gun was worst-case scenario in anyone's book.

Darrell glanced in the rearview mirror. "Shut your trap. You want everyone to know where we're heading?"

Shivering, Ashley tried to push her luck by reaching for her jacket, but as she reached over, the redhead pushed her back.

"Don't. You stay still."

Ashley's heart slammed against her chest. "Cold," she said, hands raised to calm it down. "I'm just cold." The shaking lied, it was down to being terrorized, but Redhead frowned her way, then grabbed the jacket and tossed it at her.

"No going through the pockets."

She nodded quickly and slipped it on.

Redhead looked younger than Darrell. He sat with his shoulders slumped, as if to make himself smaller. Hands rested on his thighs, but he kept chewing his nails and tapping his foot.

Ashley glanced out the window. "The sleet's turned to snow," she stated. "Are we heading down into the valley? You won't make it anywhere else."

Redhead glanced her way. "We—"

"Oh don't be stupid and answer her." Darrell narrowed his eyes in the mirror. "Shut up back there."

Redhead leaned forward and placed a hand on the seat. "But I'm hungry. That coffee wasn't enough." He straightened. "Can we check her bag for cash and stop for something soon?"

"That's real smart thinking. And let people see her and her car? You're such a moron."

"But I'm hungry."

"Jesus. Shut up."

But the car slowed, and Darrell tossed Ashley's purse back. "Check to see how much is in there."

The gun sat on the passenger side, and Ashley kept sole focus on that.

Redhead opened her purse and pulled out her wallet. He took out the cash, then shoved the wallet back into her purse. "Seventy-two dollars. Is that all?"

"Teacher by trade," she said quickly, blowing warmth into her hands. "Just how much do you think we earn?"

A slight lie there. She had more than enough money. "Car's not even mine. It's rented." That wasn't a lie, but it helped.

"Fuck." Darrell glanced back. "That means someone will be looking for it eventually."

Did she give off single signs so badly that they were more worried about someone looking for the car before they would her? She wanted to groan but buried it as she pulled her body into a tight ball. She'd read somewhere that the best way to avoid attention in a kidnaping was to not be seen and draw attention, to make yourself unattractive, to co-operate if there was no way out.

"If money's what you want, I could get some."

"What, from your bank card? Leave a trail of where we're going?" Darrell shook his head. "You think we're stupid?"

She shifted closer to the door.

"What are you doing out here, anyway? You from around here?"

"What?" She frowned at Darrell. What the hell was this? "I'm here visiting a friend. His wife died. He's staying with his brother."

"Shit." Darrell slowed the car. "You telling me you're a friend of the Coulters?"

They knew Jason…Gabe? Did that mean Gabe and Jason knew them?

"Doesn't matter." Darrell shifted up a gear. "We'll drop you off soon."

"Drop her off?" Redhead asked, as confused as Ashley. Something seemed to have changed.

"Yeah. Can't afford that kind of attention. We'll drive for a while longer, then leave her roadside. We'll be miles away before they find her, but the focus *will* be on finding her."

Redhead squirmed. "We just wanted the car. We can't leave her out in this. What if it's hours before she's picked up?"

That would be fine by her. Rather out there than in here.

"What's wrong with you?" Darrell shook his head. "Moron," he muttered. "Don't worry about her. We need to get out of Wyoming."

The car turned right onto a dirt road, and a sign read Buffalo Creek Campground. The car pulled into a clump of trees a few moments later.

"Get her out." Darrell pulled his cap low on his head and got out.

Redhead reached across her, opened the door, and gave her arm a shove, then he scooted across the seat and stepped out behind her. The rain was still falling, and he lifted the collar of his jacket. "You want to leave her here?"

"Yup. As good a place as any."

"I still don't like it." Redhead shifted from foot to foot.

Darrell peered over at him. "I still don't give a shit. Grab her purse and blanket." He adjusted his cap again. "I want no personal items of hers found in the car."

"They'll have DNA, won't they?"

"Jesus, you think this is an episode of *Criminal Minds*? The idiots around here can't trace shit from a cow let alone missing cattle from a herd."

Darrell got in the car and Redhead followed his lead, giving a glance back her way.

As they kicked up snow and drove away, Ashley picked up her blanket and stared after them, wondering what the hell had just happened. Then the chill cut into her bones, and she turned a full three-sixty, the threat of exposure and hyperthermia kicking her in the gut. In the car with them or out here in the middle of nowhere, she was no better off, and she fought the bite at her hands to get at her phone.

No signal.

"Goddammit."

Chapter 27

Gabe shouldered off his coat, glad to finally make it back home, then shut the chill of the evening out as he closed the door. The meeting with Pam had gone well, and they'd gotten the process under the wildlife conservation and habitat protection bills to send a cease order for development on the land Sam had sold. He'd also contacted ranchers around here to let them know what was going on and to keep an eye out for any trouble. He wouldn't put it past Evans to look at ways to reduce the bird population here before everything could be finalized.

It had been a tough day, with heavy flying in bad weather, and he'd pushed his landing times harder than usual to get back here, taking a slam dunk approach to landing over a slower descent. He hoped he'd make it back in time to meet Ashley, but quiet played around the reception hall and her the car he'd given her wasn't in the courtyard.

He tugged out his phone and thumbed in her number, but Caller Unavailable came up.

Gabe shook snow from his hair. Cell service was a game or Russian Roulette on the best of days, but he couldn't help feel a tug at not hearing from her. He sent through another text, and buried a smile, refusing to count her one to his...overbearing, overprotective Id that ruled his Superego. He'd looked up the Freudian terms while he'd been away and in many ways. Yeah: he agreed with her.

A call came through a moment later, and as he made his way to the kitchen, needing to talk to Jason, he answered. "Here."

"Boss, I've got the names of the hikers who found Sam." Clay read them off. "The sheriff's with them now. No sign of Sam's car yet. Logan pieced together where he gambled and with whom the night before the ransom note arrived, and everyone is starting to talk. It should only be a matter of time before Sam's Lincoln's found, unless Sam remembers something more that's helpful. But y'know, I can't help but feel that his kidnapping is nothing to do with Evans, They're not that explicit. They already had Max working on the inside."

Yeah, that was where Gabe had gone and had mentioned to Megan. "You're thinking opportunists?"

"Maybe. Logan does too."

"Okay, good to know. Thanks for the update." He turned the corner to the kitchen, then jolted when Ruth knocked the wind out of him as they collided.

"Gabe." Her breathing was heavy, hard, panic lacing her eyes.

"Hey, what's wrong?" Gabe took her by the elbow to steady her.

"I've just got a call from Ted." Ruth tapped her phone. "Ashley drove to Sally Talltree's hours ago, and she's not made it back."

Gabe started to back away, the lack of texts hitting home a little more. Ashley had sent one to ask him to stay safe as he flew out. He hadn't received one on the way home, when he knew she wouldn't let arguments or heat get in the way of her fears over flying and wanting people safe. He pointed at Ruth. "Wherever Jason is, get a call through. Tell him what's going on and that I'm over at Talltree's. Get some thermos flasks ready as well. I need to sort First-Aid and emergency foil blankets in case she's broken down and stranded." He hoped to God she'd dropped her stubbornness and taken a coat this time.

"On it," said Ruth as he made it back down the hall.

***

State route forty kept driving to a crawl as Gabe headed for highway nine. By mind map, he knew where Sally Talltree's shop stood in the foothills. He'd been there several times to grab a slice of pie and a cup of coffee when Sally and Ray volunteered on his campaign for governor.

Snow littered the windshield, and the wipers worked double time. He knew his cars. No one lived around here without thinking breakdown, so he had a mechanic always keeping check on tires and engine. That didn't say something couldn't fail, but it was less probable. That left driver skill or whatever came out onto the road to disrupt it. Ashley was a smart woman and used to driving, but not around mountainous areas, so it gnawed hard in his gut that *something* had taken her off the road.

"Christ." Gabe swerved to miss a branch that lay a little too innocently in the road, reminding him to pay attention. West of Dayton, the snow fell heavier. The road didn't lead to any large towns, and the few residents who lived here would have to wait for the weather to warm and the snow to melt before the roads were clear again.

A few miles from the turnoff to Sally's, a Lincoln sat by the side of the road, so he pulled in next to it and got out. One tire was flat, and he kicked at it, wondering why it bothered him. It wasn't Ashley's car. Snow blocked the license plates, and he crouched down and dusted off the back plate.

Gabe wiped a hand over his mouth.

Sam's. This was Sam's Lincoln.

This couldn't be coincidence playing out here. Lose one car, find another.

Gabe got to his feet and checked the door. It opened, and he found fast-food wrappers and paper cups littering the interior. He pulled out his phone, only to find he had no service.

"Damn it." He got back into his car, hands shaking slightly. This potentially put the kidnappers in the vicinity of Ashley and Sally Talltree's.

No cars were parked in Sally's lot, but the lights burned inside. After locking his car, he headed on in. The shop was empty, but Sally's voice drifted from the back.

"Be out in just a sec." She came around the corner of an aisle, looking like she'd been on a break outback with the mug of tea in her hands. "Governor Coulter." She smiled and came over to rest her mug on the counter. "What are you doing out this way so late?"

Gabe kissed her on the cheek. "How's Ray?"

She grinned. "He's here somewhere. You need to talk to him?"

"No," he said, glancing around. "I'm looking for a woman who might have been here earlier today. Ashley Roberts. About five seven, blonde. She was looking for an anniversary gift?" She could have broken down before she got here, and that worried Gabe more as he hadn't seen anything on the way over. She could have taken a wrong turn.

"Oh yes, she was here. Bought a lovely quilt, then asked to take pictures of Ray and me." Her eyes widened. "What happened? Is she all right?"

So she'd been heading back to High Peak Lake. "She hasn't arrived home yet. She's unfamiliar with the area, so I hoped she may have stayed put when the snow started." But then she'd have called to let Ted know.

Sally shook her head. "She was here for over an hour. Picked out a quilt and then enjoyed a cup of coffee and piece of pie. But that was hours ago."

Gabe's stomach twisted. "Could I use your land line?"

"Sure, right this way." She led Gabe to a small office, then closed the door behind her when she left.

Gabe punched in Jason's number.

"Gabe? What's going on?" Jason sounded out of breath. Panicked.

"I'm at Sally Talltree's. Get a message over to Sheriff Logan that I Found Sam's car a few miles east of here." He gave him the name of the road. "It's got a Flat tire."

Quiet hit the line and Gabe could almost hear Jason working it out. "She's out in the vicinity of the kidnappers?"

"Yeah. Ask Logan to connect with the sheriff in Dayton. I'll give the highway patrol a call to see if I can speak with Bill Thornton." Bill was an officer and friend and hopefully he could push to get things moving from there. "I'll wait at Sam's car until someone gets there." It was his only lead.

After finishing his calls, he opened the office door and found Sally waiting for him in the hall. "Tell Ray I'll stop by for coffee some other time."

"Just let us know when you find her, please."

"I will."

Collar turned up, he made it back to the Tahoe and grabbed a scraper from the back and cleared the window screen. By the time he turned onto the main road, he could hardly see out his windshield, the snow was heavy and the wind punched the Tahoe, making it difficult to handle. If it had been snowing, why hadn't Ashley stayed there until morning? Stayed safe?

Gabe pulled in behind the black Lincoln as car lights rounded the curve of the road up ahead, full beams broken into a mosaic by the falling snow. Gabe wiped at his window to get a better view and tension eased in his body as Clay pulled his car onto the opposite shoulder.

After tugging on a thick hood, Clay jogged over and climbed into the Tahoe. "I followed as soon as I heard." He rubbed his hands together, soaking in the warmth that Gabe turned up. "None of this makes any sense. Not unless it is the kidnappers, and with Sam's car broken down, they needed to jack another car."

Gabe stayed quiet.

"Sam got out alive, Gabe. Don't go there, okay."

Gabe shook his head. "He got lucky. Hikers found him."

"We'll find Ashley too."

Gabe snorted, hating the bitterness behind it. "Jason called Logan, I handled Thornton. The sheriff will be here soon, and Thornton will put a bulletin out on her and the Coulter Creek SUV she was driving." He looked out into the darkness. "Jason's no doubt on his way too."

Another set of headlights came around a curve in the road, and Gabe and Clay stepped out of the Tahoe when the car pulled alongside Sam's.

"Hey, Bill, you got here fast." Gabe shook hands with his friend.

Thornton nodded to Clay. "Still have my winter tires on. Besides, I was close, dealing with a drug's bust. What's this about someone missing?"

Gabe explained about Sam's car, Ashley, and the concern over how it all put the kidnappers close to her.

Thornton reached for the radio he was wearing and added more information to the bulletin that he'd no doubt put out earlier.

"Okay, let's get you back to the local sheriff's office," Thornton said to Gabe. "See what they have."

"I'm not—"

"Leaving her out here?" Thornton pointed back to Gabe's car. "Ex-governor or not, you will. You know search procedure on the ranch. It's no different now. We don't do anything until a grid search and team is put in place. I don't need anyone else out there going missing tonight. We clear? Get your head into gear and keep it there."

***

Trying to bury his anger, Gabe pulled in next to the small sheriff's office in Dayton as Clay headed to the cabin to see Ted to make sure Ashley wasn't broken down somewhere along that road.

"Governor. Bill." Sheriff Logan met them at the door before turning down a hallway. "C'mon. I'm assisting Sheriff Reed here in Dayton, and he asked me to take the lead on this. Let's go in here." He led them to a meeting room full of deputies. "When was she last seen at Sally's?"

Gabe glanced down at his watch as he stopped by a table with an iPad showing a map. "About four hours ago."

"And she was heading east?" Logan ran a finger over the main roads.

Gabe nodded. "She's not from around here, and I'd set the satnav with the quickest route there and back. Even if she lost signal, I gave her a map. She was heading back to High Peak Lake."

"And you're sure that's Sam Frasier's car up there?" Sheriff Logan pointed to where it had been parked. "About here, right?" He looked to Thornton for confirmation.

Thornton nodded. "I ran the plates to make sure it was Sam's."

Logan didn't look happy. "That would have taken her close. Could you tell how long Sam's car had been there? It could be the kidnappers had moved on long before that."

"No." Thornton gave a heavy sigh. "Engine was cold and food had been eaten, so I couldn't judge from that. But it means they could have been getting desperate to carjack."

Logan nodded. "What are you doing here anyway, Bill?" He a few keys on his iPad.

"Drug issue." He headed for the door when he got a call through. "Fill in me on the grid, I've got to take this."

"All right." Logan looked to Gabe. "Do you have a photograph of Ashley? If not, we need a full description."

Gabe cursed under his breath. For all the photos Jason had taken, that she had, he'd not taken one of her.

After noting her details down, Logan started to read out coordinates. Gabe went to move out out as well, but Logan pulled him to a stop.

"I can't let you go out there, Gabe. You know that right?"

"I've handled enough staff going missing on the ranch land, not to mention cattle."

Logan shook his head. "This may involve kidnappers, and I draw the line at anyone but my staff handling this. Stay here." He gave him a frown. "Keep close to the radios and you'll be the first to hear if…when we find her."

Gabe felt sick to the stomach. He'd promised he'd find her after he got back.

"You're no good in this state, Gabe. You'll do her more than good, especially if she thinks you're out here running headlong into this kind of grief. Go get a coffee. Try to let us do our job."

Gabe rubbed at his head, then started to walk away. "You got any news on the whereabouts of Sam's foreman?"

Logan shook his head. "Nothing yet. An alert's out."

"You don't think Evans is anything to do with this, do you."

Logan offered a small smile. "Gut instinct says no. But I don't discount anything until the evidence proves otherwise."

Tired and frustrated, Gabe nodded then headed for the conference room just as a commotion in the hallway had him looking over.

Jason rushing toward him. "Where is she?" he stammered, out of breath. "You found her?"

"Tell Jason to calm it down and get comfortable," Logan called from the next room. "He's going nowhere either."

"*What?*"

Gabe stood and backed Jason into the conference room, making sure he found a seat. Jason threw out his arms, and Gabe levelled a finger his way, warning him off.

They were both forced to wait. It was all they could do.

***

Shivering into the darkness, Ashley sat a picnic bench not far from the road, caught between keeping an eye on the road and glancing back at the campsite's concrete building and offer of a restroom. The air had cooled and the jacket that had been so warm earlier offered little barrier against the wind, so she sat wrapped Kathryn's quilt around her shoulders.

Sense told her no one would be driving out at this hour, but the more she stared, the more she kept willing *just one more minute*.

But darkness was thick and heavy around her, and she didn't like the snaps of branch and call of wildlife behind her. Strange how they took a meaner soul when the lights went down.

She checked her watch, exhausted. It was stupid to stay out much longer, but if she hid in the concrete building an someone did come by, they'd miss her.

Giving a frown, she slipped everything from her purse into her jacket pocket, then left the purse in full view on the park bench with a note attached to it. It was a small chance, but not many resisted an unattended purse in her neck of the woods, and if someone did, on the small chance, drive by, they might catch it out here. That meant she could take shelter and make sure to stay awake if a car did drive by.

Blowing warmth into her hands, she got to her feet and walked over to the concrete restrooms as the bitter chill gripped harder.

The smell wasn't pleasant, but she huddled in a corner, closest to the windows and road to listen for passing cars.

She'd lived alone for so long, she'd gotten used to it. But faced with dying alone? With the possibility of no one finding her to ease her own daughter's mind...? A tear slid down her cheek, and she wiped it roughly away.

Stay awake. She just needed to stay awake. Listen.

***

Jolting under the blanket, Ashley woke and scooted farther into the corner of the restroom, pulling the quilt tighter around her when she realized she'd woken. She stared into the darkness, waiting for her gaze to adjust to any light that might make its way through the tiny opaque window. She tried to think of Gabe, hold on to the good in life: her daughter, Jason, Cody... Lisa...but nothing but desolation kept her quiet and staring. She'd never been afraid of the dark, but then she'd never faced it like this either, how it seemed to breathe down her neck, waiting for her next screw up that pushed her deeper into its kiss.

The sound of a car's tires crunching gravel twisted her ear to the window, and she pulled her body into a tight ball. Her first thought was Darrell, Redhead, then a Ted Bundy wannabe who'd caught her note, and she scrambled to her feet and ran into a stall, locking the door, backing away until she connected with the wall. Breathing came hard, heavy, and she tried to stop it, to not make any noise.

"Professor Roberts?" A light shone underneath the stall door. "I'm Meredith Chandler, highway patrol."

Letting out a breath, Ashley listened for a moment longer. She'd not left her name on the note, so it wasn't a Ted Bundy wannabe, and she'd told Darrell she was a teacher, but even knowing that, she didn't move.

"Gabe Coulter spoke to us over the radio. He said to tell you he's still a close…friend."

Choking out a smile, Ashley rushed the door, but it took two attempts to unlock it her hands shook so badly.

"How… how did you find me?" She shielded against the light that shone in her eyes. There was still every chance it wasn't a cop, but as the light shifted off to the left, the flash of police car lights eased her breathing.

"This place was on our search grid." Chandler held up Ashley's purse and a smile came her way. "But this gave it away a little too." She looked it over. "Not the kind you see around here."

Ashley hugged the quilt tighter around her and smiled a shaky thanks as her purse was handed over.

"C'mon, let's get you into some warmth, huh?"

"Oh God…yes please."

Chandler took her arm and helped her over. As she got in, Chandler pulled out a foil emergency blanket and wrapped it around Ashley's shoulders, then reached over for a bag. "You hurt anywhere?"

Ashley frowned at the look that came her way.

"Not hurt, no. My car got jacked with me in it, but they dropped me off here. They seemed in a rush to get out of the county when they heard I was a friend of the Coulters, mostly to use it as a distraction away from them so they could get *out* of the county."

Chandler nodded, then offered her a bottle of water after she unscrewed the cap. "Take a drink, then rest on the way back before talk anymore, okay?" She said something into her radio as she went around to the driver's side. "I have a couple of protein bars if you're hungry."

Ashley took a drink of water, but kept it to small sips. "I'm good. Thank you." It took her two tries to screw the cap on the water bottle, and how she started to shake a little more hit home how bad shock could be. "Just want to get home."

"We get you looked over first, okay?" Chandler smiled her way. "The local doc's on his way to the sheriff's office, he'll meet us there."

Chapter 28

Sat on the chair in the conference room, fingers crossed, elbows on knees, Gabe kept his look levelled solely on the door. Shadows passed under the rim, footsteps coming and fading away with whispers, sometimes quiet laughter, and each time it drove his look lower until all he heard was the tick of the clock on the wall in time with fall of goddamn foot on concrete outside.

"I can't do this *bullshit* anymore." Giving a snarl, he got up, and Jason came in, stopping getting another coffee and pushing him back.

"You're no good to anyone in that state let alone *her*." Another shove made him sit back down. "Calm it."

"I know these mountains better than anyone. *You* do. Why the hell did you let Lisa give her the address to come out here on her own?"

Jason looked down, folded his arms. "You moved into shifting blame already?"

Gabe dipped his head and ran a hand through his hair. "Christ, sorry," he said quietly. "I feel so useless."

Jason crouched by him. "Sometimes there's nothing you can do. Most times we're all just crash test dummies waiting for the next smack into the wall."

Gabe looked up and cupped Jason's neck. "I'm sick of the repeat," he said quietly. "I couldn't do anything for you when you were hurting, now Ashley…?"

Jason offered him such a soft smile. "My hurt's not yours to take away, Gabe. It's a part of mine and Susan's history, and I claim all rights to that. You wanna know why?" A tear slipped his cheek. "Because she was the very best kind of hurt in all its shapes and colors."

"Christ." Gabe roughed a thumb at Jason's cheek. Younger brothers...yeah. "The best kind of hurt."

Jason nodded. "You wait, you watch, because it's the best thing for Ashley," he said, patting Gabe's neck. "My turn to remind you,"

The door came open and Gabe eased to his feet with Jason as Thornton entered.

"We've got her," he said quickly, a smile Gabe's way.

"Is she okay?" Gabe had already covered the distance to him as he tugged his jacket on.

"Chandler reported shock had set in, and we'll get her looked over by the doc who's just come in." He held the door open for Gabe. "There's no sign of the SUV, but we'll pick up their track in the morning. Snow's buried most. Miss Roberts should be here soon." Thornton said, then followed the younger officer down the hallway.

Gabe didn't stay around to hear anymore. He'd wait outside in the falling snow if he had to.

***

An arc of SUV police lights lit up the parking lot, and ignoring any ounce of cold as he'd stood there waiting, Gabe bolted over and skidded to a stop as the SUV's engine died.

"Ash..." Gabe tore off his jacket and opened the door before wrapping it around her shoulders. "Christ, c'mon." Her face was pale as she shivered, fingers looking almost painfully arthritic as she gripped the foil blanket around her. The heater had been on full blast in the SUV, and as he glanced around at the bloated fall of snow, he was conscious of how it assaulted her system, throwing her back into being out there alone.

"I'm good." She didn't sound it as she hid her face in his shoulder away from the onslaught of snow. But how she avoided looking out at the offer of pitch blackness found over the road in the line of trees that maybe kept her hidden more.

"Yeah, enough," said Gabe, his arm going around her. Jason came out a moment later, and he took to her other side, rubbing at her arm, whispering repeatedly into her ear.

"Thanks." Gabe threw a long look back at the patrol officer. A nod came his way as she took care of shutting the SUV down.

"Over here." Thornton waved them to a side door where a man stood with him. "Miss Roberts, you going to be okay to answer a few questions as we get you checked over?"

Ashley nodded and a hand on Gabe's chest stopped him from barking *no*. She wasn't okay. He could see that. Jason too from how he glared at Thornton.

"Details." Ashley turned into his ear. "I gotta do this why I remember the details, Gabe."

Gabe searched her eyes for a moment as they walked, and tightening his jaw, he gave a short nod. "Doc first, okay?" Whoever had taken her had gotten into her head, scaring her, and he'd spend a lifetime trying to ease that look in her eyes. But he also needed to know if anyone touched her in ways she should *never* be touched, because he'd spend a lifetime hurting them for it too.

***

Ashley sat in Gabe's SUV, the heater on full and sedating life outside the car window. Gabe had been right, it hadn't been a good time to talk, and she'd managed to give the basics and Darrell's name before letting her look at Gabe say she'd had enough. He stood talking to Jason outside in the snow, and occasionally looks drifted her way. She closed her eyes against it and rested her head against the window. She didn't think it had hit too hard until she gotten in the police car, but the drop in adrenaline and headache that tore through her gave her a serious reality check on bravado. She wanted home now. She wanted bed, to shut out the world and hide away from it a few hours.

Gabe climbed in next to her, and it shifted her about. He quickly closed the door before a look came her way, then he was putting the SUV into gear.

It stayed so quiet, and Ashley frowned out at the darkness, not sure why his grip was so hard on the steering wheel as he focused on the road.

"You angry at me?"

He flicked her look.

"With needing time away." She shrugged. "That I drove out alone?"

"What?" Gabe pulled the car over to the side of the road, slipped it into neutral—then pulled her in close, his hands running through her hair. "No, Christ. I…" He gave such a hard sigh. "Just tell me who needs hurting, and I'm all theirs."

Ashley choked a smile and rested her head against his. "Just be mine tonight?" She frowned seriously. "Please?"

All tension drained from Gabe's body, and he brushed a kiss at her cheek. "For as long as you'll have me."

"Deal," she said quietly.

She eased back, and the gentle pull on the SUV almost lulled her back into sleep as they slipped through the darkness. It seemed to take an age to pull up among the trees, and Ashley frowned as she glanced out the window.

"The cabin was closer," Gabe said gently as he switched the engine off, then he got out and came her way. He took her by the hand, and kept her close as he led the way to the cabin porch.

No lights came on as they entered, and Gabe glanced back, throwing a soft smile her way as he took her through to the bedroom.

She tensed, not ready for anything more than holding, and he brushed gently at her cheek before he took care of the blinds, made sure heating started to warm the bedroom, then came over and helped Ashley unbutton her shirt when the shaking in her hands started up again. After she stepped out of her jeans, he pulled back the covers and tugged her down, his hold saying nothing but...*here for you*.

Right now, in this darkness, wrapped in his hold, it was all she needed to feel as grief tore through her into his shoulder.

Chapter 29

Gabe stirred as the early morning sunlight eased through the gaps in the bedroom blinds. Ashley lay asleep beside him, and he stayed curled around her, needing to keep the world outside away from her a little longer as he stroked a distracted thumb gently over her upper arm.

He was lost, still unsure with what to do, how to react beyond this, beyond holding her. It didn't seem enough. It didn't *feel* enough. Part of him wanted him out, dragging Darrell out of the SUV, branding into his skin how he didn't come near her again, but the other? It didn't want to move in case Darrell came close to her here. Then he didn't want to move simply because he held Ashley and needed her to sleep and not wake to how much it hurt.

Give him a hammer, he could fix a fence, give him a conference table, he could talk bills to help cut taxes.

But give him Ashley?

Gabe gave a long sigh, then kissed gently at her shoulder.

Breakfast. She was going to be hungry.

Keeping it quiet, he eased the duvet off her and tentatively put foot to floor and made his way to the restroom.

It took him a while, but after sorting through Ruth's stock, Gabe had sausage and bacon cooking on the hob as he sat on the deck overlooking the lake, a cup of hot, strong coffee in his hand

A cool, crisp nip in the air from the fallen snow kept him company as the sound of water running came from the bathroom, and he gave a small smile, loving how Ashley moved about his home as if she'd always been there.

Ashley came out a few minutes later, and as she toweled her hair dry, she smiled his way.

"Morning." He offered his coffee over. "You think you're up for some breakfast?"

Saying nothing, Ashley came over and gently shifted the coffee away. Her movement light, she straddled Gabe's lap, jolting him as she framed his face with her hands and brushed a gentle kiss at his lips.

"Woah," breathed Gabe, and he put the coffee down to ease a gentle touch at her hips, fingers digging into the slim cut of her suit pants. She always took his breath with how…intimately she owned these quieter moments between them.

"My thank you," she said quietly, kissing at his lips again. "For being—"

"A friend?" He cocked a brow, and she dipped her head into his shoulder, laughing softly. She measured the distance between thumb and finger, widening the gap.

"For being you," she managed to finish. Cupping his face, she searched his eyes. "So, so scared yesterday, Gabe."

He frowned and brushed a thumb at the back of her neck. "I know." He pulled her down and kissed her lips, cheek, throat. "Logan will catch the bastards."

"Hm. Don't want to talk them." Ashley exposed her throat for more kisses, but she still fought grief over last night, only this time she needed it burning out of her another way as she slipped a touch down to the clasp on Gabe's jeans.

Gabe hissed, biting into her shoulder. She'd taken hold of his cock and eased a stroke along his length, tip to root. "You know breakfast's cooking?" he said quietly, needing to make sure she had something to ground her for a moment.

She started to kiss her way down his chest, nip and licking at skin as she undid each button. "Muesli gal here." She kissed above the V of his abs, her long hair drag-racing his cock. He reared up, grabbing her hair, loving the feel. "'I see we need to work on this—" She licked a little lower. "—friend connection."

Gabe eased her back up, her body flat on his, a hand on her ass as he took a gentle grip in her hair.

"Just a little," he whispered, winning a groan off her as his body rose into hers. "For as long as you can take me."

Her eyes came alive at the sexual innuendo he'd challenged her with, but that was Ashley: all fight and fire once you got under her skin, and he wanted to see the fight back in her, just how long she would be able to take him before her body cried no more.

***

Gabe cracked eggs at the stove, and Ashley grinned as she trashed the burned sausages and bacon over by the sink. All best laid plans aside, the fire alarm had cut play for a minute, and they'd taken to the table, floor...up against a wall, back to the bedroom. Quiet played around them now they were burned out too, and a look came her way as Gabe picked up the muesli and poured her a bowl at the table. He was learning, but so was she as she finished off the coffee, adding one sugar to his, two to hers. The contrast between the hell of last night, the heat this morning, and the calm that followed was startling, but she held on to all three, not wanting last night as an excuse for sleeping with Gabe.

She'd wanted him, he'd wanted her, and that was all it needed to be, all grief and hurt given a place, but not owning and losing them in the process.

A thud came from outside, and she refused to jolt as Gabe looked up, then eased past her, a finger raised her way asking her to stay where she was. A knock came as he reached the door.

"Ted." Gabe stepped out the way and threw an *it's okay* smile back her way as he came in. "Mornin'."

"Mornin'." Ted nodded his way, then came over to Ashley and kissed at her cheek. "You okay, lass?" He dipped his head, searching her eyes, looking for truth and nothing but.

Ashley blushed. "I'm good." She held Gabe's look for a moment. "Definitely getting there."

Ted Glanced over his shoulder. "'Bout time." He pulled back. "I've bought some extra firewood over." He thumbed behind him, then gave a sniff and looked around the kitchen. "My God, you didn't let Gabe cook for you, did you?"

Ashley buried a laugh as Gabe came over and leaned against the table. "He got distracted and—"

Wood.

Just where had Ted been cutting wood this morning, and for how long?

Gabe snorted a laugh, the *awkward* rub at his neck and look anywhere *but* at Ted seeming to question the same thing.

Just what had he seen? Heard?

"Let me get you a coffee." Gabe shifted and grabbed another mug. "We're heading back to the ranch dinner time, so the wood's gonna come in. Thank you."

"No worries, but forget the coffee. I've got work to do. Just wanted to know this lass is okay and that she's being looked after." Ted headed for the door, then glanced back as he opened it. "And if you're wondering, I waited until long after you switched the fire alarm off. Peeping Tom and his son lives at the cabin further down. I just get the warning back at mine if the fire alarm goes off here."

Ted left them standing there, and as Gabe came over and tugged Ashley in, she buried a laugh in his shoulder.

Chapter 30

Gabe pulled up to the ranch and Cody was the first out of the barn.

"Hey." He skidded to a stop Ashley's side and opened the door. "You okay?"

"I'm good," She got out and Cody shot a look Gabe's way as if to make sure. Ashley fought saying something. She wasn't up to scratch, but it didn't make her glass about to break.

"How about you get us a coffee, huh?" Gabe came and patted Cody's arm as Jason came out next, wiping paint from his hands. Looked like he'd been in Cody's studio, and he made a beeline for them too.

"Sure, sure." Cody picked up their bags, "You let me know if you need anything else, okay?"

"Hey, you." Jason swung and arm around Ashley's shoulders and pulled her in to kiss at her forehead. "How you doing, kid? He look after you last night?"

Ashley stayed in Jason's hold, but sent a soft smile Gabe's way. "Yeah. Yeah he did."

"I'm…" Gabe was back to looking so awkward. "I'm gonna go check in with Logan, see if he's asked if Sam knows this Darrell." He came over and kissed at Ashley's cheek. "You gonna be okay?" he whispered in her ear.

She nodded, then returned the kiss, this time finding a brief touch to his lips.

Jason watched him go, then eyed Ashley up.

"What?"

"Nothing."

"Nothing?"

Jason drew fingers across his lips. "Not saying a word."

"You just did. Four of them."

He laughed and tugged her back in, keeping his arm over her shoulder as they walked to the ranch.

"Just glad you're okay and that he's stopped being enough of an—"

"Asshole?"

"—an idiot in heat, I was going to say." He grinned at her. "But asshole sometimes works too."

Ashley sobered up. "Any news this morning? Do they know who Darrell is? If he's tied to the missing foreman?"

Jason kept his look on Gabe's office as they headed in. "This one's Gabe's to handle," he said quietly. Then he looked at her. "You are." He winked at her, looking so much like Gabe in that moment. "Does this mean you might stay longer?"

"I've got to get back for Nathan and Kathryn's anniversary party, but I…" She smiled down to her feet. "I might be convinced to come back."

"Good." Jason held the door for her as they went in.

"Here you go." Cody came into the reception hall with two coffees. Ashley took one and let it warm her to the core. Then she took Gabe's.

"I'll go hand him this."

"Tell him Ruth sent you," called Jason. "If you're struggling for a reason to see him again so soon…like."

Ashley buried a smile, then flipped Jason the bird without turning around.

"Language," shouted Jason. "From such a lady too. The shame of it. Watch you don't spill that coffee there."

***

"Ah." Gabe steadied Ashley as he knocked into her in the hall outside of his office.

He'd just come out, so she handed him his coffee before anymore ended up on the floor and gave Jason more fuel to play with. She buried a groan with that thought.

"Sorry," he added.

She sucked at a burned finger, and he shook his head, making her narrow her eyes at just how low his mind seemed to go.

"Any news?" she said into the smile he gave.

"Not much." He gave a sigh. "According to Logan, so far there's been no sighting of Darrell, the redhead, Sam's foreman, or our Coulter Creek vehicle. He also spoke to Sam. He's adamant he doesn't know anyone called Darrell, but from what you were saying last night, those who took you weren't too smart. Darrell could have worn a mask with Sam. It could tie in with how he knew about the area and us. He just didn't know us well enough to know Sam's in financial difficulty and couldn't pay a ransom."

"So not tied to these development people?"

"I don't know for sure, but the two don't match up. Not with how Max has disappeared."

"The kidnapping could have been a distraction." Ashley took a sip of coffee. "They've all disappeared, right? What if they wanted focus on Sam and his kidnapping in order for it all to go through, like they wanted to use me to distract you looking for them?"

"Maybe," he said quietly. "But something feels off with connecting the two." Then he shook it off. "When's Nathan's anniversary event again? I'm losing you this time, right?" He seemed so sad.

"Oh, the twentieth." She took a deep breath, blushed. "I was wondering if you'd like to come?"

He grinned. "To Cincinnati? With you? As a…friend?"

She laughed and measured it up. "A small one, with benefits."

He chuckled and kissed her, sharing coffee and heat. "God yes. Then you could show me around." He cupped her chin. "Thank you for inviting me. I was worried about losing you." He ran a thumb across her cheeks. "After that, maybe you could come back to the ranch for a while longer as—"

"A friend?" She winced.

"However, you'll have me," he said gently. "Just put a copy of your schedule for the anniversary trip on my desk? I'll arrange all the flights."

"Oh wow." Ashley batted her eyes. "From friend to lover to...*I'll pencil you in*, in just a few short breaths."

"Hey." He feigned hurt, a hand on his heart. "Everything else is written here, but—"

"But you need a little help from time to time to remember the fine detail, huh?"

"Maybe," he said, kissing at her lips. "It's the company. She makes me forget things."

"Good recovery." She patted his chest. "Damn good recovery. Gabe." She headed off with a soft smile.

"Before you go..."

She glanced back, and he came over.

"There's a Rancher's Ball later this month. Will you come with me?"

"This an official date?"

"By that time, I'm hoping it's just us doing the normal stuff together."

She brushed a touch to his cheek. "In that case, I think I'd love to."

Gabe caught her hand and held it down by his side. "Then get going. Go call your daughter too. Let her know your safe."

Christ. Ashley hadn't even... Giving a frown, she turned away into Gabe's office and tugged out her phone.

Waiting for her call to be picked up, she sorted through the drawers for Gabe's diary. He seemed the type to back up what he had on his iPad with a paper record.

As her fingers brushed a file, she came to a stop, a frown creeping in as she read the name across it.

***

Gabe headed down the hall, and Jason looked up from talking to Cody. "Everything all right?" Jason shifted a look around, no doubt searching for Ashley.

Gabe nodded as he took a sip of his coffee and stopped by them. "I'm taking some time away with her for this anniversary."

"What? You and Ashley? Seriously?" Cody widened his eyes. "Dude." He offered a fist bump, and Gabe took it with a proud grin.

"Go." Jason turned him away. "Find that studio of yours." Cody did, still managing to throw in a double thumbs up Gabe's way. Gabe laughed and Jason shook his head.

"Don't encourage him. Lisa's enough to handle."

Gabe lost his playful side. "You and her okay?"

Jason sighed. "She didn't want to talk, so I took the hint and sat through a movie with her instead, all fleece blanket and popcorn."

Gabe cupped his neck. "Next best thing, bud."

Jason nodded. "So, a trip away?" He waggled his eyebrows. "You *and* Ashley?"

"Yeah." He let a grin ease in. "She's just in my office, sorting—"

Gabe stilled, his coffee mug frozen before it touched his lips.

The files Clay had put there this morning.

"Gabe?"

"Fuck." He pushed the coffee at Jason. "No, no no no. *No.*"

***

Gabe skidded around his office door, coming to a stop as Ashley stood looking down at the file she held.

"Ash." Christ. He ran a hand through his hair as he took a few steps over. "You—"

"A background check?" Ashley looked up. "You had Clay run a background check on me?"

"After… Christ, I swear it was just after I met you, after—"

"A fucking *background* check, Gabe." The file landed at his feet, paper scattering over the floor. "I've known Susan most of my life. I've known Jason—" She stopped herself. "You know what, the hell with this, and the hell with *you*."

She shoved him off as he tried to catch her arm.

"Ash?" Jason blocked her way, but as she looked at him, he backed off, raising both hands. "What the hell's gone on?"

"Ask him." She flicked her head back Gabe's way. "Better still, get Clay on the line and ask him to check CCTV to give you the rundown. Why you're on, you better ask him if I've picked a few pockets or stolen the silverware from Ruth's underwear drawer whilst you're on."

"Ash—"

"*No,*" she shouted at Gabe. "You don't get to question my integrity. You don't get to question my principles around friends. You sure as hell don't get to run a background check on me as if I'm that one hired hand you'll never really trust."

She pushed past Jason, and as Gabe tried to follow, he got shoved back in to the office by Jason as he came nose to nose close.

"What the *hell* have you done now?"

"Get out of my way."

"*Tell me.*"

Gabe eased him aside. "I will, I promise. I need to talk to her first."

***

Gabe took the stairs two at a time and didn't bother knocking at Ashley's door. It stood open, and as she shoved clothes into her case, he went over and tugged her around.

"Back off." She shrugged out of it and grabbed her jumper. "You don't get the final bullheaded word here."

"Ash, I swear to God I did that before I got to know you. I—"

"*Goddamn* it, Gabe." She slammed the lid shut and looked at him. "You don't get to do *that* period. What the hell were you thinking?"

"*I wasn't, all right*?" He let out a frustrated sigh and threw out his arms. "I haven't been thinking right since you came here."

She shot him a hard look. "Don't you damn well blame me for that."

"I'm not. It's all on me, I know that. But dammit. You felt so good that night I kissed you, when there was no complications. Then I thought...I thought you and Jason were together, and it took me bad places. I wanted a reason for you not to be his, even of that meant stopping you from *being* his."

Ashley screwed her face in distaste. "And what? You think that alpha bullshit is sexy? In whose world other than Stockholm Syndrome county did you ever think that was okay?"

"Ash, please." He stepped a little closer, then pulled back in the next breath. "In my world if a fence is broken, I drive a car out to fix it, then wait around for the next fence to fall. There's no great plan, no grand scheme, just ticking over until the next storm that takes us under. I didn't think, and that's the whole goddamn issue here, Ash. I don't have a hammer to fix it this time. I don't know where to start trying other than to say I wish to God I'd never done it."

Ashley tugged the case off the bed. "Ask Clay. He's your foreman around here, right? I'm sure he'll know how to run a search to find a How-To for you."

He took her arm, pulling her to a gentle stop. "Stay. Let me find a way to make it right."

Ash frowned and looked around her bedroom, back out into the hall. "Too much hurt, Gabe." She looked back at him. "Too many ghosts throwing us all out of the game. You're not ready." She shrugged and a tear fell. "I don't think I am anymore, not with you. Let me go, please."

Searching her eyes for a moment, Gabe let his world fall as he let go of his hold. He loved her, he knew that, but never to the point he was the one hurting her.

She turned away, and he could do nothing but watch her leave.

Chapter 31

Staring out of his office window, Gabe sat at his desk, losing track of what Sheriff Logan said on the other end of the line. "Sorry, what was that?"

"I said we found your SUV and ran some prints. Darrell turned out to be Lonnie Tucker, a friend of Megan's ex-husband. The ex was the one who set up the kidnapping and ransom scheme, although at this time we have no proof. But as he's been out of the loop for a while, it stands to reason he won't have known about Sam's financial difficulty. I want him for the kidnapping of your friend, but Sam has said he'll ID them to save dragging her through anymore unless we need to."

Gabe rubbed at his forehead. "Thank you for that. She's been through enough." He looked back out at the patches of snow. "Anything on the foreman, Banks? Pam's managed to get an order to stop any development on the land, but I'd love for him to be picked up for his part in skimming money from Sam too."

"Still can't find him. But Evans Development has closed their office here, and I've sent a report to the attorney general's office in Cheyenne, listing Banks and that Harris man you mentioned. Maybe they will have more luck."

"Thanks, Matt. I'd appreciate you keeping me updated on this."

"You've got it." The call was cut and Gabe let the silence crawl over him. It seemed that's all there was around here lately. Silence.

Jason's anger and quiet he could put up with. Cody's…Lisa's.

But Ashley's?

Gabe frowned.

She'd refused his offer to fly her home, and the best part of him wished to God he knew what she was doing.

He ignored the worst part of him that needed to find out, because too much damage had been done for him to look its way anymore.

***

Nathan met Ashley at the baggage carousel, giving her a hug before grabbing her luggage. "Kathryn would have met you, but she's busy getting ready for the party. I didn't realize this thing was going to be such a big affair. But you know Kathryn. She loves to entertain." He smiled. "Jason mentioned Gabe might be coming with you when I last called."

Ashley stood looking around the airport, everything coming full cycle, and she frowned at Nathan. "He couldn't make it."

Nathan gave her an odd look, then took her cases. "C'mon. Let's get you home, yeah? Then you can let me know why Jason had to call and tell me about the kidnapping."

She hadn't told him, but then everything felt too close.

Jason sighed as they headed outside. "Or we'll just get you home, no pressure."

No pressure she could handle, and she settled into the car, her head resting against the window as he pulled away.

The drive into Cincinnati didn't take long, and Ashley didn't realize how much she needed to be home. She'd drop by the university later in the week, maybe have lunch with a few friends. Patch work. It's what she'd called it after her ex-husband left: patching the dead space with different colored fabric to fill the void, get through it, and she didn't think she'd be sitting here again, forced to go through the motions again. "I'll get through it," she mumbled.

"What?" Nathan pulled the car into the driveway of her modest two-story home.

She shrugged. "Nothing." She gave him a smile. "Do you mind if I just head on in with no interrogation? I'll give you a call later."

"You sure you want to be alone?"

"I'm sure I don't want to talk, not just yet."

He nodded and helped her get her luggage out of the trunk before taking them to the door. "Thank you. For coming to get me." She hugged him, but he hugged her more.

"Anytime. You know that. Give me a call if you need someone to sleep on the couch tonight, watching the door."

Odd, but today she felt safer being back home in a city of strangers compared to the expanse of nothing Darrell had exposed her too. "I'll be fine." She gave a deep sigh, then watched him head back for his car. Then she pushed on through and left her bags in the foyer as she started to check her mail. More patch work, but it was a distraction.

The doorbell rang, and she put the mail on the table and reached for the door.

"Flowers for Ashley Roberts." The man offered over a large bouquet of red roses. Frowning, she took them, but before she could respond, he was gone and her phone was ringing. She took the flowers into the kitchen and left the, on the unit before picking up her phone.

She let out a long sigh.

Kathryn.

Jason hadn't been gone five minutes and he'd called in the patch work troops. She called her back. "Hey."

"Hey you. You coming by the house later? I have wine, lots of it."

She snorted a smile. "Nathan said you're busy getting things ready for the party. You need to focus, and I'm too tired after the flight. I'm having an early night. Keep the wine on hold, though? I'll see you tomorrow."

"You sure?" Quiet. "I can come over, bring it with me. Order in more?"

218

She laughed softly. "I'm good, just really tired."

"Okay. Come by in the morning after Nathan's gone to work. About midmorning?"

"Bit early to drink wine, you think?"

"My anniversary with your brother's coming up. I need to commiserate—I mean celebrate. I meant to say celebrate with the only other woman who knows my hell."

That one won more than a chuckle. "Oh sure you did." She said her goodbyes and hung up, her look on the roses. After pulling the small envelope from the holder stuck in among the flowers, she opened it and took out the card.

I miss having you with me, Ash. So damn much. I'd take friends, even just small ones.

Love,

Gabe.

Love.

"Christ." Ashley let her hand fall into her lap as she shook her head and looked around the kitchen.

She couldn't do this. She really couldn't do this. Not anymore.

Leaving the card and flowers there, she took her cases through to her bedroom and patched up life by throwing a few things into the washer, then looking through the cupboards as she pulled a pen and pad from a drawer to make a list of items she needed to pick up. She was distracting, more building up the nerve to call Abby and let her know she was okay without breaking down.

She slumped on her bed eventually and pressed Call.

"Mom? You gonna tell me why I heard off Uncle Jason about what's gone on? Why the *hell* didn't you call me?"

Ashley closed her eyes and lay back on the bed, all fight draining from her body.

***

Rubbing at her head after a rough night, Ashley sat in Kathryn's kitchen, hugging a cup of hot coffee. She didn't need any wine to add to this.

"You all right?" Kathryn pulled out the chair across from Ashley. "I know you're not and it's a stupid question, but...?"

Ashley nodded. "It was a gorgeous place to stay until..." She frowned, then offered a shrug. "All that."

As Kathryn sipped her coffee, she tilted her head slightly. "But you're okay, though? Really?"

"Getting there."

"Because Abby called this morning. She mentioned something about Gabe. About you and Gabe." Kathryn put her mug down. "This isn't just about what went down with this Darrell, is it?"

Ashley shrugged. "It's about me always trusting the wrong sort."

Kathryn nodded, and for a moment she ran a finger over the rim of her mug. "You both went through a lot, you know that, right? From what Abby said, there was the land bill the ranchers were trying to get passed, you getting grabbed, Lisa's pregnancy possibility *and* Cody's fall, a brother who was still grieving the loss of his wife. A friend—"

Friend.

Ashley raised a finger, stopping her there, not wanting to step so close to the details. "It's still you back to making excuses for him," she said flatly. "It's still me sitting here on my own, talking for hours on end trying to reason why it hurts so much without him being here. I *know* I care for him, I *know* I want more than friends, but every goddamn time I try, he pulls some other stunt that thumps me in the stomach."

"Okay, okay," Kathryn said quickly, reaching over and stroking her hand. "No excuses. Not anymore. Let's make this about forgetting, about moving on." She raised her mug. "To absent *not* friends. To moving...over their ass with a car if they try to hurt you again."

Ashley choked a smile, but it hurt how Kathryn mirrored Gabe in that moment, how when it hurt, his response had been…who do you need hurting.

"The party's tomorrow night." Kathryn winked across at her. "That's the perfect time for forgetting and moving on"

"I'll just take the offer of a glass of wine thanks. I don't want anything more." And she really didn't.

Chapter 32

Music and laughter filled the ballroom, and Ashley made a point to mingle with everyone. This she could handle. Being alone at a party hadn't ever bothered her. She'd spent too much time with her ex over wondering who and where he'd be off speaking too, divorce came with freedom, a weight off shoulders where worry no longer mattered. So this? It brought back her old self, how mingling came with no complications, and these were friends and family here. But a look at her watch told her the time for her to give a toast to Jason and Kathryn approached, and she glanced over her shoulder to find Nathan talking with a group of men.

As Ashley joined them, Nathan turned and put his arm around her shoulders and drew her in. "All of you know my sister, Ashley, except you, right, Paul?" He looked at her. "Paul joined our firm a month ago. I thought you two might have a lot in common. He graduated from Xavier."

Paul Walker was a lean, good-looking man in his mid-forties, and he edged closer to Ashley. "Nathan tells me you are a history buff too. I'd love to know your go-to list." Taking Ashley's arm, forcing a look back at Jason, a shake of head off her, he steered her toward the drinks and away from the group. "Can I get you another glass of wine?"

"Actually, I was about to give a toast to the happy couple." But she held her glass out to him. She needed a top up for Dutch courage.

"Tell me about your work at the university," he said, taking her glass.

Ashley buried a smile. "Are you really interested in history?"

Paul grinned. "Yeah, a little. It's why I went into law. I got hooked on the Constitution."

Ashley winced. That was more than a little light reading. She went to say something, but Sue Ann Bolton yelled her name as she pushed through the crowd and came to Ashley's side. "Ashley Roberts, I can't believe it's you. How long has it been?" She placed herself between Ashley and Paul, and Ashley mouthed a *sorry* his way. Tact had never been Sue's strong point, and Paul waved her off, adding a *catch up with you later* wave. Ann continued her litany of complaints of why she hadn't gotten together with Ashley sooner, and Ashley had to cut the conversation short as she headed over to the mic to toast the couple. Gazing around the room at the crowd, she was surprised at the sudden loneliness she felt.

***

Seemed she'd been waking up the past few mornings with a hangover, and today didn't disappoint. Although Ashley didn't understand why. She hadn't had *that* many glasses of wine at the party last night. Okay she knew why, and most of it was to do with the unanswered text messages that Gabe had sent her way. He never had an issue with keeping in touch, she just needed to stay away from any excuses he sent her way. They only added to her own that kept trying to creep in. Snuggled up in bed, she buried a pillow over her head.

Turn the tables when it came to Jason, when it came to anyone looking like they were about to step into Susan's shoes, it niggled, started to gnaw deep that she might not have handled it as well either. Okay she didn't have the means to run a background check, but she'd have damn well ghosted the woman's Facebook page way back to when she'd first joined just to see who'd she'd dated and if she had a habit of going after grieving young men.

And yeah, maybe her inner bitch would have clicked in too, right along with the asshole Gabe had been. Could she really judge him so harshly?

She groaned. This was her, back to making excuses and hating herself for going there.

Her phone rang and she picked it up off the nightstand. "Hello?" She sounded angry even to her own ears.

"Hey, Ashley, it's Paul Walker."

Paul? Ashley pulled herself up to a sitting position and stuffed her pillow behind her, trying to chase the rest of the name.

A soft chuckle came over. "I made such a good impression, huh? I'm Paul, the one from the party last night?"

"Oh…" Ashley winced. *That* Paul. "Sorry."

"No problem. I'm calling to see if you're interested in dinner?"

Dinner? She gave a heavy sigh, more interested to know how he'd gotten her number and why Nathan was trying to play matchmaker. "Look, I—"

"You'd be doing me a favor." Paul sounded like he was smiling. "If only to get your brother off my back."

Ashley laughed and rested her head in her hand. "Sorry, he's—"

"Just looking out for you with…patch work, I think he called it."

Ashley looked up and gave a heavy sigh. _Nathan, you ass_. It's what they both called it.

"You up for it?"

"Yeah. Maybe I am. Thank you." She liked Paul. He was a good-looking attorney in her brother's firm, but she was rebounding, she knew that. It didn't stop her accepting. She needed something to stop herr thinking excuses.

Chapter 33

Paul pulled into Ashley's driveway around midnight. Kathryn had invited them back to stop by for a drink, and they'd sat on the deck talking and enjoying the warm evening. But that was it. Their night. Not uncomfortable, but not anything else either.

Sat in the car, Ashley glanced across at Paul. It wasn't right to drag him into her mess. He was a decent man and she liked him. He deserved better.

"Least I can do is walk you to the door, right?" Paul smiled her way. "Keep Nathan from hunting me down for the rest of the night over not seeing you in?"

Ashley buried a smile. "Yeah, that'd be good. Thank you."

He got out and a moment later her door came open. Only Paul hadn't made it around the hood, and his look fixed her way, on her open door.

A hand came her way a moment later, and she eased out, not taking it.

Gabe levelled his gaze on Paul. "Who's that?"

"That's—" She looked back Paul's way, then at Gabe. "That's none of your business. What the hell are you doing here?"

Gabe's look never left Paul's. "Take a walk for a minute, mate."

"Stop it." Ashley backed him off a few paces to try and get him to break the deadlock. "Go home."

"No. I came to try and straighten this out." His look found hers.

"You're failing—badly." She pushed him back another step. "You don't do this, not with a friend."

His look came her way, and Ashley took a steady breath. "Go on, say it," she said in a low voice. "Say he's more than that. Because that would be you back to reading every goddamn wrong signal going."

Gabe seemed to shake something off and frowned down at her. "He caught me off guard, is all."

"Go. Just go, Gabe, please. I can't do this again."

"I flew down to say sorry, no texts, no bullshit." He shrugged. "Try to mend broken fences without a hammer." He smiled bitterly. "But I still came in too heavy, huh?"

Ashley shrugged back at him, it hurting too much, and he nodded as if that was all the answer he needed. Then he kissed at her cheek as he breathed a *sorry*. He nodded at Paul a moment later. "Make sure she gets in safe, okay?"

"Will do." Paul gave a small salute, but he kept his distance as Gabe turned away.

Ashley went to say something, but she pulled back, fists clenched at her sides over his bullheadedness. He wanted this his way, when he thought she was ready. Life didn't work like that. *She* didn't work like that, because she wasn't the one who needed to take a step back and clear aggression levels. Tonight proved that.

Chapter 34

Gabe tossed his jacket over his office chair and slumped in his seat. He couldn't get his head right, but in the same angered breath, he didn't want it putting right either. Switch roles, put a woman getting out of Gabe's car in the middle of the night, Ashley would have reacted *exactly* the same. Okay, he had the rest of his bullshit to throw on top of that, but last night caught him out, nothing more. He hadn't expected…what? That she'd have friends? *Male* friends that could just be friends?

He groaned, wiping a hand over his face. He didn't stop his groan as Jason pushed through.

"Sam's out of the hospital and back at home." Jason came around and leaned against the desk. "T.J. hired a foreman who's good at handling the books. Logan also said he'd picked up Megan's ex for questioning."

"You know—" Gabe pushed out of his chair and went over to the drinks cabinet. "I really don't give a fuh—care at this point."

Jason frowned as Gabe took a swig of whiskey. "Not even if I mention you got a message through from your kid? He's hoping to come up over the holidays."

Gabe glanced back, all anger falling. "Seriously?"

Jason smiled. "Yeah. Sounded good to hear from him. I think he has a girlfriend."

Gabe gave a sigh and took a second drink over to Jason. Jason took it as he sat down.

"From the look on your face, you'd have thought you'd lost the ranch." Jason took a swig of his drink. "What happened with Ash?"

Gabe snorted. "It was me, handling Ashley. How the hell do you think it went?"

Jason winced. "I told you to give it some time. Let her breathe. You too."

"Yeah, well." He got to his feet, not quite sure where he wanted to go. "Seems I've fucked it up again and have a lifetime of it now. I just would have preferred to have spent it with her, y'know?"

***

After watching Gabe go, Jason took his whiskey and headed down the hall to his own office. For a moment he stood looking out the window, wiping a hand over his jaw. Letting his gaze rest on a picture of him hugging Susan on a skiing holiday, he pointed her way before taking a swig of whiskey. "I know, I know," he added quietly. "They're both struggling."

He tugged out his mobile and thumbed in a number.

Someone picked up eventually. "Jason?"

"Ash." He gave a heavy sigh. "We okay to talk a while?"

Quiet. "Don't offer excuses for him, okay? I'm so sick and tired of thinking excuses."

"I wouldn't," he said quietly. "I just want to talk time. Maybe knock both of your heads together a little when it comes to losing it..."

***

Ashley stood in the guest bedroom, feeling a little strange with being back at Coulter Creek, the familiar sights and scents making her briefly close her eyes for a moment. Still felt like home, but it hurt how it did.

"Haven't see Gabe since breakfast." Jason came in, carrying her bags.

"He didn't know I was coming?"

Jason put her cases on the bed. "No," he said softly. "He needed a few days out of his own head, so I threw every—"

"Broken fence at him?" finished Ashley.

Jason laughed. "Something like that, yeah. It's why I flew you down."

"Good." Ashley went over and kissed at his cheek. "Leave him alone without one to fix and we could plant him on Sam's land as a landmine, all hothead and—"

"There's love there, I see." Jason peered a little closer, just to make sure.

"There's time," she said softly. "That's enough for now, right? A last chance to use it before she reminds us she'll ultimately call enough?"

Jason glanced down at her cases, then offered a nod. "More than." Then he winced. "But we're talking Gabe here. It might take a few more last chances. But he's harmless, I swear. All big soft puppy with teeth who's still not out of teething trouble yet. He bites at everything."

Ashley laughed and started unpacking her case. "Do you know where he is?"

Jason glanced at his phone. "Heading for the library from the look of things." He flicked her a look. "Knowing Clay has its perks."

Didn't it just.

Ashley left him there and headed down to the library. Quiet played around her, and for a moment she listened for any sign of life, then made her way over to the small bar and poured herself a glass of wine. Dutch courage...again, but she needed it. The good echoed too much around these walls, and she smiled privately, remembering the last time she'd had a couple of glasses of wine here.

Footsteps behind her made her glance over her shoulder, and Gabe didn't see her for a moment. But as she shifted, he came to a stop, eyes startling.

"Ash... What...what are you doing here?" He was back to looking unsure over what to do, how to react, whether to drop Cody's math book he'd picked up to return, come over...stay...bolt. Ashley kind of loved how she made him look so...chaotic.

"You said you wanted to talk?"

"Yeah, but...?" He took a step toward her, then stopped, running a hand through his hair. "You're here..."

Ashley smiled down to her feet. "Can't get past that one, huh, cowboy?" After resting her glass down, she went over but kept a little distance between them. "This is me. Here. So talk."

He frowned her way and a lot of hurt came with it. "I'm..." He shrugged. "Sorry."

She dipped her head a little to try and understand the bluntness. "That's it? That's all you got?"

He nodded. "No excuses. Just my fault. My sorry. No promise to try and make it work, because if you have to try and make something work, your heart's not in it from the beginning."

"And your heart has been. From the beginning?"

He shrugged again. "Maybe twenty minutes after, when you had the guts to get in my plane and take the ride with me despite being so damn scared of flying. Maybe thirty minutes after as well, when you reached back to grab your camera and your skirt road a little higher, showing me those long legs of yours..."

She laughed and hit his shoulder. "No love at first sight, then?"

"Twenty...thirty minutes... Still counts, right? Takes me a little time to sort through all those...broken fences to see the wood through the forest fire I stoke."

She gave a hard sigh and went in close, her arms draping his shoulders. "Good recovery," she said gently as he slipped a hold to her hips. "Damn good recovery."

Gabe closed his eyes and rested his head against hers. "Not enough, though. I forgot about the background check," he said quietly. "With everything, it slipped my mind. Clay put the paperwork on my desk just before we got back. It didn't register, not until you went in there."

"You never read it?"

He shook his head. "I shouldn't have *asked* for it." He gave such a rough sigh, and Ashley pulled away a little, stroking at the back of his neck.

"Thought it over a little when I was away," she said to him. "When it comes to Jason, to the kids…" She winced. "I might have just done the same thing with a new woman on the scene."

Gabe choked a laugh. "Seriously?"

"Seriously."

"Then God help him if he finds anyone else." He winced. "Might be best to tell him we're looking out for him that kind of way. Avoid the same screw ups."

Ashley patted his chest. "You get that job. I'm hiding when you do. He's a Coulter."

"Damn right." His kiss touched hers, and it lasted an age. "Friends," he said gently. "Just small ones?" He even measured it between finger and thumb.

Ashly shoved his hand away and backed him up against the wall. "Gabe," she breathed as she flicked at the clasp to his jeans. "It's about time I told you something." She gave such a wicked smile. "You make one hell of a lousy friend." She nibbled at his lips, him at hers. "So I'll take the lover, thanks."

ABOUT THE AUTHOR

E.H. Hunter is an educator in the Pacific Northwest where she lives with her family She enjoys traveling, new adventures, and writing angsty romances.

Connect with E.H.:

instagram.com/ehhunterauthor

www.BOROUGHSPUBLISHINGGROUP.com

If you enjoyed this book, please write a review. Our authors appreciate the feedback, and it helps future readers find books they love. We welcome your comments and invite you to send them to info@boroughspublishinggroup.com.

Follow us on Facebook, Twitter and Instagram, and be sure to sign up for our newsletter for surprises and new releases from your favorite authors.

Are you an aspiring writer? Check out www.boroughspublishinggroup.com/submit and see if we can help you make your dreams come true.

Love podcasts? Enjoy ours at www.boroughspublishinggroup.com/podcast